"Good work! All right, let me go fetch someone. Heh...heh-heh-heh...... Hey, Alice, Six, we'll be splitting credit evenly, right? Right??"

D1209681

SNOW

A diligent woman who rose up from the slums to become captain of the Royal Guard. She's very ambitious and zealously seeks credit for accomplishments.

■SNOW'S VIEW
I was gracious enough to give them a shot at glory. They should be grateful for any credit at all!

HIS VOLUME'S MAIN HEROINE

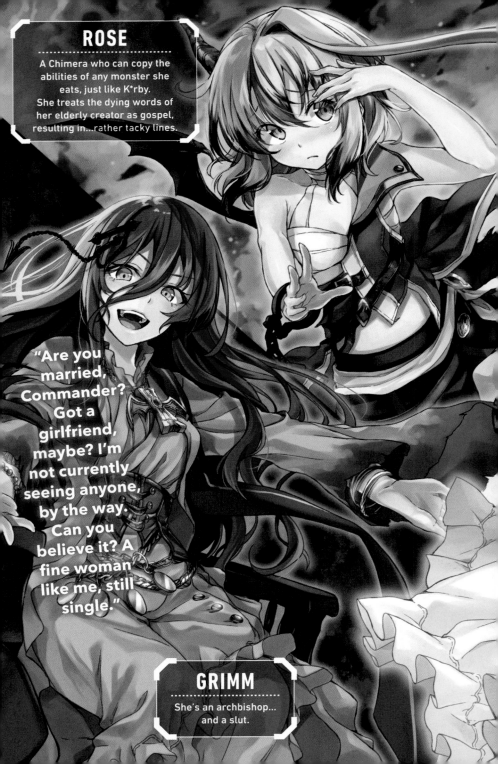

ROSE

A Chimera who can copy the abilities of any monster she eats, just like K*rby.
She treats the dying words of her elderly creator as gospel, resulting in...rather tacky lines.

"Are you married, Commander? Got a girlfriend, maybe? I'm not currently seeing anyone, by the way. Can you believe it? A fine woman like me, still single."

GRIMM

She's an archbishop... and a slut.

"The name's Rose. Artificial Humanoid Battle Chimera Rose... You think you can handle me...?"

"I am the Kisaragi Corporation's high-spec pretty-girl android: Alice Kisaragi. No need for formalities. We're the same rank."

ALICE KISARAGI

A high-spec android developed with the latest technology the Kisaragi Corporation has to offer. Her internal reactor will melt down and self-destruct if exposed to excessive levels of violence.

■ ALICE'S VIEW

There's nothing wrong with self-destructing.
It's the dream of every great villain.

■ ROSE'S VIEW

...But Grandpa said...

■ GRIMM'S VIEW

Hey! Why is my intro so much worse than the others?!
O Great Lord Zenarith, I beseech thee!
Deliver disaster unto this page's creator!
May they choke on a fish bone and suffer!

INTRODUCTIONS

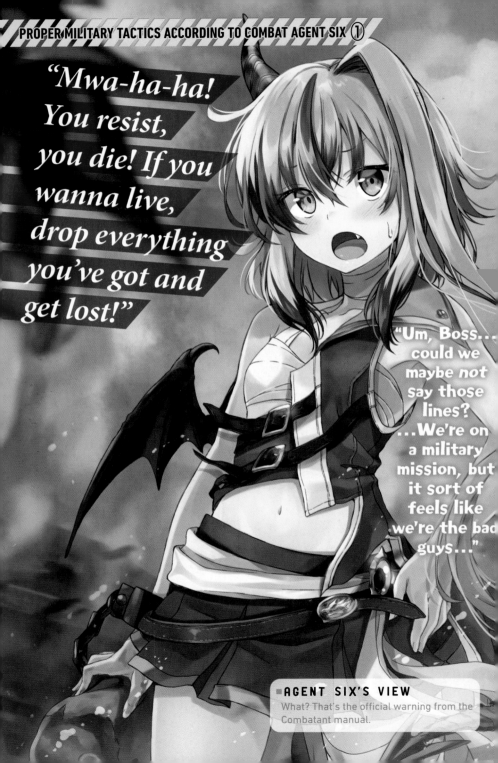

"Mwa-ha-ha! You resist, you die! If you wanna live, drop everything you've got and get lost!"

"Um, Boss... could we maybe *not* say those lines? ...We're on a military mission, but it sort of feels like we're the bad guys..."

AGENT SIX'S VIEW
What? That's the official warning from the Combatant manual.

"Okay, next let's try leaning back on your arms, spreading your legs, and lowering your hips.

Hey now! Get that hand out of the way. Hands *behind* your legs."

"""Yikes..."""

HEINE

One of the Demon Lord's Elite Four, also known as Heine of the Flames. She has huge boobs. If you like dark-skinned demi-humans, this demoness is definitely your type.

■HEINE'S VIEW

Six...! You sick bastard! I'll never forgive you!!

PROPER MILITARY TACTICS ACCORDING TO COMBAT AGENT SIX ②

HERE AND NOW !

PROPER MILITARY TACTICS ACCORDING TO COMBAT AGENT SIX ③

CONTENTS

Prologue
P. 001

COMBATANTS WILL BE DISPATCHED!

COMBATANTS WILL BE DISPATCHED!

1

Natsume Akatsuki

ILLUSTRATION BY
Kakao Lanthanum

YEN
ON

NEW YORK

Natsume Akatsuki

Translation by Noboru Akimoto
Cover art by Kakao Lanthanum

SENTOIN, HAKEN SHIMASU! Volume 1
© 2017 Natsume Akatsuki, Kakao • Lanthanum
First published in Japan in 2017 by KADOKAWA CORPORATION, Tokyo.
English translation rights arranged with KADOKAWA CORPORATION, Tokyo through
TUTTLE-MORI AGENCY, INC., Tokyo.

English translation © 2019 by Yen Press, LLC

Yen On
150 West 30th Street, 19th Floor
New York, NY 10001

Visit us at yenpress.com
facebook.com/yenpress
twitter.com/yenpress
yenpress.tumblr.com
instagram.com/yenpress

First Yen On Edition: September 2019

Yen On is an imprint of Yen Press, LLC.
The Yen On name and logo are trademarks of Yen Press, LLC.

Library of Congress Cataloging-in-Publication Data
Names: Akatsuki, Natsume, author. | Lanthanum, Kakao, illustrator. | Akimoto, Noboru, translator.
Title: Combatants will be dispatched! / Natsume Akatsuki ; illustration by Kakao Lanthanum ; translation by
    Noboru Akimoto ; cover art by Kakao Lanthanum.
Other titles: Sentoin haken shimasu!. English
Description: First Yen On edition. | New York : Yen On, 2019.
Identifiers: LCCN 2019025056 | ISBN 9781975385583 (v. 1 ; trade paperback)
Subjects: CYAC: Science fiction. | Robots—Fiction.
Classification: LCC PZ7.1.A38 Se 2019 | DDC [Fic]—dc23
LC record available at https://lccn.loc.gov/2019025056

ISBNs: 978-1-9753-8558-3 (paperback)
978-1-9753-3151-1 (ebook)

10 9 8 7 6 5 4 3 2 1

LSC-C

Printed in the United States of America

Prologue

"…Would you mind telling me again where you're from?"

"Japan. Nippon, Nihon, Japan, please use the name that's easiest for you to pronounce."

"…My apologies, it's just that I've never heard of a country named Japan…"

"I understand. It's a tiny island country in the Far East."

"I see… Now, I see on your résumé that you previously worked for an organization called the Kisaragi Corporation. Would you mind telling me a little bit about it?"

"I'm afraid I can't. I'm bound by a nondisclosure agreement of sorts."

"I…I see. Um…well, I notice that under the skills section of your résumé you list something called an Omnidirectional Vibrating Blade Bad Sword…? Um…what exactly is that?"

"It's my Finisher."

*   *   *

"...Finisher?"

"Yes, it's a special technique I've used to finish off many a Hero."

"...And when you say 'Hero,' you mean...?"

"The enemy."

"I...see. I apologize for the constant stream of questions. So... would it be accurate to say that you're something of a fighter?"

"Yep, that's fine by me..."

"—I was a Combat Agent after all."

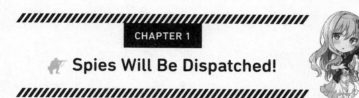

1

The Kisaragi Corporation. A global corporation known to every man, woman, and child on Earth. And I'm sitting here in a conference room in the very heart of its company headquarters.

"—That about covers the basics. I trust you have no questions, Agent Six?"

"Got it, Agent Six?"

"I think I misheard you. Would you mind going over that again?"

The faces in front of me sigh, presumably in exasperation at how thickheaded I'm proving to be.

"…Very well. Agent Six, your assignment will be to infiltrate the target as an advance scout for the Kisaragi Corporation. Your mission will be to survey the local fauna. If you encounter any aboriginal inhabitants, you are to gather intelligence on their military capabilities. Your overall objective will be to assess whether the target has the resources and territory with sufficient strategic value to justify an invasion."

"...I see."

The mission makes perfect sense. It's something I've done countless times before.

"Your target will be an alien world. You got that?"

"Yeah, you got that?"

"...No, I can't say I do," I immediately reply, and the expressions of the pair in front of me sour in puzzlement.

The first is Astaroth the Ice Queen. A slender woman with hip-length black hair that shimmers like obsidian. She possesses an ethereal, otherworldly beauty that inspires fear more than anything else.

The other is Belial the Great Flame. A flame-haired bombshell, she dresses in an outfit that leaves little to the imagination.

The Ice Queen and the Great Flame both have a preference for skimpy clothing and share a hobby of using their unique titles in daily conversation.

Astaroth the Ice Queen lets out another sigh, preparing to describe my assignment for the third time in as many minutes.

"...Just what is it that you fail to grasp here, Agent Six? There's nothing about this mission that should cause you any confusion. All I'm telling you to do is to infiltrate the target as a spy."

I notice Belial the Great Flame nodding along in agreement.

"I understand the mission. But you keep losing me at the 'alien world' part. Look, I've learned to play along with your cosplay outfits and corny titles...but I've gotta admit...a pair of grown women going on about alien worlds is a bit much, even for me."

"H-how...how *dare* you call our uniforms cosplay outfits?!"

"Tacky...?! Agent Six, is that how you've thought of us all this time?!"

The pair in front of me flush and become noticeably more animated.

"Well, I mean…it's not exactly rare for the two of you to make statements that are a bit…out there. But you're breaking new ground today. Have you been watching too much of those *isekai* anime about people being reincarnated in other worlds?"

"Silence! That is enough of your impudence. You *are* aware that we, the Kisaragi Corporation, are nearing our goal of world domination, correct?"

"Well, yes, of course."

I try not to notice the bulging vein on Astaroth's forehead as she patiently resumes her explanation.

World domination. For the Kisaragi Corporation, this doesn't refer to dominating a particular industry or market. It's literal, and Kisaragi happily describes itself as an evil secret society on the "about us" page. The corporation's primary business is the planning and execution of evil schemes.

As for me, well, I started working here as a Combat Agent while in high school. Soon after they hired me, they cut me open and installed some weird body enhancements, making me a glorified errand boy—a role I've been stuck in ever since.

Ordinarily, you expect a corporation to retain plausible deniability about aiming for world domination, but we became so big that we stopped trying to keep it a secret a long time ago. We're now a multinational criminal organization, focusing on mayhem, death, destruction, and plunder. There isn't a military force on the planet powerful enough to oppose us, and I've been told that the handful of countries holding out hope with economic sanctions were on their last legs.

"Very well. Now, what do you imagine will happen to you operatives when we finish conquering the world?"

I don't understand what Astaroth is asking, and I tilt my head.

"...? We, of course, become the new rulers of the world and indulge in a life of decadence and debauchery, right?"

"No, you fool. We're looking at a massive restructuring of the organization."

""..Say what?""

Belial and I respond with one voice to Astaroth's response.

"...Restructuring? Is that your way of saying you're gonna start firing people?"

"That's right."

The conference room goes deathly quiet.

"...Wait, wait, what? You can't just... After all that I've done for you! You coldhearted bitch! First, you make me do all your dirty work, and now you're just gonna toss me aside?! I'm basically unemployable and undatable given all the modifications you've made to my body. You *owe* me. So let me move in with you! Please! I promise I'll make a good house husband!"

"Hey, am I on the chopping block, too?! Is my position as the Supreme Leader in charge of military operations going to get eliminated?!"

Both Belial and I cling to Astaroth, but true to her title, the Ice Queen doesn't so much as flinch...

"Calm down, both of you... H-hey! Agent Six! I'll explain the plan! Just don't grab my top! It's slipping! Stop, stop, stop! My outfit's too skimpy to be pulled like that!"

...Astaroth pulls away from us, panting in panic, wrapping her arms protectively around her top to hold it in place. She scrambles away with teary eyes to secure some personal space.

"I can't believe you two. Listen! First, Belial, you're one of the Supreme Leaders in this corporation. Your job is safe. We will still need a military after we finish our conquest. As for you, Agent Six..."

Belial lets out a sigh of relief, but I, the lackey, find nothing reassuring about Astaroth's answer. As if reading my mind, Astaroth shifts her gaze to me.

"Unlike Belial, you're just one soldier in our great army. With that said, you have been with us since the very beginning. Whatever your title, we consider you one of our own and think of you as part of our leadership."

"…Does that mean I can get a raise? I've been working here since I was in high school, but my pay hasn't changed since I was a temp."

"However! If we provide special treatment only to you and ignore the other operatives, we risk alienating the rank-and-file members and having the corporation fall to pieces."

Astaroth makes no indication that she heard anything about my pay as she continues her spiel.

"…Then how will you decide who stays and who gets canned? If you say, 'By drawing lots,' I'm gonna give you a taste of the modifications you've made to me."

"F-fool, that's why we're talking about your new assignment!"

Apparently recognizing that my patience was wearing thin, Astaroth backs up into a defensive crouch.

"Basically, Agent Six, the idea is that once we conquer Earth, we look for another planet to attack. The layoffs were new, but we've been discussing our next target for a while now. We have to govern what we've conquered, and without a war on, there's no money to spend on an excessive military," Belial adds from next to Astaroth.

"So that's why you're going on about alien worlds? But we don't have the technology to get there. If we had that kinda tech, I'd have fled to the planet of big-breasted beauties by now. We'd have to start by getting people to Mars or Venus," I say to them with a pitying glance.

"…We should continue this discussion in Lilith's room. Come with us, Agent Six."

Astaroth, with her icy visage back in place, turns on her heel and leaves the room. The most I can do is tilt my head in confusion and follow.

The third of Kisaragi's three Supreme Leaders is Lilith the Black. Her lair at Kisaragi headquarters, a research laboratory, is always filled with machinery with no clear purpose. Yet, today my eye catches a new object in the center of the room.

"Agent Six, do you know what this is?" Astaroth asks, waving her palm toward a jumble of large technological equipment attached to a great glass pod.

"It…looks like a teleporter straight out of a sci-fi movie."

As soon as the observation leaves my mouth, I hear the lab owner call out in reply, "A keen observation, Agent Six! You're certainly sharp for a meathead!"

The harsh appraiser of my intellect is a beautiful young woman with dark hair in a bowl cut and dressed in a white lab coat as she triumphantly struts around the object. Lilith the Black, the Kisaragi Corporation's resident mad scientist and the one who applied the various modifications to my body.

"Wait, you're serious…? You've actually achieved teleportation? With a pile of junk like this?"

"Junk, you say? How rude! This is the answer to humanity's prayers. A magnificent device that will solve every problem plaguing our world today. One of my greatest inventions if I do say so myself!"

The ordinarily taciturn and antisocial Lilith is in a fine mood. Even Astaroth's poker face cracks a little, thin frown lines creasing her brow.

"A lab coat again, Lilith? You *are* one of the leaders of this organization. You should wear the proper uniform every once in a while."

"You're kidding, right? Why would I want to expose myself like that? I'll go ahead and say it—Astaroth, you and Belial look like you're auditioning for a cosplay porno."

"Oh, good, I'm not the only one who thought so!" I comment.

""Wh-what?!""

It appears this observation is news to Astaroth and Belial, who freeze in place…which, honestly, is the least of my concerns right now.

"…So this is an actual working teleporter? That's…one hell of an invention. I figured the people in the organization calling you the world's greatest scientist were just sucking up to you. Your lab always did seem like a black hole that just ate up our budget."

"…I—I see that you're still not afraid to voice your opinion."

Ignoring the tomboy nerd's forced smile, I continue examining the pod.

"How does this relate to my assignment?"

I tilt my head in curiosity. Lilith's face brightens at my question.

"Do you believe in aliens?"

"I bet they exist, but it's not something I've spent too much time thinking about."

The corporation counts mutants among its ranks, and then there's those oddities called Heroes. I wouldn't be surprised if there were other things out there, given the size of the universe.

"To date, modern science has confirmed the presence of thousands of planets similar to Earth. They have things like water, atmospheres, and what appears to be plant life. These planets are at the right distance from their stars, are the right size, and made of the right material… and so this is a reward for all the hard work you put in each and every day."

…*Reward?*

At my puzzled expression, Lilith turns to stare intently at me.

"Think about it. There is literally an astronomical number of stars in this universe. Billions of stars with planets like Earth. There are so many worlds that counting them is a waste of time."

Lilith grows more reverential and animated, sweeping her arms outward in a grand gesture as she continues her sermon.

"And with these infinite worlds come infinite possibilities. Worlds where the inhabitants are still in the primal stages. Worlds that have made wondrous technological advancements. There's even the possibility that some of them have actual magic, like the swords and sorcery books you're so fond of. Don't you want to explore those possibilities?"

"So there might be worlds where everyone adores me without question or I'm the very image of beauty or, heck, I'm the only man, and this teleporter will help take me there? I'm sold. Fire it up."

Lilith edges away at my monologue, gesturing toward the back of the laboratory.

"E-excellent. I'm glad you're so eager to go. Of course, we won't be sending you in alone... Come on in, Alice."

A little blue-eyed, blond-haired girl dressed in a white flowered dress enters the room in response to Lilith's summons.

She looks like a sixth grader.

She's carrying an enormous backpack much too large for her small body, wobbling slightly with each step.

"Who's the brat? I should probably mention that I hate kids."

"Just who are you calling a brat? You're not exactly royalty yourself."

....

"...Oh-ho? Is this what we're doing? Who does this damned brat think she is? I'm a soldier for an evil organization. No one mouths off like that to the Kisaragi Corporation and gets away with it."

"If you attack me, my reactor core will melt down and vaporize everything within a considerable radius. If that's what you're after, be my guest. And my designation is not 'damned brat,' it's 'high-spec pretty-girl android.'"

...An android? Seriously?

I suppose that explains why the girl seems...off. Now that it's been said out loud, I can kind of see it.

"Well, it looks like you two will get along splendidly. Let me give you a proper introduction. This girl is Alice. She's a high-spec android specifically designed to support you. She ranks up there with the tele-porter as one of my greatest inventions."

"Unlike you disposable lackeys, the corporation has spent an enor-mous sum of money on my development. You'd better take care of me. I've been warned you're a meathead. Leave the thinking to me."

"...Can I return her? I don't really need a dangerous, mouthy pile of junk following me around."

I check my equipment, stepping in front of the pod.

The comforting weight of my trusty sidearm on my right hip. Plenty of spare magazines on my belt. On my left hip rests my lucky combat knife, purchased with a bonus I got a few years back.

If I'm being honest, the whole set doesn't really amount to much, considering I'm walking blindly into an alien world...

"Well, I see you've made your peace with going."

Astaroth has recovered from the shock of being called a cos-play porn star, and her icy expression has been replaced with a gentle smile.

...It's the smile that charmed me into signing up with a shady company calling itself an evil organization after that complete con of a recruiting poster tricked me into applying.

The smile that convinced me it was worth it to participate in evil schemes and take on the entire world.

"I'll go. I'll go! I mean...I'm the one you chose out of all the corporation's Combat Agents to represent Kisaragi in this new world, right?"

Astaroth, of course, backs me up enthusiastica...lly?

"Huh...? O-of course! Most certainly! There's no one else we could trust with such an important assignment!"

"Wait...how did you pick who to send? Belial? How did you choose the scouting party?"

I ask Belial, still sulking in the corner, rather than the unconvincing Astaroth.

"They're not skanky... The Supreme Leader outfits aren't skanky...hmm? The scouting party? Astaroth rolled a die..."

"We're counting on you, Agent Six! N-now go on. There's not a moment to waste!"

Astaroth interrupts Belial and shoves me toward the pod.

...When I get back, I'm going to demand a Supreme Leader–level salary. Just you wait.

"Oh yes, I almost forgot. If you need any weapons or other supplies, write down the request and send it with this mini-teleporter. The chips we've implanted in you and Alice will let us know your coordinates."

Lilith gives what I assume is supposed to be a reassuring smile, then hands Alice and me a pair of devices resembling wristwatches.

Well, that takes care of my concerns about equipment. So long as I have access to Kisaragi Corporation equipment, it really doesn't matter where they end up sending me.

The mouthy pile of junk follows me into the pod.

"What was your name again? Alice? You mentioned your reactor might melt down if you get hit. You sure you can handle this? I can't have you blowing up on me."

"Isn't it the dream of every evil minion to self-destruct and take the enemy with them? Don't worry yourself. Evidently, I was built to support you, so you ending up dead is out of the question. I'll make sure to pick the right time and place to explode."

That's not reassuring. I'd rather she not self-destruct at all.

"Agent Six."

Astaroth calls to me with the cold expression worthy of her title... which is quickly replaced by a look of concern.

"...Well...you've been with us since you were still in school. As

I mentioned earlier, I consider you to be one of this organization's Supreme Leaders. It's true."

This is hardly the place or time for this. It's true that I started working here as a part-timer back in my first year of high school. It didn't take long for us to conquer half the world. One minute we were facing off against various militaries, the next we had spandex-clad weirdos calling themselves Heroes coming after us. We even faced off against a giant robot made of smaller interlocking robots, which was as big a waste of technology as I've ever seen. This whole situation has been utterly ridiculous and terrifyingly dangerous. I've lost count of the times I've threatened to quit…but still…

"I've enjoyed my time with everyone here at the corporation. I'm even looking forward to this next assignment in spite of everything. I can't promise I'll come back safely, but I'll do my best not to disappoint you. When I *do* get back, would you mind giving me a decent raise?"

"You fool. That's where you're supposed to swear you'll make it back home. The three of us will be waiting to welcome you home. In fact, when you get back, we'll promote you to the fourth Supreme Leader… The Four Supreme Leaders, or perhaps the Elite Four has a good ring to it."

Astaroth's lips curl in a daring smile at my reminiscing. I don't have the heart to tell her that at nearly twenty years of age I'm a bit too old to call myself a member of something like the Elite Four.

"*Sigh*… I wish I could go. You're so lucky, Agent Six. I should've sneaked in the weighted die."

"…Weighted die? Belial, you were on the list of candidates?"

Belial laughs as though my question was particularly absurd.

"Of course! Astaroth would go on a one or two, I would go on a three or four, Lilith on a five, and you on a six. Astaroth made it pretty clear we had to pick from a small list of trusted people, so that's how we came up with that list. Of course, when your name came up, she threw a fit, insisting it was too dangerous, and demanded that she go instead."

"V-very well! Are you prepared, Agent Six? I will now formally give you your assignment!"

Astaroth, flushing from her face to her ears, interrupts Belial's little story with a hurriedly off-pitch order.

Aw, so they really do consider me a member of the inner circle. And they're worried about me, too. ...*Sniff.* Huh, there must be something in my nose.

Astaroth tries to compose herself even as her cheeks stay stubbornly flushed.

"...Astaroth, do you mind if I give you a hug?"

"Here is your assignment! Your mission is twofold. First, secure a base of operations, assemble a teleporter at this base, establish two-way travel from between the target to Earth, and return safely. This task will primarily be Alice's responsibility."

Belial smirks as Astaroth tries vainly to dodge my question.

"Agent Six, this sort of occasion calls for more than a hug. Kiss her already. I'm sure Astaroth wouldn't mind..."

"Don't you dare, unless you want to be frozen! We're getting off topic... Your second objective is to gather intelligence on local military forces, resources, and soil. This objective is intended to determine if the target is a suitable solution to pressing issues such as continued employment for our Combat Agents, food shortages due to population growth, land pollution due to war, and the reduction of habitable land due to rising sea levels. You are to determine if the target planet is suitable for human colonization."

...Huh?

"This assignment... It's not just about the future of our organization, is it? It's one that concerns the fate of Earth and even humanity itself."

"Of course. That's why failure isn't an option. I mean, if you fail at this assignment, you'll be stuck there, so be careful. As Lilith said earlier, if you have any need for equipment, make a request in writing. For now, it'll have to be small enough to fit in the pod."

...*Ah*. So the corporation will back us up and provide unlimited use of company equipment.

"Also...make sure to send a progress report at least once a week... Let me know how you're doing, all right?"

That smile again.

Before I can throw my arms around her, Astaroth kicks me into the pod.

"...All right, then. All set?"

With Alice and me inside the pod, Lilith goes through the final preparations.

Next to her, Astaroth has her eyes focused on the ground in front of her, arms crossed across her chest. Belial clings to the glass pod, staring intently at me as though trying to etch my features into her memory.

"Uh...could you maybe back up a little? The staring is making me nervous."

At my remark, Astaroth looks up. "...Right. You're right, of course. Now that you've made up your mind, having us fuss over you is just going to make you anxious... I'm praying for your safe return, Agent Six."

Astaroth looks at me as though she's never going to see me again.

"You're blowing this all out of proportion. I won't be gone too long. I mean so long as we find a suitable building, we'll have a teleporter up and running before you know it. Then we can just zip back and forth."

"Sorry, can't help it. We're not even sure if the teleporter works properly."

Despite my attempt at levity, there's a sadness to Belial's gaze.

"There's nothing to worry about. Lilith wouldn't make something that doesn't work. She's the world's greatest inventor, right?"

""………""

Astaroth and Belial exchange a wordless glance. Next to them, Lilith silently continues the preparations.

"Um, Lilith…? Just what is the success rate with teleportation? How many times have you used this thing? When you say you're sending us to a known planet, are you able to place us accurately onto the surface?"

"The success rate for teleportation is currently at one hundred percent. The number of attempts is classified. So are details about the accuracy of the teleportation process."

"Um…on second thought. I'd like to decline this mission."

Alice grabs hold of my arm as I try to get out of the pod.

"Hey! Let go of me, you piece of junk. I need to step outside the pod for a minute."

"What are you so afraid of, lackey? Did you forget to make a backup this morning?"

…*What is this junk pile going on about?*

"…You *do* understand that humans can't just save and load from a backup, right? And if you don't stop calling me *lackey*, you're going to suffer an unfortunate accident when we reach our destination."

"Thtop ith! Leth goff oth my theek! You're gointh to thretch my thkin! I'll stop calling you lackey if you call me Miss Alice."

"Well, this isn't getting anywhere. We may as well send them out now."

As I pull on Alice's cheek, Lilith makes her chilling remark, and the pod begins to fill with smoke.

"Wh-what's going on? Lilith? What's with this weird smoke?"

"Ah. We're making sure we're killing off any microbes and viruses that might be stuck to you and Alice to avoid infecting the natives. Oh, bear in mind that you're not allowed to come back if you get infected by something while you're over there," Lilith adds.

I make an effort to break out of the pod, but Alice keeps me from making contact with the glass.

"...Agent Six! With your enhanced body and your power armor, you should be able to handle any environment you find yourself in. We're praying for your safe return."

"We believe in you, Agent Six! Don't forget to bring back souvenirs!"

"Wait, wait, wait! Shouldn't we take a bit more time to test all this? Come on, now!"

I shout vainly in response to Astaroth's and Belial's good-byes.

"Listen, Agent Six. To date, this device has a hundred percent success rate. But if we keep testing it, there might be accidents, and the success rate will fall under one hundred percent. If the success rate goes down, that puts you at an increased risk."

...I take a moment to think through Lilith's logic.

"What the hell are you going on about?! That risk calculation makes no sense! There's no way you're a genius inventor! You're nowhere near that fine line between genius and insanity! You're just a mad scientist!"

"You need to learn a little restraint when you're upset. There's no one else on this Earth who would say something so rude to a woman of my intellect. Anyhow, enjoy your trip, Agent Six! Don't forget to write!"

Lilith breezily activates the teleporter...!

"You tomboy nerd! I'll be back for my reven—!!"

2

The moment the teleporter fires, I take a full blast of cold wind to the face and reflexively shut my eyes. After a moment to steel my nerves, I sneak a peek and see—

"That idiot! I should've known better than to trust her! I don't wanna die, Idontwannadie, donwannadieeeee!"

"Could you shut up and stop panicking? Based on visual estimates, we're about thirty thousand meters in the air. We have a bit more than two minutes before we hit the ground."

Yes, it turns out I've been teleported so high off the ground that objects below appear blurry.

"What about this situation suggests I stop panicking? Alice! You're a high-performance android! You have a flight mode, right...right?!"

"Actually, my only internal feature is the self-destruct."

"You pile of juuunk!"

My falling speed increases as gravity grabs ahold of me. The wind rushing past my ears and life flashing before my eyes make it hard to hear much of anything. Halfway between my first steps and my first bike ride, I notice Alice matching my fall speed and offering me the backpack she'd been carrying.

"Put that on. Lilith and I are smart enough to plan for this possibility. If you set the target too close to the ground, even the slightest error means you and some dirt end up occupying the same space. Even your meathead brain can understand that's much more fatal than a little fall, right?"

The pack is a Kisaragi Corporation standard-issue parachute. It's specially designed to allow for parachute drops wearing even these stupidly heavy suits of power armor. Doing as I'm told, I hastily place the pack on my back, double-checking that the straps are all in place. As I finish, Alice wraps her arms around my waist.

"You don't have your own?"

"We don't have the budget for it. Have to save with the little things. I'll leave the deployment timing to you, but you better be careful. Remember, if we hit the ground too hard, the explosion will vaporize everything within a few miles."

That's really not a reminder I need right now. I can't shake the feeling that being followed around by this walking nuke is meant to be punishment.

Once the parachute is securely attached to my person, my anxiety drops from panic to mild concern. I take a moment to scope out the ground below me.

"Check that out, Alice. Looks like a city of some sort."

"Huh. Most of this land is untouched. There might be intelligent life but not a lot of it."

I catch a glimpse of something that looks like a walled city a distance away from our landing zone.

A castle sits at its center, which is then surrounded by the city proper and some farmland. Enclosing the city, farmland and all, is a massive wall that's an impressive sight even from this altitude.

Outside the walls of the city stretches a vast plain of red-brown dirt. The plains reach out toward the horizon and disappear into the woodlands, and it looks like the rest of the world itself.

I make these observations on our leisurely trip down. After a while, Alice and I make contact with the ground. I take a moment to savor the feeling of solid earth beneath my feet, then let out a slow breath.

"…All right, Alice. Send our coordinates to those idiots in charge. Screw securing a base. We'll put the teleporter together here and head back to regroup. As payment for the sudden near-death skydiving experience, I'm gonna grope that tomboy until she cries."

"Sorry, no can do. The teleporter is a really sensitive piece of equipment. It needs to be assembled in a clean room. We need to let the connection stabilize for at least a month. So if getting home's important to you, you better get cracking on securing a base of operations."

......Seriously?

"...Not again. Do you know how many times they've done this to me? You know what they told me before modification surgery? 'If you get these modifications, you'll be blowing through missions with ease. Promotion, reputation, money, and women—it's all yours for the taking,' they said. Do you know how much I actually make?"

"I don't know, and I don't care. But cheer up! Teleporting so close to a settlement is pretty lucky. It's not a bad start at least. Let's begin by heading toward that city we saw on the way down."

Alice starts rapidly walking in the general direction of the walled city. I suppose it's better than making a scene here in this barren wasteland. Throwing a tantrum won't bring me any closer to a base. Still, this is going to take a while...

"Hey...things were a bit hectic earlier...so let's redo introductions. I'm Agent Six, the longest-surviving Combat Agent in the Kisaragi Corporation. I've made it through every hellhole and battlefield imaginable, and I intend to keep it that way."

I reintroduce myself as I hurry to catch up to Alice.

"I am the Kisaragi Corporation's high-spec pretty-girl android: Alice Kisaragi. No need for formalities. We're the same rank."

"Hey, that's my line! You do know I still have seniority, right? Oh, whatever. So what is it you can do? I can't really do anything but fight. Oh, hey! Speaking of fighting, we could use more equipment. Lilith said to use these mini-teleporters to order what we need, right? Even if we can't get a teleporter, we can order a buggy to drive around in."

I catch up to Alice, but she stops dead in her tracks and turns to me.

"Oh, right. I need to explain that part to you. Six, how many Evil Points do you have?"

Evil Points.

It's one of the things that allows the Kisaragi Corporation to function as an evil organization.

Each individual member of Kisaragi is implanted with a chip that tracks that member's Evil Points. You'd think that doing evil for evil's sake shouldn't be our highest priority, but our leadership takes our role as villains really seriously. So they've set up a system where they track our villainy. You can then use your accumulated Evil Points to get equipment or exchange them for reward money.

People who are model evil minions have lots of Evil Points. The more you have, the better equipment you can buy, and better equipment means better performance on the battlefield. That, in turn, leads to promotions, which ultimately net you even more Evil Points.

Unfortunately, I've never been particularly good at villainy. At most, the things I do are petty nuisances rather than truly vile schemes. That means whatever my abilities on the battlefield, the other members of the corporation view me as a poseur.

The Supreme Leaders believe there's an art and science to villainy. They expect Kisaragi Corporation members to be charismatic super villains rather than mere beasts or thugs. I admit I don't understand what the hell that even means.

"My current score's about three hundred."

"That's a bit low to be invading a fortress city like that. All right, we'll walk there to save on points and infiltrate the city as spies."

Come again? We're starting with the assumption of invading? That's a little scary.

"…Wait, are you saying we need to buy equipment with points? Just how evil is our corporation? I thought this was a giant, important undertaking!"

"There's a literal universe full of candidate planets. You may be the first scout, but they'll eventually send out others. We don't have enough resources to spend generously on each and every planet. We haven't even finished conquering Earth yet."

...This is starting to feel like one of those RPGs where they give you about as much money as you'd get from bagging groceries and expect you to use that to defeat the Demon Lord.

"It's not like I have a lot of leverage given my limited skill set. Sigh... I have to admit it's almost impressive how evil our corporation can be."

"If you don't want to get fired, you need to focus on the job. If it turns out this planet is a good candidate for colonization, we'll have plenty of things for you to do like fighting life-forms that threaten new settlements. So far, the atmosphere is breathable; that's a good sign so far as this world is concerned."

Alice continues her explanation as she starts lightly tapping at my neck.

"That seems like a good reason to provide equipment instead of this nonsense about Evil Points. I mean, with the right equipment, Mr. Six can easil... Ow! The hell are you doing?!"

"I've injected you with immuno-boosting nanobots to protect you from unknown diseases. Anyway, let's hope the inhabitants of this fortress city are pushovers. We did pick a world as close to Earth as possible, so there's a good chance the locals are *Homo sapiens* like you. I didn't notice any skyscrapers, and given the amount of undeveloped land, it should be easy enough to slaughter and subjugate them."

Well, if I had any doubts Alice is an android, that settled it. That cool expression as she casually discusses slaughter and subjugation? Yeesh.

3

I've lost track of how long we've been trudging along these plains.

After staring at a hazy blob on the horizon for what feels like an eternity, I can finally make out some details of the walled city—Wait, what the heck are those...?

"Liar! I thought you said this place was like Earth! Those things don't exist on Earth, dumbass!"

"Stop whining and start shooting. There's a lot of them."

We find ourselves surrounded by a mob of grotesque four-legged monsters.

I draw the pistol from my hip holster, thumb off the safety, and take aim. Alice, meanwhile, takes shelter behind my back.

"The hell are you doing? What sort of robot hides behind a human?"

The pack spreads out to surround us, rearing up on their hind legs in a show of strength. I carefully squeeze the trigger, methodically taking the monsters down one at a time.

"I told you, I'm a high-spec android. As a high-spec model, they put extra effort into realism. So I have the same combat abilities as a similar-size human girl."

"You useless pile of junk! You're definitely **not** a high-spec model! You better treat me with respect from here on out!"

Just as I yell out to Alice, one of the four-legged monstrosities pounces. Thinking (incorrectly, as it turns out) that its mouth was at the front of its head, I brace for a bite. Instead, the creature's back splits open, revealing two glinting rows of razor-sharp teeth...

"...It's gonna eat me!"

I grab at each jaw with my hands, flexing every bit of cybernetic, power armor–boosted muscle to keep the jaws from snapping shut.

"Alice! Alllliiiice?! You may not believe this…but this thing's jaw is as strong as I am! Quick, help me out here!"

What the hell is up with life on this planet? I've got both enhanced muscles *and* power armor on, and I can barely keep the jaws open.

"I'm sorry I can't be of help, Mr. Six. I'm a useless pile of junk incapable of solving this problem."

"Look! I take back everything I said earlier! Just help me out here! Please!"

I struggle to keep the jaws of the first monster pried open as a second and then a third lunge toward me. I manage to fight each creature back with desperate, flailing kicks, but it'll only be a matter of time before I'm dinner.

"Well…I suppose I can help you out. Buy me a shotgun with your Evil Points?"

"Okay, okay! Just hurry up and help!"

Alice quickly sends over the order as the four-legged monsters appear to have come to the conclusion that attacking one by one is a losing proposition. They're ready to attack all at once.

"●●●●,●●●●!"

What sounds like words with some sort of meaning attached to them comes from the direction of the fortress city. Turning my gaze toward the voice, I see what appears to be a group of horseback cavalry heading in our direction.

More precisely, it's a group riding mounts that look like horses with single horns on their heads.

Yes, it's a unit of armored warriors on what appears to be a bunch of unicorns heading toward us and yelling something.

"It's here, Six. Just remember who it is that's saving your hide."

Alice pops out from behind my back, taking aim with her newly acquired shotgun and squeezing the trigger.

The shotgun blast sends a creature flying. It lands with a wet squish, tumbling along the ground with a final whimper before going still.

With my arms freed up, I bend down to pick up my pistol and quickly squeeze off a shot at a convenient target.

The monsters, caught off guard by the shotgun blast, didn't take long to finish off—

"●●●,●●●●●●●● is it?!"

The woman at the front of the unicorn cavalry calls out to us.

She's wearing full armor, so it's hard to tell her figure, but just based on her face, she's the sort of strong-willed beauty who's right up my alley.

The woman, her light-blue hair flowing behind her, dismounts from her unicorn, drawing her sword and pointing it at me.

"●●●● me! What ●●● are ●●●●? Where did you ●●●●!!"

I don't quite catch her meaning, but based on her expression and tone of voice, it's clear she's demanding, rather than asking for, answers to her questions.

"What do you think we should do, Alice? She looks about ready to shove a few inches of steel into my gut."

"Why don't we just wait and listen for a while longer? We can figure out what to do after."

Listen to what exactly? It's not like we can understand what she's saying.

"Just where is that ●●●●● from? I've never ●●● anything ●●● that!"

…Wait, what?

"And it looks like you're not carrying a ●●●●. Answer me! Who are you?"

……

"Hey, Alice, I think I may have acquired some new abilities on this planet. For some reason, I'm starting to understand what they're saying. Pretty amazing, isn't it? I'm already powerful, and now I might be gaining the ability to instantly understand language."

"I have no idea what you're going on about, but the reason you can understand her is because I'm analyzing the words and sending you the translation data through the chip implanted in your head."

......

"Wait, the chip in my head can do that? That's news to me! Honestly, that's pretty creepy."

"It's not particularly relevant right now. Just be quiet and let me take care of this."

Alice brushes aside my objection and turns to the woman barking questions.

"Fair knight, I shall answer all your questions. Please quell your anger."

I completely fail at my attempt to hide my surprise as Alice answers fluently in the local tongue. For a moment, I'm convinced she's an innocent little girl.

According to the story Alice is giving the knight, I was once a relatively important individual in my home country. I commanded armies and fought to protect people, leading an intense life of traveling from battlefield to battlefield.

Unfortunately, that life of conflict caught up with me, and I picked up a particularly nasty, traumatic head injury in battle. So accompanied by my guardian Alice, I was on a journey of self-discovery to heal my mental and physical wounds.

Due to my post-traumatic stress disorder, I'm prone to fits of odd behavior and outbursts. This means I can't function in polite company. As Alice would have it, it's not something I'm doing intentionally—so she beseeches the knight to treat me with compassion and ignore small indiscretions along the way.

As for how we wound up where we are now, Alice explains that a large band of beasts attacked us as we emerged from the woodlands near the city. We managed to fight our way out of that situation, but in the process, we had to abandon the wagon carrying most of our belongings.

The knight listens to Alice tell what is honestly a ridiculous tale and nods solemnly without interrupting.

"I thought you might have been bandits or fugitives, not travelers. Forgive me for the harshness, but understand it's part of my job. Witnesses in the city saw something fall from the sky. We were on our way to investigate when we found you."

Ignoring the pitying looks from the knight, I grab Alice by the arm and drag her out of earshot.

"...What the hell, Alice? Why are you making me out to be some sort of head case? What did I ever do to you? Do you have a death wish?"

"I based it on the data Lilith provided me. Look, let's be honest, Six; you're a meathead. There's no way you can stick to a story over the long haul. At least with this story, we can get away with your ignorance of local customs and lack of common sense. Any odd behavior on your part can be explained away as mental illness, and people will just treat you with pity."

Alice explains her reasoning without so much as a flicker of expression.

"Also consider the fact that you're black haired and brown eyed. It's a stretch to pretend we're siblings. So we'll say you saved me from a pedophile. When you were saving me, you suffered another head injury. Your brain was already scrambled, but the injury made things much worse. Blaming myself for your condition, I resolved to accompany you as your innocent and brave young guardian. Got it?"

"Got what exactly? Just what sort of monster was this pedophile?

And why do you keep insulting me in your explanation? So I'm crazy, and you're the brave young girl?"

The whole story pisses me off…but I can't think of a better one. I hate to admit it, but Alice makes a good point.

No, not about there being something wrong with my head. It *is* a lot more convenient if everyone thinks I have issues with my memory.

The knight regards our whispered conversation with a touch of suspicion but turns away.

"…Very well, I understand your situation. Ordinarily, I'd find it hard to believe you came through the Darkwood, but having seen that… Well, the only thing left is to welcome you to our kingdom… Of course, that's if you want to stay once you learn the situation."

I couldn't shake a bad feeling at her faint smile as she gestured toward the dead monsters with her chin.

4

On the road toward the fortress city, the armored woman gives us the rundown.

"It came without warning. The demon nation that neighbors our kingdom of Grace declared war upon us without provocation."

The other members of the search party were off investigating the object that fell out of the sky—which was probably me and Alice. Once deployed, a heavy-duty parachute is a bit of a hassle to lug around. Which is why Alice and I had decided to leave it at the landing zone. I try to push any concerns about it being connected to our appearance to the back of my mind as I turn my attention back to our guide.

"Well, that got dark really quickly. So what exactly are they after? Resources? Food?"

The armored woman shakes her head no in response to my question.

"They're after land. I don't know what it's like where you're from, but around here, there's a limited amount of habitable land. There's a giant monster called the Sand King that's turning their country's land into desert. But at the same time, they're hemmed in by the Darkwood. Which is likely why they've decided to focus on our kingdom."

Sand King, monsters, evil forests—I'm not hearing a lot of encouraging keywords here. Is this planet really worth invading? At the very least, it seems more than the locals can handle.

"The demons are probably aiming to conquer our kingdom, take over our lands, enslave the population, then use the slaves to settle the Darkwood. However, there's an ancient prophecy that's been passed down for generations in our kingdom."

"Prophecy...?"

In spite of all the dangers, I feel a giddiness welling up in my heart.

"That's right, a prophecy. When mankind faces the wrath of the Demon Lord, the gods will anoint a champion with a mark on his hand. After facing many travails, the Chosen One will defeat the Demon Lord..."

I remove the power armor gauntlet and show off the top of my hand.

"Well then, it would seem that I am your Chosen One."

"That's a mosquito bite."

Alice lets out a soft snort of exasperation, but my expectant gaze was never meant for her. I look up at the armored woman hopefully.

"...Um...well...I hate to dash your hopes...but the mark has already appeared on one of the kingdom's princes."

Dammit...

My shoulders slump, and my eyes droop. The spring in my step is gone as I trudge along the road. I suppose the armored woman noticed my disappointment; she speaks up, trying to change the subject.

"H-hey…so I don't think we've been properly introduced! My name is Snow. I command this kingdom's Royal Guard. What are your names?"

"Combat Agent Six."

"I am Alice Kisaragi, the high-spec pretty-girl android."

……

"You know…you should probably rethink the whole calling yourself 'high spec' and 'pretty girl' thing."

"At least I'm using a name. Have you been called Combat Agent Six for so long that you've forgotten your actual name?"

Snow tilts her head after our introductions, repeating our names several times to herself as if trying to sound out the words.

"Com-ba-day-jent Sicks…? Ah-liss Key-sarah-ghee…? And what is an android exactly?"

It appears that my full code name is actually kind of hard to pronounce in the local language.

"You can just call me Six."

"You may simply refer to me as Alice. That will suffice."

"Very well. So do you understand the situation our kingdom is in? We have no issue welcoming you as guests if you're willing to put up with the war. If you're short on travel funds, I can at least find you some work. I mean, I'm sure our meeting isn't just a coincidence; I'd like to think there's some higher purpose at work."

Snow smiles at us in what I assume she thinks is a reassuring and gentle way. For someone in my line of work, it's not hard to see through that expression and sense there's more lurking beneath the surface. Alice, of course, chooses this moment to break into my thoughts in Japanese:

"<Hey, Six. This is a great opportunity. Ask her to find you a job. It'd be a good chance to evaluate the average combat skill of the natives. It's also a lot easier to sabotage the castle's defenses if we're living there.>"

"<You're pretty ruthless, even for an android. But it would be nice

to have a source of income while we conduct our survey. And it looks like we can avoid the need for identification if Snow's our way into the country.>"

Snow looks at us suspiciously as we converse in what is, to her, a foreign language.

"My apologies. This man is a bit…dim, so I was explaining the situation to him in our native language. Please don't worry about his combat abilities, though. What he lacks in brains he more than makes up in brawn."

"Could you stop sneaking in insults at every opening? …Oh, whatever. As Alice says, I'd be happy to work for you as a mercenary or such. Just tell us what you need."

In response, Snow flashes that shady smile of hers. "Of course! We'd be happy to have you. I'm looking forward to seeing what you're capable of…heh…heh-heh-heh."

"Open the gates! It's Snow, Princess Tillis's personal knight and captain of the Royal Guard. I've brought a pair of travelers we encountered on the road."

In response to Snow's command, the soldiers open the gate and salute.

"Welcome back, Captain! And travelers? That's a welcome surprise… Where did they come from, and how did they get here, I wonder…? Regardless, I'm sure you're all tired; please head to the castle and get some rest."

We enter through the gates and are greeted by an unexpected sight. Alice, riding behind Snow on the unicorn and cheerfully cleaning her shotgun, also pauses to stare at the same object.

The city itself is a collection of what appears to be pretty solid buildings of brick. Given the lack of power lines, it doesn't look like they're using electricity yet.

The people milling about the city are diverse, with a wide range of skin and hair tones. Judging by their clothes and the things they're carrying, it seems pretty safe to assume that this country is as technologically advanced as you'd expect from the castles and armored knights we've seen so far.

However...

"Hey, Snow...what is that exactly? It looks like a tank to me."

Sitting on the road just inside the gate is a rusted scrap heap that looks like it was once a battle tank of some sort.

"...Wait, you know what that artifact is? That's an ancient weapon that once saved this kingdom from a giant magical beast. It was back before the city's walls had been built. The weapon stood its ground here, stopping the magical beast in its tracks. They tried to save its technology and preserve it using magic, but as you can see, the years have taken their toll."

If this is an ancient weapon, that means there used to be a civilization advanced enough to build tanks. That probably means it was at least as advanced as Earth is now. All this talk about Demon Lord prophecies and armored knights got me into a fantasy world mood, but suddenly it seems like we're in a postapocalyptic sci-fi setting. This bears investigating... Hey, wait a minute!

"Magic...? Did you just say there's preservation magic cast on that thing?"

"Wh-what are you all excited about? I mean, I can't use it myself... Hey, don't look so disappointed! I can't help it! The use of magic is a rare skill, after all."

This planet has magic...... I suppose that makes sense if there's a Demon Lord and magical monsters. It makes perfect sense. Still...

I raise my hands to the sky and yell out.

*   *   *

"EXPLOOOSION!"

......

"You did mention his…strange outbursts… Is this one of them?"

"Exactly right. He engages in odd behavior like this from time to time, but when he does, it's best to simply leave him be."

Snow and Alice whisper behind me as I stand there with my arms held high.

5

"Welcome back, Snow. Thank you for undertaking the mission… Perhaps you could introduce me to your companions?"

Once inside the castle, we're taken to the largest room at the very top of the building and introduced to a blond-haired, blue-eyed young woman. I get the sense she's the calm, quiet sort.

"Of course. I encountered these two while carrying out my mission, Your Highness. They say they are foreigners who come from beyond the Darkwood. I was not able to determine the truth of their claims, but when I found them, they had slain a pack of Deadly Heggs. At the very least, they are skilled enough to navigate the forest."

Hearing Snow's report, the young woman covered her expression of surprise and mouthed *Oh my…*

"Lower your heads. The lady before you is Her Highness, Princess Cristoseles Tillis Grace, princess of the realm and your new employer."

"That name's a mouthful."

"Y-you insolent cur!"

Snow glares as I blurt out my opinion, while the young woman in front of me lets out a soft chuckle.

"I see you're one who readily speaks his mind. Clearly, you're not from any of the neighboring kingdoms... I doubt anyone who knows of my reputation would behave this way in my presence."

The young woman chuckles in amusement, letting the implications of her statement remain a mystery.

"How should I address you? Princess Grace? Or should I refer to you as Princess Cristoseles?"

"Please call me Tillis. There is no need for formalities or titles. I ask that you act as naturally as possible."

"...L-Lady Tillis, surely that is going a little too far...?"

Snow seems to have more to say, but Tillis is breezily unconcerned. The Supreme Leaders at our corporation are pretty quick to comment about my attitude, but it appears this princess doesn't need constant reminders of her status.

Snow whispers into Tillis's ear. A moment later, the princess nods and turns back to Alice and me.

"...Sir Six and Lady Alice, is it? I'm told that you commanded armies in your homeland, Sir Six?"

"I sure did. I led countless Combat Agents in vicious battles against all sorts of enemies from around the world."

Snow shoots us a skeptical gaze typically reserved for scam artists, while Tillis chuckles in her artful way.

Eesh. For once, I'm telling the truth.

"Currently, our war with the demons has left us with a shortage of qualified soldiers. Given your abilities, we would appreciate it if you could lend your strength to us, if even for a short while."

Tillis clasps her hands together as if in prayer, then gazes up at me.

"W-well...I can't very well refuse the request of a princess. D-don't think I'm accepting just because you're easy on the eyes..."

"Six, stop being a creep. You're just going to complicate things."

Hearing my response, Tillis lets out a soft sigh of relief and smiles at me.

*   *   *

"Honestly…I know you're a foreigner, but there *are* limits! Her Highness is kind enough to ignore your indiscretions, but don't think the other nobles are so tolerant. I don't mind you losing your head, but you're likely to take me down with you!"

After our interview with our new employer, Snow takes us to the next part of the hiring process. Even though Tillis has given us her blessing, they still need to interview us, if only as a formality. It looks like bureaucracy's strict adherence to protocol is a universal concept.

"Please forgive him, Lady Snow. Six is certainly a fool without a shred of common sense, but when it comes to battle, he's a professional. He'll prove his worth soon enough. His accomplishments will be a credit to you, I'm sure."

"Well…"

Snow's string of complaints cuts off as Alice highlights our potential.

"Oh! I get it now. Since you're in the middle of a war, I'm sure you want every able-bodied fighter. Seeing the corpses of those whatchamacallit monsters, you thought we'd make quite the catch. I see, I see… You made a big deal out of your generosity in giving us work when what you *really* wanted was to get your hands on my sexy body!"

"We're not *that* desperate! And your body? Don't make me laugh! I'll be honest with you. My three greatest loves are money, glory, and high-quality swords!"

I'm caught a bit off guard as Snow drops all pretense and essentially declares herself a megalomaniac.

"Look, Six. There's something about you that makes me think we have something in common. Normally, they wouldn't just hire a foreigner. I've got some authority, too. If anyone gives you crap for being a newcomer, I can use my position as captain of the Royal Guard to crush them. We're on the same side, you and me. I'll try to give you some backup from here on out. I'm counting on you!"

Snow has just admitted to being a social climber and accused me of being the same thing, and I'm still reeling from the sudden revelation when Alice suddenly pipes up.

"...Say? Snow, what might *that* be?"

As we pass the castle courtyard, we come across another sight that, like the tank, looks completely out of place in a stonework castle. There's a box-shaped contraption around three meters to a side sitting there in the courtyard. Alice stares at it, examining it in detail.

"Compared to the tank, this appears to be in much better condition. Seems to run on solar power. What is this for?"

We stop to examine the object, and Snow lets out a sigh at our curiosity.

"This is another of our kingdom's artifacts. It's a legendary relic that makes rain. Every year, during the dry season, one of the members of the royal family offers a prayer to the device, and it brings rain to the kingdom. As you might have noticed, it's currently not operating. It's safeguarded here, protected by layers of preservation magic, but someday it, too, will be lost to the sands of time..."

Snow trails off at the last comment. From her expression, it's clear she's equating the fate of the device with the fate of the kingdom.

"If it's not too far gone, I might be able to fix it. May I open it up?"

"T-truly? Even if you can't fix it, I'll take full responsibility. But please, give it a try!"

In response to Snow's hopeful expression, Alice produces a toolbox seemingly out of nowhere and starts repair work on the device.

"Where the heck did that come from?"

"I carry the tools I need to maintain my own body. It's like how you take care of your health," Alice responds airily.

She can repair herself, hmm? She might be more useful than I thought.

Snow shifts impatiently as she watches Alice work.

"Well…? Can you fix it?"

"Yes, ma'am, it looks repairable. Some of the wires are worn. It should just be a matter of replacing them and restarting the device."

Snow's face lights up as Alice explains the repair process.

"Good work! All right, let me go fetch someone. Heh…heh-heh-heh…… Hey, Alice, Six, we'll be splitting credit evenly, right? Right??"

Snow breaks out into a bewildering fit of giggles as she dashes off in a random direction.

"…Split the credit? But she didn't do anything."

"You haven't done anything, either, you know… There, that should do it."

Alice pushes what appears to be the on switch, and a mechanical voice speaks up.

"Commencing reinitialization process. You will be prompted to set a new password once reinitialization is completed."

Password?

Ah, so that must be what Snow was talking about when she mentioned saying a prayer to the device.

"Reinitialization process complete. Please set a password."

The device announces that it's ready to accept a new password.

"Dick festival."

"Password set."

"…What the hell are you doing?" Alice blurts out, momentarily pausing as she puts away her tool kit.

I wag my finger and tut. Alice is an android; she should have seen this coming.

"Think about what Snow said. Every year when they need rain, a member of the royal family says a prayer. That means Tillis. Imagine that beautiful, well-mannered princess saying that obscenity. In public, to boot! Each time Tillis is forced to embarrass herself to the masses, I'll also get some Evil Points."

"Clearly you didn't think this through. Snow said *a* royal. That means it doesn't have to be Tillis. Tillis is a princess. That means there's an actual king. So you've made it so that every year a middle-aged guy is going to say that idiotic password in front of a huge crowd of people."

......

"Crap. When you put it that way, I'm starting to think this wasn't such a great idea."

"Well, it's too late now. Six, get them to send us some plastic explosives. We can blow up the machine and erase the evidence. Then we tell Snow, 'We couldn't fix the machine. I thought it was fixed, but it blew up.'"

That's a wonderful idea. I can see why Alice is classified as a high-spec android.

"Excellent, let's go with that!"

"And what, pray tell, is so excellent?"

A familiar-sounding voice interrupts me from behind.

Tillis is standing behind us with a forced smile and a fan clutched in a death grip. An uncomfortably silent Snow stands next to her, sweating bullets and trembling.

The chip in my head chooses that moment to chime in with a familiar notice.

<Evil Points acquired.>

6

"Stop squirming! You're in the royal presence!"

"Oh, come on! You said you'd take all the responsibility for any-thing that went wrong! Liar! Sadist! If you couldn't handle one little screwup, you shouldn't have asked us to fix the damn thing in the first place!"

After Snow and the other soldiers take us into custody, we're dragged into what appears to be the audience chamber in front of the king himself.

"S-silence! I told you to fix it...not do...*that*!"

Snow shoves me, hoping to shut me up. Our arms bound, Alice and I are thrown onto the carpet in front of a dais and forced to kneel. The gentle-looking man sitting on the throne in front of us gazes down at us with a look of curiosity.

"...And these are?"

"Your Majesty, these were travelers Snow recruited to serve as officers in our military. They came upon the artifact in the courtyard and claimed they could repair it...and ended up doing just that."

A woman who appears to be a secretary or assistant describes our misdeeds, prompting the man's brows to rise in surprise. At this point, I'm pretty sure this man is the king himself, after all...

"Hey, Alice, I don't think I've ever seen someone who looks so... kingly. Look at that beard! He'd make Santa Claus jealous! Do you think he'll let me touch it?"

"Six, that is the ruler of this country. If you must spout mindless drivel, can you at least whisper? You're practically shouting."

Ignoring our exchange, the secretary continues her explanation.

"Unfortunately, in the process of repairing the artifact...they changed the prayer into...well, an obscene phrase."

"An obscene phrase? And what phrase would that be?"

The secretary is an attractive woman with a calm, collected demeanor.

What is it with this planet anyway? All the women I've met so far are superhot. Now that I think about it, the knights who were accompanying Snow were all pretty easy on the eyes, too...

"Um...it's...dick festival..."

"Ah...forgive me for making you say that aloud."

I can't help but feel another pang of regret as the gravity of the situation sinks in.

But wait a second...all those women were riding unicorns...

"We cannot understand why anyone would do such a foolish thing. You there, do you dispute anything the secretary has said so far?"

...If I'm remembering my mythology right, unicorns only accept the company of virgin maidens. Say, does that mean...?

"You! Answer His Majesty's question!" Snow's face breaks into my thoughts.

"Whoa! Too close! I see what you're trying to do! Taking advantage of my reverie to steal a kiss!"

"What...?!? What are you talking about?! Do you realize where you are?!"

The king breaks in with a polite cough and repeats his line of questioning. "You, is it true that you changed the prayer into an obscene phrase?"

I recall my current situation with a start and glare at Snow.

"It's true, but *she* said she'd take all responsibility."

"Y-you son of a... He's lying, Your Majesty! I only ordered him to fix the device..."

The king appears at a momentary loss for words as I try to press responsibility onto Snow...

"We appreciate the fact that you repaired the artifact. For that, we will forgive your indiscretion and provide you with a reward. You may take that reward and make your way—"

"Father, a moment please." Tillis, wearing a calm smile that just manages to cover whatever emotions were roiling beneath the surface, interrupts the king and enters the audience chamber. "I would like to take those individuals into my service. They are, after all, capable of wiping out a group of Deadly Heggs and repairing artifacts. It would be a pity to lose their services over such a trifling matter."

"V-very well. If that is your judgment, I will support your decision, Tillis."

The king nods frantically in agreement to Tillis's suggestion. Alice and I have an aside in Japanese.

"<Six, it looks like the true center of power in this country is that princess. The king strikes me as more of a doting, doormat father.>"

"<Ah, so we should cozy up to Tillis. Brownnosing is one of my best skills, leave it to me.>"

"<You are something else...>"

Snow waves her hand grandly toward us as she processes what Tillis had just said.

"Your Highness! We should banish this man! Think of what he's done to our artifact! He might very well be a spy planted to bring ruin to our kingdom! Please rethink your decision!"

"Oh? Spies, huh...? What does that make the person who talked up our potential and got us hired?"

Snow explodes with rage. "You dare accuse me of treason? No one is more loyal to the princess or this kingdom than I!"

"Ah, looks like I struck a nerve... People get really defensive when the accusations against them are true. The truth hurts, doesn't it?"

Snow responds to my taunting by drawing her sword and lunging at me. "You bastard! Give me one good reason not to use my beloved Flame Zapper to cleave your head from your shoulders!"

"Ah, resorting to violence against a helpless opponent just because you're losing an argument. I guess chivalry really is dead! You sure you wanna kill someone your boss is interested in hiring? There's something else you ought to be doing, isn't there?"

Snow, cheeks flushed with rage and ready to take my head off with a single swipe of her blade, freezes in her tracks.

"...Something else I ought to be doing?"

Alice explains to the bemused Snow. "Well, you told Six and me, and I quote: 'I'll take full responsibility.' Our part has been swept under the rug, but that doesn't change your role in all this."

Snow begins to tremble uncontrollably, sword slipping from her hand and clanging against the floor. Cringing, she turns her gaze toward Tillis. The glimmer of hope in her eyes is quickly extinguished as the kingdom's true ruler directs a gentle smile toward the knight—

I stretch as I leave the interview room, and Alice comes up to me, speaking in Japanese.

"<Hey. How did your interview go? Since they're already planning to hire us, I'm assuming they just asked some easy background questions.>"

"<Yep. They asked about Kisaragi, my Finisher, and even a couple questions about Heroes.>"

After the audience with the king, they had me write a résumé for a quick interview for appearance's sake. I'm just giving a rundown of the interview to Alice.

"<So I'm now a knight of the kingdom...not bad. If I can't be the Chosen One, I'll settle for being a knight.>"

"<Just don't forget you're a Kisaragi Combat Agent first and foremost. Our mission comes first.>"

"So that language you sometimes break into, is that your native tongue?"

*   *   *

A voice breaks into the Japanese conversation between Alice and me.

"You again?"

It was Snow, finally having changed out of her armor and revealing that the outfit was hiding one seriously nice body. The outfit, which I assume is some sort of knight uniform, is pretty heavy on blue tones. The color accentuates the whiteness of her slender legs that peek out from the skirt, and judging by her looks, Snow would give a supermodel a run for her money.

"What do you mean, 'You again?' I'd prefer not to be here, either."

She's weirdly hostile. I mean, I suppose I've given her a few reasons to hate me, but still.

"And…? What do you want? We were just on our way to the barracks." I'm pretty salty myself, and I'm not even trying to hide it.

Snow's brow twitches. "I've been assigned to take you to those very barracks…and tend to you while you're there."

"…Say what?"

The moment the question leaves my mouth, Snow straightens and snaps off a smart salute.

"I've been assigned to your unit, effective immediately. From here on out, I'll be serving as your executive officer."

…It appears Snow is now part of my unit. Wait, how did it come to this?

"…You're saying my first assignment is as a unit commander?"

Snow maintains her salute, but her expression turns to a look of annoyance.

"…W-were you even listening to Princess Tillis? We've lost most of our veteran commanders and knights in our war against the demons. That's why you see women serving as soldiers. It's also why so many knights and officers are barely older than children. We have a critical shortage of commanders. You have experience leading units in your home country, right? So starting today, you're being placed in charge of your own squadron. Even if the group is only at squadron level, this is still a leadership position."

Ah. I see this kingdom's higher-ups appreciate my talents, making me a squad commander so quickly.

"With that said…I consider you a figurehead. When it comes to actual combat, I'll issue the orders. Stay out of my way."

What the hell is this woman going on about?

"Hey! Don't let that whole knight-captain thing go to your head. I've got a pretty good record as a commander. Definitely better than your kingdom's losing streak to the demons."

"…I *do* appreciate that you repaired the artifact. But in the process, you made it abundantly clear that I can't trust you. I'm on to you now, so don't try anything funny."

Snow turns on her heel and starts walking without so much as a backward glance. Her body language makes it clear she's not planning on making friends, but Alice and I don't intend to just let her march off without getting in a barb or two of our own.

"Taking out your anger on us because you got demoted… Don't you have any shame? Some people!"

"Some people!"

"…I—I haven't been demoted! I'm…I'm here to make sure you two don't do anything suspicious. And since you're basically an amateur, I've been assigned to support you. You'd best understand where you stand."
Snow turns back toward us and gives a hurried string of excuses.

Her eyes are bugging out way too much for us to believe her. Alice and I turn to each other and shrug.

"…Pretty sure she's the only one who thinks she's being assigned to watch us…"

"Of course. After letting *that* happen to a national treasure like that artifact? I'm pretty sure a screwup that big would normally call for seppuku. Poor girl, deluding herself into thinking she's getting an important assignment."

"You…you bastards!"

7

"This will be your room. We've furnished it with the basics. Now, what shall we do about Alice…?"

After a brief argument, we've finally made our way to the barracks and been led to our rooms. Here, for whatever reason, Snow has decided she needed to complicate the discussion.

"What do you mean, 'What shall we do about Alice?' Did you have something special in mind for her?"

"…Well, ordinarily this barracks is off-limits to nonpersonnel." Snow looks a little nonplussed.

"Excuse me? You think you can exclude me *now*? I'm a member of Six's unit, dammit. Seriously, that's why you got demoted, dumbass."

Alice suddenly launches into a tirade. Her expression isn't much different from usual, but I get the impression she's miffed.

"Wh…what? A-Alice…wh-where did you learn to speak so disrespectfully?"

The sudden burst of venom from Alice, who by all appearances is a child, sends Snow reeling back, wide-eyed.

"I don't need any lectures about respect from *you*. Check yourself before you criticize anyone else, got it? Now go and ready a room for me, you cheapskate!"

"…Y-you…insolent little brat! Squadrons have five members. Each member has a specific role. Usually, there's three knights as front liners, with a mage and healer as the back line. Six and I would be knights in this case. Meaning we need at least one more front liner, a mage, and a healer… What can you do, Alice?"

Snow looks at Alice skeptically, but if Alice is troubled by it, she's not letting it show at all. She scowls as she presses her face up at Snow.

"What can I do? As a high-spec model, I can do anything. My specialties are planning, strategizing, and devising tactics, but I can also use nanomachines to provide medical attention to those in need. It's technology far beyond the comprehension of you troglodytes. So I guess you can tell that healer or whatever to hit the bricks. Their services are no longer required!"

Alice unilaterally declares healers to be superfluous extras, then stomps her way out of the room in a manner not befitting a presumably emotionless android.

"...Can she do that...?"

Snow mumbles her concern, momentarily looking less like a cynical knight and more like an insecure teenager.

Snow makes arrangements for Alice's room, then leads us to the exercise yard in front of the barracks. Snow mentions that there's currently a group of soldiers awaiting assignment, carrying out training exercises there.

"Eyes up! We will now begin the recruitment of two members for a brand-new squadron. If you think you're up to the task, step forward!"

In response to Snow's announcement, the soldiers stop sparring and gather around us.

"You haven't been here long enough to know what each soldier is like, so I'll be choosing our squad members. However, feel free to peruse their résumés if you'd like."

Snow shoves a pile of papers into my hands, then waits for the soldiers to assemble. If she actually wants our input, she's doing an amazing job of hiding it. Anyone can see that she's just putting on a show by waiting for everyone to gather before announcing her preset choices.

"Hey, Six, look at this."

Alice pauses filing through the résumés and holds a set up for me to look at.

"'God of War, Alexandrite Gravekneel.' Good pick—he sounds like a badass."

"No, not him. Just look at his age. That geezer is over eighty years old. I'm talking about these two."

With a title like God of War and the experience from surviving into his eighties, I'm pretty sure Alexandrite's got all the qualifications of a badass, but Alice is intent on the pair on the next page.

"'Artificial Humanoid Battle Chimera: Rose,' 'Grimm, Arch-bishop of Zenarith'...? These names sound like trouble to me. What's so great about them...? Hey! 'Mirei the Clumsy Ally-Killing Mage'! Let's go with her! I want a clumsy mage on the team!"

"There's no way that a clumsy mage is anything but a ticking time bomb. Besides, just look at the kill counts for the two candidates that I found. They're way higher than the others."

I go through the résumés again after Alice makes her point. Sure enough, those two have a lot more kills than the others.

Still...

"But if we're talking about kill count, Alexandrite has ten or twenty times their number. Might be better off going with him..."

"Forget about the old guy. We can't have a soldier that might keel over from a heart attack mid-mission. Besides, these two have more interesting titles. I have no idea what an Archbishop of Zenarith is, but a Battle Chimera sounds like a perfect fit for the corporation."

...That's true. The title does make her sound like some sort of mutant.

"I see you've all assembled. Now, I'll announce the choices for the squadron. First..."

Alice interrupts Snow in the middle of her announcement without so much as a *by your leave.*

"Hold up, Snow. These are the two we want."

Alice hands the chosen résumés to Snow.

"Uh…wait, not these two… Can we at least swap one out for Sir Alexandrite?"

"Do the two of you have a geezer fetish or something? Just call them forward already."

It's hard to shake the feeling that Alice has Snow firmly under her heel, and the knight mumbles complaints under her breath as she summons Alice's selections. A young girl steps in front of me, looking a little older than Alice, at maybe fourteen or fifteen years old.

"…Well, each résumé describes the soldier in question, so you can read up later. Rose, go ahead and introduce yourself," Snow orders.

"The name's Rose. Artificial Humanoid Battle Chimera Rose… You think you can handle me…?"

Covering one eye with her hand, Rose glares at us with a look of deliberate disinterest to rival Alice's.

A closer look reveals a lizard tail peeking out from the hem of her skirt and a little demon horn protruding from behind her silver bob. Each of her eyes is a different color, and the combination does in fact bring a Chimera to mind.

I mirror Rose's pose.

"Combat Agent Six. Cybernetic killing machine. I buried my past with my old name. Pleasure to meet you, Artificial Humanoid Battle Chimera…"

"I'm Alice Kisaragi. Don't worry, our corporation deals with so many cringeworthy nutjobs, we've got HR policies to help special snowflakes like you. We'll make good use of your abilities."

At our introduction, Rose freezes in place, covering her face with her palms. She falls into a trembling heap, evidently hoping that we might have mercy and forget about her weirdly haughty intro.

"Alice, you could have at least *tried* to play along. Look at her;

she's so mortified, she's shivering. You'll probably make her cry if you call her cringey again."

"Why would I play along with her dumb antics? ...You there, stop acting like that if you find it so embarrassing."

"Y-yes, ma'am... I'm Artificial Humanoid Chimera Rose. P-pleased to meet you."

Rose slinks toward us, her face beet red.

"Try to look past her oddities; she can't help that her creator raised her this way."

"My creator...that is, my grandpa, told me to do this when intro- ducing myself... *Sniff, sniff...* I didn't want to do it, but it was my grandpa's dying wish..."

Rose starts crying after Snow's explanation. This strikes me as a good time to look away for a bit, so I turn my attention to Rose's résumé. I note the basics: age, assignments, kill count, and special abilities...

"...Whoa, what's this? You can absorb the abilities of things you eat?"

"Huh? Y-yes, sir...as a Chimera, I'm pretty easily influenced by the things I eat... It can't be just a bite or two, but if I eat enough of a monster, I start manifesting its abilities. Lately, I haven't eaten much other than meat from one-horned ogres and fire-breathing lizards. That's where this little horn and tail come from..."

Alice and I exchange glances.

"<Alice, she's a mutant initiate.>"

"<We definitely need to secure this one.>"

"...Wh-what's going on? I can't understand a word you're saying... but it doesn't sound particularly pleasant... Um...say...you wouldn't have any unusual foods on you, would you? Something smells really tasty..."

Rose's initial panic at hearing Japanese is replaced by curiosity, her nose twitching in response to a scent. I haven't had time to eat a proper meal since we were teleported, so I started snacking on a ration bar on my way to the barracks. I take out the partially eaten ration bar and show it to Rose.

"Did you mean this? It's everyone's favorite, delicious, nutritious ration bar, Calorie-Z. You can have it if you agree to follow all my orders without exception."

"S-seriously? Oh...but it just smells too good to resist."

"Tsk... Six, you know you look like a pedophile trying to tempt a little girl with candy, right? ...Still, that is useful information for the future."

Rose's mismatched eyes follow the ration bar as I wave it from side to side.

Snow's attention remains on the gathered soldiers, looking for a specific face. When she finds her mark, Snow calls out, "Grimm, wake up and get over here!"

In response, a woman in a wheelchair wheels her way over to us. Seated barefoot, the slender woman looks to be about eighteen or nineteen years of age. She has sleepy brown eyes on a faintly pale face framed with beautiful straight brown hair. The first word I can think of to describe her is *frail*, and I can't help but wonder if she's actually fit for combat.

"I'm Combat Agent Six, your new commander."

"Staff officer and medic, Alice."

Grimm listens to our introductions with a bright, shining gaze.

"It's a pleasure to meet you! My name is Grimm. I have so many questions for you! But let's start with the most important one. Are you married, Commander? Got a girlfriend, maybe? I'm not currently seeing anyone, by the way. Can you believe it? A fine woman like me, still single."

"In spite of my rugged good looks and charming personality, I'm still single, as well."

"This is a military squadron, not a dating service! Fraternization within the same unit is strictly prohibited! Focus, Grimm!"

Snow works herself into a righteous frenzy, but Grimm appears unfazed by it. If anything, Grimm shifts from side to side in her chair, almost giddy.

...I suppose I should pick something combat-related to talk about. What do I ask first? *Who or what the hell is Zenarith? Do you really need to be heading out to battlefields when you're in a wheelchair?* There's a whole lot of questions that keep bubbling up, but the most important question comes first.

"Grimm, are you a magic user? If you are, could you tell me a bit about your abilities? I'm a novice when it comes to magic."

Of *course* I'm going to ask about magic first. Especially since Grimm's résumé lists something as creepy as curses in her Special Abilities section.

"Well, if you want to go into specifics, I'm not a magic *user*... Instead, as an archbishop, I serve as a conduit for the great Lord Zenarith. He uses me to manifest his blessings upon this world."

A conduit for blessings? What the hell does that even mean?

"Uh...so just who or what is this great Lord Zenarith?"

"Lord Zenarith is the God of Undeath and Disaster. I, Grimm, am a humble servant and worshipper of the great Lord Zenarith."

God of Undeath and Disaster...?

"...So...a dark god?"

"Blasphemy! Watch what you say, or Lord Zenarith might smite you!"

Ordinarily, I'd ask that she demonstrate, but the whole "curse" thing makes me a little nervous. I suppose I'll see it in action soon enough on the battlefield.

... I don't quite know what's gotten into Grimm, but suddenly she shifts in her wheelchair, hugging her knees to her chest with a playful grin. Her long skirt lifts in response, and the hemline creeps up along her legs...

"...Tee-hee...hey, big boy. Are you interested in what's going on *down here*? If you repent for your sin of calling Lord Zenarith a dark god, we can initiate you...and then maybe I'll let you have a little pee*EEEEEK*!"

<Evil Points Acquired>

I lose patience with Grimm's teasing and hike up her skirt.

I'm forced to reassess my opinion of Grimm as her panties come into full view—she's wearing a black G-string. Far from being a frail, reserved beauty, it seems that Grimm has a rather naughty side.

"I had no intention of actually letting you look! You'd better take responsibility for this and put a ring on it! You'll be supporting me for the rest of my life! I'm never letting you go!"

I take that back about her being naughty... Any way you slice it, this chick is *crazy*.

"Easy there, Lady Butt-Floss. You're partly to blame for teasing Six like that."

"Don't call me Lady Butt-Floss! I only started wearing this underwear because *Gothmopolitan Magazine* said it would make it easy to get a boyfriend!"

The hell is *Gothmopolitan*? Some sort of dating magazine?

"If seeing panties was enough of a reason to marry a woman, I'd have my own harem by now! I'll show you my underwear later, and that'll make us even, Madame Butt-Floss?"

"Don't you dare equate your dirty boxers with a maiden's panties! And you'd better stop using that nickname, too!"

Snow lets out a deep sigh as she watches our exchange.

"*Sigh*...of *course* he'd choose the biggest potential headaches... Still, at least they're useful in combat."

I take another look through the résumés at Snow's remarks. It's not just the old man or bumbling mage or these two weirdos. Every single candidate has one problem or another. So this must mean...

"Well...anyway, I suppose we'll just have to do our best as the cream of the reject crop. Any chance of us becoming friends is pretty much dead, but I'll at least try to keep you alive."

Snow wears a sullen look, turning her back to us and waving her hand dismissively...

...Hey, who the hell is *she* to call *us* rejects?

I mean, sure, we've got a thong bishop in a wheelchair, a perpetually hungry monster girl, along with a Combat Agent and android from an evil organization, but...

...Okay, yeah, we're definitely a bunch of social rejects.

...Hey, wait a second.

"That means they thought you were a reject and sent you to join us, doesn't it? Makes sense given your personality..."

Snow twitches and shoots us a look of pure venom.

"Wh-what are you going on about...?! Of course that's not the case! I'm here to watch over you!"

"Hey, Six, not only did she get demoted, but Tillis decided to use the opportunity to get rid of her. Ha! Re-ject! Re-ject!"

"Ha-ha! R-re-ject!"

"Whoo-hoo! Serves you right!!"

Drawn in by Alice, even Rose and Grimm join into the taunts.

Snow clenches her jaw, squeezing her knuckles tightly enough that the color drains from them entirely.

"S-say what you will! You just need to listen to my orders! Under my command, we'll produce results and I can get myself promoted out of this mess!"

Snow glares at us with a mixture of hurt and determination, likely due to her shattered pride as an elite soldier.

"Did you hear that, Six? She just admitted this unit is a mess! After all that talk about being assigned to us as a guardian."

"Hey, you're right. She finally admitted that she got demoted... which reminds me, why do we need to listen to Captain Demotion again? I've commanded units myself."

The taunting from Alice and me has Captain Demotion at the end of her rope, and her brows rise in anger.

"Don't call me Captain Demotion! You've never fought in this country before, so that's why you listen to *me*. Just what the hell is up with your armor anyway?! There's something...*off* about it. It's black and evil looking...like something a low-ranking demon would wear, not a knight!"

"Watch it! My armor's got nothing to do with it. I'll admit the power armor looks a bit prickly, but I don't have to put up with remarks like that from *you*!"

The power armor I'm wearing is an older model and heavy as hell, but it's been my constant companion for years and saved my ass more times than I can count.

"I've had enough of you! Just the fact that our commander is some shady-eyed, scar-faced bastard from parts unknown... prone to strange antics, to boot...that's enough of a stain on our reputation!"

"Wha—?! You little..."

Oh, so that's how it's going to be, huh? I start going easy on her, and she decides it's an invitation to walk all over me.

"What's more, you look like an ignorant bumpkin! What kind of schooling did you even receive? I have a degree from the kingdom's top university!"

"...Grrr."

I didn't go to college. Hell, I was so busy with my job as a Combat Agent that I never even finished high school!

"Do you get it now? Do you see why you should just shut up and listen to me? Swear you'll listen to my orders, and I'll at least make sure you're not embarrassed on the battlefield!"

Oh, this little— ...I'll show her...!

"What's with that look? Going to resort to violence now?! Fine! Ignore the fact that I'm a woman and give it your best shot! Assuming you have the balls! Well?! Come on now!"

You...!

"You biiiiiiitch!!"

Snow drops into a fighting stance at my yell. I approach the knight, poised and ready for an all-out brawl...and grab hold of her breasts. Yes, Snow's ample bosom that swells out from the front of her uniform. The whole room goes silent, the rest of the squad just gaping. I don't think I'll ever forgive the sheer look of incredulity that Snow wore as she stood there frozen in a fighting pose.

<Evil Points Acquired>

8

"Help! Someone help! This chick is crazy!"

"Who are you calling crazy?! If anyone's messed up in the head, it's *you*!"

This is a new experience for me. I've never had a woman chase me around like this before.

"Calm down! I told you I was sorry! I'll apologize again if you want! Just put down that sword!"

"It's way too late for apologies! I should've sliced you in half the moment I saw you!"

Okay, so when I say "chase me around," in this case, I mean a wild-haired woman is chasing me around with a drawn sword and murder in her eyes.

"Drawing your sword in response to groping *definitely* makes you the crazy one!"

"A sane person doesn't just grab a woman's breasts without any context or warning, you lunatic!"

So…accidentally groping a woman's breasts is a pretty common trope in manga. So, too, is getting chased around by an angry woman in response to an accidental grope. But…

"Can't you at least blush while you're chasing me? Or swing something less lethal?! There's nothing pleasant about being chased by a raging berserker! Not even a little bit!!"

"Of course it's unpleasant! I'm trying to kill you!"

"Someone, heeeeelp!"

What the hell? This is *not* the clichéd rom-com development I thought it would be.

I continue running through the halls of a castle, turning a corner and hoping against hope for some deliverance.

Wait…is that?

"Tillis! Just the person I wanted to see!"

I catch sight of Tillis walking in our direction.

"Why, Sir Six, what a pleasant surprise. I was just about to… Wh-what are you two doing? Is something the matter?"

"Can we talk about that later? I really could use your help right now."

"Your Highness, I'll be lopping off this bastard's head. Please look away."

Snow's eyes glint with murderous intent as I tremble in fear behind Tillis. A woman of Snow's age shouldn't be mentioning lopping off heads so casually.

"I…I'm not quite sure what transpired between the two of you, but the use of deadly force within the castle will end with you shackled in the dungeon, Snow! Calm yourself, please!"

Curling her lips in a disappointed scowl, Snow lets out a frustrated grunt and sheathes her sword.

"…You better watch your back on tomorrow's mission."

Snow makes clear her intent to murder me tomorrow and storms off toward the barracks. She definitely missed her calling. Rather than being a knight for some Royal Guard, she'd fit in way better at the Kisaragi Corporation.

"Thanks, Tillis… I didn't expect her to take getting groped *that* personally."

"Sir Six…wh-what possessed you to do such a thing? Snow has no sense of humor. Unlike the noble-born members of the Royal Guard, she could never afford one. She rose from a life of poverty in the slums to her position as captain of the Royal Guard by way of honest effort. That's why she seems so serious…"

Oh…I thought she was of noble birth, given her pride and arrogance…

"By the way, didn't you mention you wanted to talk to me about something?"

"Yes. It was on the subject of a room for Alice."

"Well, I guess this is fine. Thinking logistically, it's better that we share a room anyway. Just don't get any funny ideas because I'm pretty. I'm not equipped with any reproductive functions, so we couldn't do anything even if we wanted to."

"Don't be ridiculous! I wouldn't lust after an android! How the hell did we get into this situation anyway?"

Due to our sudden hiring, they could only ready a single room for me and Alice to share. It made sense from the castle's point of view; after all, we'd been traveling together for some time. Something I hadn't thought about when coming up with our backstory.

"If you do get any urges, I'll gladly leave you to your own devices for a bit. I'll also make sure to knock and wait a few moments before opening the door."

"Don't put yourself out! I'm not some horny monkey!"

I glance around the room we've been given. Thankfully, they've prepared two beds for us. The furniture is rounded out by a simple table with chairs and a single chest of drawers. Aside from that...

"Check that out, Alice; there's running water. And that's not an oil lamp, is it? There's no place to pour the fuel. There's also something that looks like a cordless TV hanging on the wall. I thought we could just bring some technology over and be worshipped as gods by the primitive locals, but I guess we'll have to scratch that plan."

"Best not to underestimate this world's technology level. That lamp and sort-of TV are probably powered by magic. Add the fact that they can create artificial Chimeras... And then those artifacts. The list of things to investigate is getting longer by the day."

I spread out the items we've brought from Japan and let out a sigh of relief. At least it looks like we'll be able to sustain ourselves here for the time being. I strip off my power armor and flop down on the bed.

"Say, Six. Snow made it clear that we'll have a combat mission tomorrow, but don't forget our main objective. We can support this kingdom so long as it helps us achieve our goals, but if things start to look bad, we should cut our losses and leave. Hiring us as knights, then lumping us in with the social rejects... I don't know who came up with that, but it's a decent bit of petty villainy. We shouldn't underestimate them."

Alice begins polishing the shotgun I bought her. She seems oddly fond of it now, making a habit of polishing it every chance she gets.

"I know, I know. But think about our audience with the king. They took my knife but left my handgun. That means guns aren't common knowledge here. They called the busted tank an artifact... If they're still mostly using swords and bows, then we have plenty of options. We've found ourselves some work and a place to live, so why don't we go make a name for ourselves and establish a proper base of operations...?"

CHAPTER 2

Ravage Our Rivals

1

The next morning.

"How dishonorable. The enemy only assigns the weakest demon to staff their supply caravans. There's no glory in slaughtering errand boys."

Grace Kingdom's knights assemble in the exercise yard to be briefed, while we find ourselves on the periphery, left to fend for ourselves. Evidently, the plan today will be for the army proper to take the fight to demons and monsters gathering on the outskirts of the kingdom. It's an opportunity for honor, glory, and riches…and the kingdom's commanding general is giving quite the speech in front of the assembled soldiers.

As for us? Well, we've been told to "use our discretion," which is a polite way of telling us to get lost. We're now in the process of debating our own plan of attack.

"Boss, if it's at all possible, I'd prefer to fight strong enemies. Grandpa made me promise on his deathbed that I'd devour the flesh of every monster in the world and become the greatest Chimera."

Ah, I guess she really loved her grandpa. When she phrases it like that, complete with a deathbed promise, I feel the faintest twinge of guilt in the shriveled remains of my conscience.

"Well, I'll do what I can to help you fulfill that promise. How about getting meat from the monsters taken down by other units?"

"If monster meat isn't eaten fresh, it won't be as tasty, so…"

…Never mind. That twinge must've been heartburn. Damn glutton.

"Rose is right! Enemy units with a lot of strong opponents will have important commanders. We can assault that unit and take the commander's head. It'll be easy. I'll take on the strong enemies, and we can wipe out the grunts using Grimm's curses. Rose, you'll come with me!"

My biggest headache right now is this glory hound. Her ambition's blinded her to anything but her next victory. So far, Snow is refusing to even consider attacking the enemy supply lines. None of my attempts to reason with her have worked. In her pettiness, Snow is still holding the whole groping thing against me.

Evidently feeling we had wasted enough time, Alice injects herself into the conversation.

"Just listen, all right? You seem to be under the impression that attacking the enemy supply's convoy won't win you enough glory, but that's where you're wrong. First, you lot have done nothing but attack the enemy head-on. That means the enemy doesn't expect you to do anything else. They won't have any substantial defense around their supply lines. And what do you think happens to the enemy units fighting at the front when they hear their supplies have been wiped out? It'll throw them into a panic."

"…Mmph."

Snow knits her brows together as she mulls over Alice's explanation.

"Second, losing your supply train in war is disastrous. A win on the battlefield is pointless if your soldiers starve. If we get rid of their supplies, the enemy goes home even if our knights lose in battle. A single squadron changes the course of the war. Is that enough glory for you?"

"Hrm...I suppose."

Snow listens to Alice's explanation without argument. I can't help but be irritated by the change in her attitude.

"Finally, consider this. If we take out their supplies once, the enemy will be wary of additional attacks. That means they'll start defending their supply lines. This, in turn, means fewer soldiers on the front. And that happens even if we never attack their supplies again."

Alice is right, of course. Even if it's not a large portion of the enemy, they'll be forced to keep some of their armies back to defend their supplies, reducing their numbers on the front.

Which I'm pretty sure is one of the points I made earlier.

"...Well? Attacking the enemy supply lines is a pretty basic tactic, but you understand how it can have long-term effects, right? I get how important chivalry is to you, but this is war."

"...I understand what you're saying, Alice. But I'm not sure it'll be recognized as a great achievement... My demotion means a pay cut... At this rate, I won't be able to pay back the loans I had to take out for my beloved sword collection... If I miss a payment for my burning blade Flame Zapper, it'll get repossessed..."

Snow's eyes fill with tears as she hugs her sword to her chest.

Beloved sword collection? I guess we can add "sword maniac" to Snow's weirdo checklist.

"Well, leave that to Six. Exaggerating the results to get maximum rewards is one of his specialties."

"...Now that you mention it, he does have that look about him."

"You two really want to get smacked, don't you?"

Still, it would seem we've gotten all the objections out of the way.

"Oh... We're attacking the supply convoy?" Rose lets out a wistful sigh while rubbing her stomach. "I spend most of my pay on buying monster meats I've never eaten before... The money doesn't last very long...and since it's close to payday, I haven't been able to eat that much... I actually haven't had anything to eat today, and if I can't get any monsters to eat, well..."

I let out a sigh as the tears start to well up in Rose's eyes.

I'm seriously starting to wonder how the hell she stays fed most of the time...

"In that case, you can do what you want with the supplies we find. There's a pretty good chance it'll be mostly food anyway."

"Supply line attacks it is, then!"

2

"...Huh. Looks like we've caught them with their pants down. They're not even carrying weapons... Hey, Grimm, would you mind waking up now?"

We sit behind some bushes along the highway a few miles from the enemy's rendezvous point. Oblivious to the danger, the enemy's supply convoy rumbles leisurely along the road in front of us. Snow takes a moment to jostle Grimm awake. The archbishop has been napping since our briefing session, sleeping through our entire journey to this site with Rose gently wheeling her along.

"Mm...wh-what? ...Waking me up in broad daylight...? What did I ever do to deserve this? Someone should put that sun out of its misery..."

Grimm mutters under her breath, her head lolling to the side as she's stirred out of her slumber.

"Grimm, it's time for battle. We need you to pay attention. Seems like it's mostly small fries, but stay alert." Snow steps away from Grimm, drawing her favorite sword and making her final preparations.

"If it's only small fries, you don't need Archbishop Grimm…mm…"

"Hey! Don't go back to sleep!"

"Goddamn, you guys are loud! Look, they spotted us!"

The exchange between Snow and Grimm was loud enough for the nearby enemies to hear. They look like the orcs you'd find in Japanese fantasy manga. The creatures, pig-snouted humanoids pulling at carts, begin fussing in response. It's actually kind of odd if you think about it. Orcs are supposed to be a creature from Earth folklore, after all. Why the hell do they exist on a different planet?

…I really don't have time to be thinking about this right now…

"Well, it can't be helped if we've been found out! Let's give 'em hell!!"

Jumping out of the bushes, I let out a loud whoop, drawing my knife and licking its blade as I charge toward the enemy. I also make sure to shout the appropriate battle cry as specified in our combat manuals.

"Mwa-ha-ha! It's the end of the road for you!"

A shotgun blast rings out beside me—

Alice has joined in the charge.

"Mwa-ha-ha! You resist, you die! If you wanna live, drop everything you've got and get lost!"

"Get lost!"

We yell out the standard lines from the manual. Approaching the lead cart, I land a kick squarely on its side. The cart tips over, spilling its contents on the road and blocking in the rest of the convoy. The orcs let out a squeal of panic, scattering as Alice and I continue our assault.

Rose, who had been following a step behind, sighs after dispatching a nearby orc.

"Um, Boss...could we maybe *not* say those lines? ...We're on a military mission, but it sort of feels like we're the bad guys..."

...Hey, don't look at me. That's the official warning in the Combat Agent manual.

"Oh! Boss! What should we do with the supply crates? There's a whole lot of them."

"Take what you need, then burn the rest of it! Let's show them what happens to those who try to resist Combat Agent Six! Mwa-ha-ha-ha-ha-ha-ha! Mwa-ha-ha-ha-ha-ha-ha-ha-ha!!"

"Got it, Boss!"

As I let out a maniacal laugh, the hair on the back of my neck stands up to warn me of the sudden approach of death.

"Gotcha!"

"Whoa!"

I roll forward, barely avoiding being skewered, and find Snow with her sword arm outstretched in a lunge.

"So, uhh...what the hell was that all about?"

"...Dammit."

"Did you just curse because you missed?!"

There's definitely something wrong with this woman. I need to make sure I don't show my back to her from here on out... Actually, it might make more sense to get rid of her now... I'll make it look like an accident.

"Wh-what are you looking at? You wanna go? Good, come at me! I'll show you that grabbing a maiden's bosom has deadly consequences! Taste my steel!"

...Just as Snow and I get ready to cross blades, a rush of heat surges past my back.

"Drown in a sea of hellfire...! Sleep for all eternity! Crimson Breath!"

Behind us, Rose spews an impressive jet of red-hot flame. I can't hide my surprise and turn to Alice, remarking in Japanese:

"<...Hey, Alice, seems like that's one of her Chimera abilities... and she's an artificial one. They can't have things like her lying around in droves...can they?>"

"<I wonder if she would make a source of green energy back on Earth... I'd really like to know how that flame throwing works... It's fascinating at the very least.>"

Several orcs are caught in the flames and begin letting out high-pitched squeals, rolling around on the ground among the charred supply crates. The pleasant aroma of grilled pork begins to waft around the battlefield.

"...Drool."

Triggered by the smell of roasted pork, Rose begins drooling, the saliva smearing the soot around her mouth... Hey, now!

"Rose! Wipe that drool off your chin! And the soot while you're at it... Also, remember we're still fighting. No eating the orcs until we're done!"

"!"

Rose hurriedly wipes at her mouth with her sleeve. The orcs around her have stopped their panicked flight, picking up whatever weapons are in arm's reach. They cautiously inch forward, hoping to find a moment to strike.

"Say, Rose... Do you need to recite those words and strike that awesome pose every time you want to breathe fire?"

"M-Miss Alice, please give me a break! I-I'm sure you already know the answer to that... I'm just d-doing what Grandpa said to do..."

Rose's eyes well up with tears at Alice's teasing. The orcs, hoping to take the opportunity to attack, attempt to rush Rose...

...Only for the red, flaming slashes of Snow's sword to cut them short. With practiced ease, Snow moves among the orcs, each swipe of her burning blade splitting an orc clean in half while engulfing them in flame. Like a whirling, bladed firestorm, Snow wades through the orcs, and within moments, the entire band is down.

I hate to admit it, but when she was wielding that blade, she looked every bit the knight she claimed she was.

"<Hey, Six, she might be a run-of-the-mill, flesh-and-blood human, but it looks like she's pretty capable after all. If all the knights in this world are like that, our invasion might hit a few snags.>"

"<Tillis did mention that Snow's an elite knight. She rose through the ranks with hard work alone… I sure hope that means she's not a typical knight.>"

Snow glares at us as she notices we're standing there whispering to each other.

"Hey, you two better stay focused; we're not finished yet… Wait, where's Grimm?"

So far, we've seen Rose's abilities, but I haven't seen Grimm do much of anything. I'm actually looking forward to seeing her curses in person. So where is she exactly…?

Grimm hasn't moved from the bushes. She's curled up in her wheelchair, fast asleep…

""…Seriously?""

"Oh, for the love of— Being nocturnal is no excuse to slack off in the middle of a battle! She needs to shape up a bit. I think it's time for a little tough love…," Snow mutters darkly as she stalks over toward Grimm. I turn in the opposite direction, briefly surveying the battlefield.

"Looks like the orcs are either fleeing or roasting. Just let her be; I'll wheel her home."

Just as I say this, we're engulfed by shadows as something blocks out the sun. Reflexively, I glance up at the sky…

"The hell is that?"

Soaring above me is another creature that only exists in mythology, at least on Earth.

A griffin. No longer just an image in a storybook, the enormous and not-so-mythical creature slowly descends toward us…

3

""'Griffin!'""

Heading straight for us is a giant creature with the head of an eagle, the body of a lion, and massive wings sprouting from its back. Snow and Rose freeze, their bodies tense. Their anxiety does nothing to dampen the excitement Alice and I feel at our first glimpse of a griffin.

"It looks just like the griffins in video games and movies! Isn't it a little odd that fictional creatures like orcs and griffins exist here? By the way, we do have a digital camera, right? Let's take some pictures!"

"Well, it might not actually be called a griffin; that's just what I chose as the translation. Still…how is that thing flying? It doesn't have the wingspan or chest muscles to carry a body that large. If we can get it back to Earth, we'll be able to laugh in the faces of everyone who's ever studied aerodynamics!"

I start snapping photos of the griffin like a tourist.

"Six, what are you doing?! Stop playing around and fight!" Snow warns me.

High up above, a voice responds, "Hold it; I'm not after you lot! I just want the supplies!"

The voice belongs to an individual sitting atop the griffin. Given the pair of horns sticking out of her head, she must be a demon of some sort. The combination of other details like the white hair, red eyes, and dark skin all click into place.

*　　*　　*

"—Dammit, I shouldn't have left this all to my underlings. I come to find out why the supply convoy is so late, and this is what I find…"

The griffin's passenger dismounts once the great creature is a few feet off the ground. I get an eyeful of beautiful dark skin, as the rider's red-trimmed outfit leaves little to the imagination.

"I suppose I have you lot to thank for this disaster? You there, the guy in weird armor…I'm guessing you're in charge of this bunch. Well? What do you have to say for yourself?"

I guess she's talking to me. I'm a little preoccupied at the moment, however…

"Hey! I'm talking to you! What the hell are you doing anyway?"

This is too precious an opportunity to waste. I snap a few more pics of her bountiful brown bust.

"Hey… Hey, Six! If you're going to take pictures, focus on the griffin. Why are you taking so many pictures of that woman?"

Sulking, I put the digital camera away.

"…Yes, we're the ones who attacked this supply convoy. And what about you…? Based on your attitude and outfit, I'm guessing you're one of the Demon Lord's generals."

The buxom demoness sighs in admiration at my reply.

"My, my, you can tell I'm a general with a single glance, mm? I must say, you've got a pretty good eye. You're correct. I'm one of the Demon Lord's Elite Four, Heine of the Flames. Given your eye for strength, you must be quite the warrior yourself."

The woman who declared herself to be Heine of the Flames narrows her eyes and puffs out her chest. I try to keep my staring as subtle as possible.

"Whew…! I guess you could say that. I mean, you do have a certain…aura that only high-ranking villains possess."

It's not a lie. The upper echelons of the corporation are filled with oddballs. Seems it's a universal law that outfits become skimpier as you climb the ranks. Yep, she's got that oddball aura.

"Not bad…for a human! …Heh-heh, I like you. It'd be a pity to have to kill you. If you'll leave those crates, I'll let you escape with your lives."

Heine looks like she's truly enjoying this exchange as a creepy smile spreads across her face.

"Have you lost your mind?! There isn't a human alive who'd obey a demon's orders!"

"That's right! Even against a high-ranking demon, humans will never give up! Also, these supplies are going to be my dinner!"

Snow and Rose refuse.

"…Hey, Alice? What do you think we should do? She seems at least mutant level. We're not equipped to handle her. Think we should just go home?"

"That's why you've been stuck as a lackey for so long. At least *try* to read the mood."

Snow and Rose are staring at us in surprise.

"Y-you bastard! You're thinking about running away?! Have you no shame? I should've killed you the moment I saw you!"

"B-boss! My dinner! I'm really hungry right now; please don't make me leave all this behind!"

Heine stares as my subordinates yell at me…then breaks out into laughter.

"Ha-ha-ha-ha-ha-ha! How cute! So direct and honest! Hey, why don't you come and join us? You seem pretty strong. Once we finish taking over the human lands, we'll make you one of the rulers. You can take all the women you'd like!"

"Deal."

"Wait, Six. At least think it over… And as for you. Heine, was it? We can't have you poaching our operatives. Sure, this one's pretty dull as far as his wits are concerned, but he's still one of our main Combat Agents."

Heine turns her gaze toward Alice for the first time.

"…Huh?"

The demon continues to stare at Alice, tilting her head to the left in puzzlement.

"...You... Are you actually human...? For some reason, you reek of golem..."

Heine's muttering is soft enough that neither Snow nor Rose catch the meaning of the words.

"So what's your answer? Will you join me?"

I really, *really* want to say yes, but the glares from all around me are making it impossible. Snow looks about ready to shove her entire blade down my throat.

"Sorry, I can't. My current bosses are already scary enough." I draw my knife and drop into a fighting stance.

"...I'm going to include that in my report."

"A-Alice...that's not funny."

Heine doesn't appear to be particularly upset by the answer, briefly closing her eyes and chuckling softly.

"Figures. You talk a good game when it comes to your villainy, but deep down, you still stick with the underdog. I've got an eye for that sort of thing. Mind telling me your name?"

Wow, that's actually news to me. I'm the sort who can't betray the underdog? This woman's certainly got a high opinion of me. My resolve wavers as I recall the armored woman barking orders at me during our first meeting and the faces of my superiors who damn near got me killed by teleporting me here. Maybe I should actually... Nah.

"I'm Combat Agent Six...but you, Heine of the Flames, pillar of the Demon Lord's Elite Four, can just call me Six."

After a moment's pause, Heine breaks out in a giant grin. "A-ah! Six, eh? I'm Heine of the Flames! One of Demon Lord's Elite Four!"

...I see.

"<Hey, Alice? This woman's just like our Supreme Leaders. The sort who gets upset if you don't use their nickname and title.>"

"<That also means you can manipulate her by calling her by that name. Those types just love sticking to the script.>"

Heine lets out a joyful yelp, holding out her hand. On her palm appears an orb of blue flame.

Wait, what? What the hell? Seriously, *what the hell?!*

Is that real magic?!

"What are you two whispering about? Here I come, Six! I'll try not to kill you, but I won't make any promises! Come taste the power of Heine of the Flames!"

4

Crossing my arms, I block a kick from the griffin's front legs. A moment later, I find myself rolling forward on the ground, Heine's fireballs landing where I had been just a moment before.

"Stay down, Six!"

"Whoooooooa!"

Trying to get up leaves me vulnerable, and the griffin swings again to take advantage of that moment.

"Boss! Behind you!"

"Yiiiiiiiiikes!"

Another of Heine's fireballs whizzes past me as I somehow avoid the griffin's blow.

"Hey! Why am I the only one fighting?! We outnumber them!"

I take a quick step backward, barely avoiding losing my eyebrows to a fireball. My bangs aren't quite so lucky, and I catch the unpleasant waft of burning hair.

"W-well…I brought a burning blade this time! It's not much use against an enemy that manipulates flame. Look, keep Heine and the griffin busy! I'll go burn the supply crates!"

"A-and I'll go grab the boxes we're taking home, so Snow doesn't burn them by accident!"

Talk about useless. I find myself seriously considering Heine's offer in light of how useless my companions are turning out to be.

"Ah-ha-ha-ha-ha-ha-ha! Amazing! Simply amazing! To think a mere human is holding up against the combined attacks from me and the griffin! Just who the hell are you?"

I plan my next few actions around positioning myself so I can use Snow to shield me from the strangely giddy Heine. Turning to avoid another fireball, I mentally map out the steps required. The griffin rears up on its hind legs to pounce when…

…There is a loud noise, and the griffin is flung backward. I look to the source of the sound…

Alice is on the ground, flattened by the recoil of a big-game shotgun shell.

"…Not that I'm not grateful, but just how weak are you anyway?"

"Shut up. I was waiting for the right moment as you jumped around like a headless chicken. You could at least fight more convincingly," Alice complains, inserting more shells into her shotgun and taking aim at the griffin.

The creature whines weakly, blood pouring from the gunshot wounds all across its upper body. The sight wipes Heine's smile off her face. She freezes for a moment in shock, then eyes the shotgun in Alice's hands.

"…A mere child, intimidating my griffin? Just what is that thing…? Just who the hell are you two?!"

Heine drops down to a low fighting stance, all playfulness gone from her features. There's a new tension in the air, and it's clear from her demeanor that Heine's reevaluated how much of a threat we pose.

The animal part of my brain screams to me that this woman is much more dangerous than the griffin. Alice appears to agree, shifting her aim to Heine and keeping watch over her movements.

"Looks like the odds have shifted in our favor. Your defeat will be my greatest achievement yet!"

Snow, having realized that Heine's pinned, wraps up her arson and joins us, blade raised. What is up with this woman? Now that the heavy lifting is done, here she comes to steal the show. I try to come up with the perfect cutting remark for the insufferable glory hound when suddenly...

I hear a dull thump behind me.

It's the sound of a really heavy object landing after a long fall. I turn around, and there it is. An enormous creature stands and spreads its wings, immediately darkening my surroundings as its wings block the sun.

"...Mutant class," Alice states without inflection.

The object that fell from the sky was an enormous, horned, humanoid demon at least three meters tall. The well-built monster has a pair of large bat-like wings growing from its back. It holds an enormous metal club in its hand and tilts its head downward to stare at us.

"<Let's use Snow as bait and get the hell out of here, Alice!>"

"<Right there with you!>"

"Hey, Six, enough of that strange language; it's hardly the place or time! You're clearly plotting something!"

Snow is whining behind us, but I don't have the time to respond. Heine and the griffin are bad enough. I'm not standing around waiting to face that thing, too!

"...Mm... Huh...?"

A voice chooses this moment to speak up in a sleepy tone. At the foot of the mutant that fell from the sky is a familiar-looking wheelchair. Grimm, who had somehow managed to sleep through all the other commotion, is awoken by the sound of the monster's impact.

She rubs the sleep from her eyes, glancing around in a daze. She turns her gaze upward, staring directly into its eyes.

"G-good morning…?"

In response to Grimm's greeting, the monster lifts the club in its hand and draws back…

…The sound is a cross between a moist crunch and a wet pop. Grimm slumps back into her wheelchair, missing everything above her shoulders.

"H-hey, Grimm?"

Snow steps into a fighting stance as she notices Grimm's motionless body.

"Six! Go get Grimm while I keep this thing busy!"

Get Grimm…?

I'm pretty sure that blow was lethal.

"Um…you want me to go get her? You sure you're okay? She's just a pile of meat now."

The monster swings its club, flicking the blood off it, then kicks over Grimm's wheelchair. Grimm's body lands on the ground with a thud as pieces of the wheelchair go flying in every direction.

"Heine, why are you playing with these maggots?"

"…Tch. I wasn't playing. Whatever, the moment's ruined. You finish cleaning this up, yeah?"

Heine climbs onto the back of the whimpering griffin, patting its back. The dark-skinned demon sighs, giving us a cursory glance before the griffin takes flight and vanishes off into the distance.

My brain's having a hard time keeping up with everything happening at once.

Okay, first order of business is to do as Snow says and get Grimm.

If I think about it, Grimm's a magic user. So her current state's gotta be an illusion of some sort, right?

"Six! Get it together!" Alice smacks my back, shoving me forward.

"Oof! A-all right! Okay, Snow, I'll leave the big guy to you. I'll handle Grimm!"

As I make my way toward Grimm, Snow steps forward to engage our new adversary.

"Ha! Frail humans who die from a little poke…fighting *me*? Hilarious! Too hilarious!"

He flexes his enormous wings, blasting the area with a gust of wind.

"Urgh…"

Snow lets out a soft snarl as the headwind holds her back.

"Hey, human, before I kill you, allow me to introduce myself. I'm one of the Demon Lord's Elite Four, Gadalkand of the Earth! Remember my name! You'll remember it, right? Okay! Now let's see who else I can poke to death."

Gadalkand roars as another of Alice's shotgun blasts rings out. He throws his arms up to block his face, the shot peppering his stone skin. Unfazed by the blast, Gadalkand digs his heels into the ground and charges toward Snow…

"Fuuuuuuuuuuuuuu…"

Rose inhales deeply as Gadalkand begins running.

"Raaaaaagh! C'mere you! Don't you dare underestimate me!"

As Gadalkand steps forward to attack Snow, Rose's fire breath blasts him backward, engulfing him in flame. Seeing an opening, Snow steps forward, striking at Gadalkand with her burning blade. The flames billowing around Gadalkand intensify, and he lets out a pained cry, staggering backward.

Gadalkand roars in frustration, using his mighty wingbeats to quell the flames lapping at his skin. I reach Grimm's side and pick her up from the ground…

And freeze.

Nope, this doesn't look like an illusion at all. Grimm's body, lacking its head, has the characteristic dead weight of a corpse. It slumps in my arms.

"<Hey, Alice…you think humans on this planet can survive this sort of wound?>"

"<Get it together, Six. She's clearly dead.>"

Alice glances at Grimm's body in my arms and gives her frank assessment. I feel something inside me as Grimm's death registers. I mean, I only met her yesterday, and I don't know anything about her other than her taste in underwear…but still, she was a member of my squadron.

"You're as good as dead, you son of a bitch! Alice, Snow, cover me! Screw the Elite Four! I'm gonna rip this guy a new one! Rose, take care of Grimm's corpse!"

Snow flinches at my anger but drops back into her fighting stance.

"R-right. He's one of their top brass. Defeating him here will be a tremendous achievement."

"Ha! What are you getting so worked up about? You need to relax, learn to enjoy life more! You humans barely live that long to begin with. Are you so eager to die?" Gadalkand taunts.

"I don't care what else happens—you're *dead*. Alice, fetch me the R-Buzzsaw! I'm gonna make mincemeat out of this bastard!"

"Okay!"

Just as we all get in position to attack, a voice interrupts from above.

"Lord Gadalkand, there you are! What are you doing, sire?"

Hovering above us was a demon that looked like Gadalkand except two or three sizes smaller.

"Oh, it's you. I didn't feel like dealing with that brat Lassel lording his command over us, so I was taking my time getting to the battlefield. Heine caught these humans attacking our supply convoy and was toying with them. I figured I'd have some fun, too…"

"Lady Heine is already on the front lines, sire. The battle is already joined. Whether the supply convoy survives is not our concern but rather Lord Lassel's as supreme commander. However, if we're not at our assigned posts it will be our responsibility. Please, sire, let us make haste for the battlefield—if not for Lord Lassel's sake, then for our clan."

Gadalkand curses under his breath.

"Looks like you get to live a little while longer, humans. Go ahead and carry that corpse back to your castle and sob around it. You'll stay out of my way next time if you know what's good for you!"

And with that parting line, Gadalkand stretches out his wings and takes flight.

"You bastard! You think you can run away? Get back here!"

My taunts ring hollow as Gadalkand gains altitude, rapidly disappearing from view.

"That bastard mentioned heading toward the battlefield..."

"You planning on going after him? I wouldn't recommend it. There's no way you're going to catch up with a flying target. The battle's likely to be over by the time you get there. We'd better do something for Grimm first."

Snow stands next to me, watching the demons fly off before turning her attention back to what's left of the convoy.

"...Alice, what's the status on the R-Buzzsaw?"

"Didn't send the request since that winged bastard flew off. Want me to send it now?"

"......No, it's fine. Let's take care of Grimm's body, then make our way back. I'm sure we'll see that bastard again."

Around me, Rose continues collecting various crates and piling them on a captured cart, while Snow checks for any stragglers. I turn to look at Grimm's corpse, laid out on the supply cart, and sigh.

What a waste...

Sure, the things she said were kind of weird, and she spent most of the day napping, but still she seemed like a good person.

"Snow, what do you do with bodies in this kingdom? Burial? Cremation?"

The least we can do is give her a proper funeral.

"...Mm? Wait, Grimm didn't tell you anything?"

"......?"

I stare at Snow in confusion.

"You seem to be under the impression that Grimm is dead. She's not this easy to kill."

"...Say what?"

......

What the hell is she talking about? The last time I checked, surviving decapitation wasn't on the list of things humans could do.

"I'm saying Grimm's not actually dead. Did you not read her résumé?"

Snow points to Grimm's body on the cart, which is rapidly being surrounded by Rose's captured crates. I get that space is at a premium, but I wish Rose hadn't placed a pumpkin where Grimm's head would be... It's more than a little creepy.

"Go over that one more time for me, would you?"

Snow lets out an impatient sigh at my slack-jawed expression.

"Remember when I told you that all the potential candidates for our squadron were rejects of one sort or another? Take Rose, for example. She's got demon blood running through her veins. That in and of itself is enough to make her a target of prejudice. Despite her abilities, her previous commanders made her take on all the dangerous tasks, usually alone. An expendable pawn."

......

"Seems this kingdom's filled with people who make me look like a saint by comparison."

"That's right, this kingdom is full of men as worthless as you are."

...*This bitch*...

"Now, about Grimm. The god she serves, Zenarith, is a bit of a special case."

Snow struggles to find the right phrasing.

"Grimm is quite famous as an archbishop in the right circles...the Archbishop of Zenarith, the ancient evil God of Undeath and Disaster."

5

The knights are already back at the castle by the time we arrive.

Even considering the time we took to load the captured supplies onto carts, it's a little too soon for the main force to be back. A brief head count explains why—there's a lot fewer of them now than there were this morning. The knights who did make it back are all wounded in one way or another.

"Judging by the looks on their faces, it's safe to say they lost. That's convenient for us, really. It's a good time to talk up our success in taking out the enemy supply convoy. Go find someone important and give them a rundown. Something along the lines of 'You guys may have lost, but thanks to *our* successful attack, the enemy will be forced to retreat.' Really remind them that we saved their hides."

Alice casually suggests rubbing a ton of salt into the army's fresh wounds.

"Leave it to me! I'll make sure to repeat several times that our attack on the supply line was designed to make the enemy fall back. While I'm at it, I'll also mention the fact that the five of us tied up one of the Demon Lord's Elite Four by ourselves while everyone else got stomped."

"...I—I see you're as scummy as ever. Still, it seems you're someone I can rely on at times like this. And in truth, I don't really mind that sort of thing. Calling out elites for their failures is one of my favorite things in the world. Just the thought of savoring their delicious shame is making me drool..."

Given Snow's career, she probably kicked quite a few people while they were down. I suppose that's the attitude it takes to crawl up from the slums and join the Royal Guard, but it's not exactly an attractive trait. I try not to let Snow's blatant sadistic inclinations dampen my mood as I go to make my report.

A ways from the capital sits a small shrine. The place looks like it was once a small cave of some sort, and upon its walls are countless carvings of disturbingly dark imagery as the wind howls through it. As I glance at Grimm's body lying lifelessly on an altar at the center of the shrine, I'm kind of impressed by the fact that such a creepy spot exists so close to the city proper.

"We're gonna resurrect Grimm in a place like this?"

Still riding the high of making the pretentious soldiers feel like garbage, I join Alice and the others at the altar.

"That's right. Although resurrection might be overstating it. All we're going to do is put Grimm's corpse on the altar with some offerings. Once night comes, she'll wake up like nothing happened."

"…Offerings? …You mean that junk you've got piled up on the side of it?"

Next to Grimm's corpse are some raggedy dolls, threadbare clothing, some tools worn out from years of use, and…

"Oh, these are my favorite socks. Since they have holes in them, I figured I'd use them as an offering for Grimm's resurrection," Rose admits with a faint blush as I gaze at a pair of worn socks sitting by Grimm's pillow.

Seriously? A pair of socks is enough to bring her back to life? Is a person's life just not worth that much on this planet?

"The god Grimm serves, Zenarith, prefers offerings of items that have sentimental value to people. Items that they've had for years and treated with care. There should be enough here to cover Grimm's resurrection— Anyway, I'm going to grab something to eat and head

back to my room. There's a documentary tonight about Zolingeran knives. I've been looking forward to it all week!"

"I'm going to go dig into the vast amounts of food we took earlier!"

"I fired my shotgun quite a bit today, so I think I'll do some maintenance on it. What about you, Six?"

The others begin to head out.

"Mm…I think I'll stay here. Grimm's coming back to life at night, right? I want to see what that looks like. Plus, it sounds kind of sad to come back to life and not have anyone around…"

Dusk becomes night, and the shadows make the shrine look even creepier. There's not much to do but sit and wait, so I get comfy on the ground, hugging my knees to my chest. My attention turns to a hole in the ceiling where the wind gusts through. I'm struck by the sheer number of stars in the sky above. So *that's* what you can see when the sky isn't clogged with smog and other pollutants.

It helps that there's not a lot of light pollution, with the capital having little in the way of large buildings or lighting.

I consider snapping a few pictures to take back home. Which reminds me, pictures of the orcs and Gadalkand would've made nice souvenirs, too. My thoughts continue on this pointless track when I think I catch a bit of light shining from Grimm's body.

…No, I'm not imagining it. She's actually glowing.

A magic circle pops into existence around Grimm, and then a column of bright light rises from the altar. The column shines through the hole in the ceiling and pierces the sky, lighting up the room…then fades as quickly as it appeared.

When my eyes adjust again to the gloom, I notice the offerings on the altar are gone. Grimm flutters her lashes and sits up. She rubs at her forehead, as though dealing with a headache, and turns to me a bit sleepily.

"…Commander? What are you doing here?"

"…I was waiting for you to come back to life."

Grimm glances around the room, as if looking for something, then turns back to me with a puzzled expression.

"Wait, why were you waiting for my resurrection? …Oh. Are you here to punish me because I died before I could do anything useful?"

"Huh? No, that's not it. I just figured you'd be lonely, coming back to life with no one around. That and, well, I guess I was a little skeptical that all we had to do to bring you back to life was leave you on an altar with a pile of junk."

"A-ah… I was not aware that they treated my lifeless body so carelessly."

I probably shouldn't tell her that there was a pair of used socks among the offerings. Grimm surveys the room but stops after a few moments when she can't find what she's looking for.

She turns her gaze to me. There's no trace of her usual twitchiness or anxiety, just a calm, steady gaze.

"You're an odd one, Commander. I've never known anyone kind enough to patiently wait around for me to come back to life. "

"That might be the first genuine compliment I've gotten since coming to this kingdom."

Grimm smiles at my words, her expression softening.

"I mean it. Normally, people back away when they learn that I serve Zenarith, God of Undeath and Disaster. Then, once they've been sufficiently creeped out by my string of deaths and resurrections, they stop talking to me entirely. But you, Commander… Evidently, you can still talk to me like I'm just another girl. You're also not bothered by the fact that Rose has demon blood. How very odd."

The truth is, the mutants at our corporation are so twisted that they make Rose look perfectly normal.

"A word of warning for you, Commander. Rose and I are hard to kill, but that doesn't go for the rest of this squadron… They always send the rejects into the most dangerous places. We're expendable."

There's a hint of sadness in her smile as she tilts her head toward the stars. Since she can cheat death, she must have survived while many of her companions met more permanent ends. Her starlit smile is a beautiful, fleeting thing. In this moment, she couldn't appear more different from the lazy, good-for-nothing Grimm I'm used to.

A unit of rejects, hmm? Conscript a bunch of expendable people and send them on high-risk, high-reward missions. If they get results? Great. If they die? No big loss.

That's pretty messed up. Makes the corporation look like a charity organization. I suppose I should report this method of doing things when I get back to Japan...but I get the feeling our Supreme Leaders would turn up their noses at such an inelegant solution.

"So, Commander... This squadron is dangerous. You should quit while you're still alive and get out of this kingdom."

There's a loneliness and tenderness to Grimm's tone.

Upon hearing her heartfelt warning, I give my honest reply.

"Huh? What're you talking about? I'm not going anywhere."

Grimm is caught off guard by the frankness of my response.

"D-don't be silly, Commander. This unit's going to get treated like a bunch of expendable rejects and be forced to face the most dangerous situations."

...That's already happening!

"Where I come from, it was pretty common to be sent to battlefields where we were up against hundreds of enemies all as strong as the Demon Lord's Elite Four."

"...Wha—?"

Grimm just stares at me.

The invasion of America was especially brutal. They just had so many Heroes.

"And in spite of all that, I'm still here and kicking. Even today, I was getting ready to beat the shit out of that Elite Four bastard who killed you, but he ignored me and flew off to the battlefield."

"U-um…well, that's… Normally, one wouldn't be able survive an encounter with a monster on the level of the Demon Lord's Elite Four."

Well, that's certainly true in this case, but…

"For something of that level? With the right prep and weapon, I can take on at least five of them at once."

As a general rule, Heroes would always attack in groups of five. I remember being tossed into the fray against those teams despite being an average human… Couldn't say I enjoyed the encounters, but I won and made it out alive. My expression sours as I think back to those battles, and Grimm just goes silent.

"…Commander, just who are you? There's also that strange weapon Alice carries around…"

Whoops, I should probably cut off that line of questioning here and now.

"It's not worth worrying about. Plus, now that I think about it, I can definitely see a harem situation developing with our current squad members. You couldn't pay me to quit."

Grimm giggles at my attempt to change the subject, her expression radiating joy despite the gloom. "Ah-ha-ha… I get it. We all have things we don't want to talk about. Just try to stay alive, won't you?"

After her laughter dies down, Grimm tilts her head, her eyes fixated on me.

"…Well, it's getting pretty late. Do you have any plans, Commander? Since there was a battle today, tomorrow will be a day of rest."

"Huh…a day of rest after a day of work? That's pretty generous… Back at Kisaragi, we'd get home after seventy-two straight hours of guerrilla warfare, only to be sent on our next errand by a boss."

And that boss would be Lilith the Black, the same lazy, mad scientist who couldn't be bothered to leave her lab to fetch a few measly test subjects.

"I…see. It seems you've had a rather hard life yourself, Commander. Maybe even harder than Rose or myself."

"That wouldn't surprise me…"

Now that I've been away from the corporation for a little bit, I've come to the realization that the work environment was a bit…harsh.

"A-anyway…will you be free tomorrow, Commander?"

"Yeah, I guess. There doesn't seem to be a whole lot to do for fun in this kingdom. I wandered around the city a bit last night after unpacking, and the only places open were bars."

Okay, so I wasn't expecting to find a twenty-four-hour convenience store or an arcade, but still there was *nothing* to do! …Hang on a sec, I bet I could find a brothel if I really put my mind to it. Sadly, since I haven't been paid yet, I'm way too broke to go looking for one.

Grimm chuckles and smiles at me.

"Well then, Commander…how about we go on a date?"

6

…I don't really get it, but apparently this is what passes for a date in this world.

<Evil Points acquired.>

<Evil Points acquired.>

"Ah-ha-ha-ha-ha-ha-ha! Ah-ha-ha-ha-ha-ha-ha-ha-ha-ha-ha!!"

"Mwa-ha-ha! Faster, faster, fasteeer!!"

Grimm and I fly through the streets of the capital.

Well, to be more precise, Grimm's sitting in a wheelchair that I'm pushing around at breakneck speeds through the capital.

"Commander, this wheelchair is incredible! So light…so fast! I can never go back to an inferior model! You've ruined me for all other wheelchairs!"

"Yep! This here's a Kisaragi wheelchair. High-quality aluminum frame, run-flat tires, high-speed design! You're the fastest woman in the kingdom, Grimm!"

Apparently, back when Grimm was surveying the room after being resurrected, she had been looking around for her wheelchair. Sadly, it met a pretty gruesome end at the hands of Gadalkand's foot, so I had the Kisaragi Corporation send me a new one on the teleporter...

"Amazing! This is the best night of my life! Hey, Commander, look over there! It's another couple!"

"Brace for impact! We're going in!"

"H-hey! Stop, you twoooo!!!"

Grimm and I have been harassing lovey-dovey couples throughout the city by charging at them with the wheelchair. It looks like the city guard finally caught on, and we're now being chased by a woman in uniform.

"You there! Stop right there! I can't believe what you're doing! This is a romantic spot for couples to share a tender moment! You're ruining their evenings! If you want to wreak havoc, go somewhere else and take that thing with you!"

Not wanting the entire city guard after me, I screech to a halt. Grimm glances up at me in confusion.

"Wait, isn't wreaking havoc why we came *here* in the first place?"

"It sure is. Why's she interrupting us?"

"Wait, so you two were disturbing the peace on purpose? Well, that changes things. I'm afraid I'm going to have to ask you both to come with me."

Grimm sneers dismissively at the uptight guardswoman.

"Ah, you poor lamb. You've been forced to work late into the night. Be more honest with yourself and take a look around. Why should you give up your nights for these infernal couples? Secretly, you're seething with envy and hatred, aren't you? Let them suffer as you have suffered..."

"Um, well...actually, I have a boyfrie— Ow! Hey! Stop that! I'll toss you in jail for assaulting a guard!"

Leaning forward in her wheelchair, Grimm starts kicking the guard's shins, landing several blows with her bare heel.

"Wait…you can use your legs? Why are you in a wheelchair, then?"

"It's the backlash from a curse cast long ago. In exchange for borrowing Lord Zenarith's power, there are various…conditions…"

The backlash from a curse?

"Okay, but that still has nothing to do with why you're rolling around here and raising hell, so knock it off! …You do dumb stuff like this and then wonder why you can't get a man… Honestly…"

The guardswoman mutters under her breath, prompting Grimm to retrieve what appears to be a doll from her bosom and point at it menacingly.

"Oh, you've said it now! Commander, allow me to give you a proper demonstration of my power! O Great Lord Zenarith, I beseech thee! Deliver disaster unto this woman! May she suffer from vertigo!"

"…Gah?!"

The officer pinches the bridge of her nose, wobbling from side to side as she loses her footing.

…………

"Wait, *that*'s your power? It's a little…underwhelming, don't you think?"

"Look, Commander, curses are an art, not a science. Even with all my power, I succeed maybe eighty percent of the time. The success rate drops like a rock each time I use the same phrasing. Curses also require a sacrifice, and even then, I might fail and suffer the curse myself…like with my legs…"

Grimm looks down sadly at her legs, rubbing at them wistfully.

"…Oh, I see. So you used a curse to weaken someone's legs, but something went wrong, and you took the curse instead, costing you your ability to walk, huh?"

"…What? Oh no, the backlash from this curse just prevents me from wearing shoes."

…Now I feel stupid for pitying her.

"Wow, that ability is totally useless… I feel kind of bad for you actually, so I'm just going to let you go now…"

The guard, now fully recovered from her vertigo, looks upon Grimm with pity.

Grimm scowls in response, glaring at the officer, producing several more dolls from her top.

"Useless?! I'll show you useless! Feel the full wrath of my curses! O Great Lord Zenarith, I beseech thee! Deliver disaster unto this harlot! May she suffer the pain of stubbing her toe on a dresser!"

"…?!"

The guard cringes, closing her eyes in anticipation of the pain…

"Aaaaaagh!"

Rather than the guard, Grimm clutches at her right foot and lets out a pained scream.

"Careful! Don't squirm so much in the wheelchair or you're gonna— Oops."

"Urgh!"

Writhing in agony, Grimm tips over her wheelchair, falling to the ground and slamming her head against the cobblestones below. She goes totally limp as the guard and I stand there dumbfounded.

…I see. So this is one of Lord Zenarith's…conditions…

But…

…Does this mean I have to take her back to the shrine?

7

The next day.

"Please, no! Please, no! Please have mercy!!"

"It's all right… You'll be much stronger once you eat this."

Today is supposed to be a day off, so I'm wandering aimlessly around the barracks when I hear shouting...

"I can't, I can't, I can't! Bugs are absolutely out of the question!"

"Insects are rich in nutrients and a good source of protein. Eating insects is a basic part of survival training. Stop being such a baby and eat it already!"

I follow the familiar voices to a half-open door and peer into the room. There I find Alice trying to feed Rose a grasshopper. Meanwhile, a teary-eyed Rose is shying away and shaking her head.

"What are you two doing?"

Rose jumps up and takes cover behind me.

"Boss, help! Alice is bullying me!"

And with that, Rose cowers from Alice, peering at her from behind me.

"Perfect timing, Six. Hold her down for a moment, will you?"

"You wouldn't do that, would you, Boss? You're a nice person, aren't you? Right? Right?!"

Caught between these two, I sigh and slump my shoulders.

"Why exactly are you doing this, Alice? It's not gonna earn you any Evil Points. You should leave this sort of thing to me."

"How could you, Boss?! I can't trust anyone! Grandpa was right! Humans are inferior and deserve to be wiped off the face of the planet!"

I ignore Rose as she whimpers and smacks my back, and I focus my attention on Alice.

"I'm trying to figure out how her copying ability works. It looks like she absorbs the genetic material of whatever she eats. I figured I could gather more data through experiments."

Rose calls herself an artificial Chimera. According to Snow and Grimm, there's nothing to back it up other than Rose's own claim. The truth about just who and what she is remains shrouded in mystery. All we know is that she was found hibernating in an artifact inside some ruins...

"So what exactly is the deal with the ruins she was discovered in? Did there used to be a super-advanced civilization on this planet or something?"

"That's definitely a possibility. Which is why I want to try feeding various things to her. I'm starting with a grasshopper. If she absorbs the genes of a grasshopper, I'm pretty sure she'll become the most powerful creature on this planet."

Ah, I think I see what's going on here.

"I don't understand why that means I have to eat the grasshopper! Aren't there stronger things I could eat instead?"

I'm hit with a wave of genuine culture shock as Rose's words reveal just how little this world knows about genetics.

"Don't underestimate the grasshopper's genes, Rose. In our corporation, making mutants from grasshoppers was considered taboo."

"Exactly. Now suck it up and eat the grasshopper. If you finish it, I'll give you a special treat."

"What are you even talking about?! You two aren't making any sense!" Rose backs away from us, crouching into the corner. "B-but…what do you mean by special treat? Is it something delicious? Depending on what it is, I might consider it…"

Alice takes out a wrapped package of some sort.

"It's called silicone. If you eat it, I'm sure it'll increase your bust size."

"How wonderful! Alice! Let's order a ton of silicone. Then we can feed Rose until she becomes super-busty!"

"I don't need something like that! I'm perfectly fine with my current size!"

Hey, that reminds me.

"Say, Rose, I meant to ask you before. Why are you putting up with how they treat you here? Given your power, I'm sure you could find better employment elsewhere."

"…To learn more about myself. The kingdom's scholars are

studying the ruins they found me in. The higher-ups promised that if I kept fighting for the kingdom, they would tell me whatever the scholars learned…"

Rose then recounts her memories to us. According to Rose, the old man who created her died after delving into dark, forbidden arts. Before falling victim to those twisted energies, the old man left a series of instructions for Rose. In order to carry out those instructions, Rose is currently on the hunt for a certain item.

It's a stone of some sort, as well as the very object the old man dipped into the forbidden arts to obtain. It's said to cure all illnesses if made into medicine, to grant immortality as an elixir, or to craft the ultimate, indestructible weapon if forged. If used as a spell component, it can change the very shape of the world. And if used as an offering to the gods, the gods themselves would appear before you to grant your wishes. This ultimate stone was what Rose's creator was after.

…But listening to stories about Rose, I can't shake the feeling that Rose is a powerful artifact in her own right. I have to admit I'm impressed by how casually this kingdom's leaders use her. I mean, hell, they pay her peanuts and send her on suicide missions. Honestly, this kingdom is run by some pretty heartless bastards.

"<Hey, Alice, once we establish a two-way link with Earth, we should send some Kisaragi researchers into the ruins. Also, make sure we officially add Rose to our ranks.>"

"<I agree. She's already looks like one of our mutants. All we need to do is get her into the right mind-set and she'll make a powerful Combat Agent."

"…Um, why are you two suddenly speaking in that strange language again?"

Our sudden switch to Japanese is clearly making Rose's anxiety worse. Alice and I reassuringly put our hands on Rose's shoulders.

"Rose, from here on out, the two of us will cure you of your ignorance. Starting today, you're officially one of us."

"You're still a child, so you'll need proper indoctrination. You should feel free to think of me as your mother."

"Alice, you're younger than I am! I'm going to have to pass on the lesson. I bet you're planning on teaching me some strange things... And what is this badge?! I don't want this!"

Alice attaches an official Kisaragi badge to Rose's chest.

"Congratulations, you're now a Combat Agent in training," I tell her.

"Congrats! From here on out, not only is Six your boss but he's also your mentor. Listen to him carefully."

"Wh-what? No! You two look like you're planning something... Wait, why are you clapping? Stop it! I'm fine with the way things are right now! B-boss? What's that in your hand?! Whatever it is, I'm not eating it! You can't make me eat grasshoppers or silicone or anything weird!"

[Status Report]

Safely arrived at target destination despite being teleported to an altitude of several thousand meters.

Alice reports some substantial differences in fauna between target destination and Earth, but aside from lower CO_2 concentrations, atmosphere composition is similar to Earth.

Discovered extensive undeveloped land and civilized settlements.

Resource studies yet to be conducted, but local foodstuffs are edible and provide sufficient nutrients.

Undeveloped lands show potential to alleviate food shortages on Earth from population growth.

After a demonstration of our abilities, recruited to lead a squadron for a local political entity.

Local political entity is currently in conflict with a competitor calling itself the Demon Lord's Army.

Engaged in combat with said competitor. Confirmed presence of mutant-level opponents.

Sustained a near loss due to insufficient equipment. Requesting substantial material reinforcements. Could really, really use the latest and greatest equipment. Kindly stop being a bunch of cheapskates.

Reporting Operative:
Combat Agent 6, Who Almost Died from Lilith's Mistakes

CHAPTER 3

The Right Way to Assault a Tower

1

With our new toy…er, subordinate Rose safely added to our ranks, our squadron has been sent out on a number of assignments along the front. Although they're just minor skirmishes, we've managed to accumulate a number of victories, a welcome change from the constant losses. We've settled into a comfortable routine, and we're currently taking the day off. Alice and I are lounging in our barracks room with nothing better to do.

"Something's not right."

Alice pauses her shotgun polishing and looks up at me.
"What's wrong? Has there been some kind of strange development with the Demon Lord's Army?"
"No, this is much more important."
Alice sets the shotgun parts down on the table and leans forward, listening intently.

"…Since our arrival, we've been out on several missions, steadily getting results. It's been a couple weeks now, but it doesn't look like anyone's falling for me."

"…What?" Alice gapes, unable to believe her ears. It's an oddly human expression for an android.

"Don't 'What?' me. Listen, Alice. Except for me, our unit is all women. And then there's Tillis, the women in the knighthood, and enemies like Heine of the Flames. I even met a pretty city guards-woman, though I guess she did mention she had a boyfriend."

"That guard nearly wrote us up. Grimm's taken a shine to the wheelchair you gave her, by the way. She's been zooming around the city at night, making a nuisance of herself. There's a warrant out for her arrest. If she gets caught again, I'm pretty sure they're going to lock her up," Alice replies.

I ignore her and raise my fist before launching into an impassioned monologue.

"And yet! All these fateful encounters and no major events! We're well past the time for Snow to wander into the baths while I happen to be in there or for a sleepy Grimm to mistake my room for hers and crawl into my bed. Maybe a hungry Rose goes looking for something to eat and finds a thick, juicy sausage. But it's actually my… The point is, we're long overdue for an event like that!"

"…Wow, that last one was a new low, and yet, I'm not really sur-prised to hear you say it. Fascinating."

Alice gazes at me as though studying a particularly strange ani-mal. I continue my monologue, not minding the scrutiny.

"Before our arrival, this kingdom was on a big losing streak. Then I show up and lead the kingdom's forces to its first real win in ages! I've got a pretty substantial number of victories under my belt. Mostly small skirmishes, but still. There's plenty of reason for women to swoon over me. I've even been standing ready in the hallway making sure I can run into a woman and grope her by mistake."

"Oh, right. There've been complaints about that, actually. You're becoming a pest."

Grousing, I grab Alice's head and grind my knuckles against her temples.

"I want to be yelled at for being oblivious, for not hearing a confession of love due to a gust of wind, or for totally missing the hints thrown my way. And then…and then a group of beautiful women can surround me and demand that I choose one of them! I want drama… Hey, where are you taking me?"

"Yes, yes, confessions and hints and whatever else. Now if you'll just follow me to the infirmary so I can check your head."

I pull my arm away from Alice's grip.

"There's nothing wrong with me! Think about it! The majority of this kingdom's knights are women! How have I not been able to get a taste of the 'lucky pervert' trope even *once*?!"

Alice lets out a deep sigh, brushing aside the intense sincerity behind my words. There are times when I find her actions a little too human for comfort.

Alice grabs my right hand and places it against her chest. I stare at her in confusion, completely unable to grasp her intent.

"Ah. Ah."

Alice is stone-faced as she lets out a couple dry moans. I pull my arm away from her a second time.

"Lucky you. You got to touch a pretty girl's chest. Happy now?"

"Why would I be happy about grabbing a lump of silicone on a robot's chest? At the very least, you could put a little more emotion into it. Well, that's not exactly the part I'm miffed about! I mean, yes, I wanna do dirty stuff, but—!"

"Okay, okay, whatever. Let's go to the infirmary, okay?"

Alice does her best to talk me down and pats my hand condescendingly.

My thoughts are interrupted as someone knocks on the door.

"Just what were you yelling about?! I could hear you through the door! Anyway, a meeting's been called, and you're on the invite list, so quit the perverted ranting! Be mindful of how your actions reflect on *me*!"

Snow's cheeks are flushed red as she opens the door to drag me off to the meeting.

"The Chosen One and his party were badly wounded in a battle against Gil the Mighty and Rista the Clever, the demons guarding the top floor of the Tower of Duster. They are currently being treated by our top healers."

We're currently in the castle's conference room. After confirming that all the unit commanders are present, the kingdom's general, some crusty old fart, launches into his status update. The news of the Chosen One's defeat sends a murmur through the room.

"Quiet! Thankfully, the Chosen One's wounds aren't too serious. The healers have assured me that the treatment will be rather straightforward."

The commanders let out a collective sigh of relief at the news.

"However, as you're all aware, our kingdom is currently being pushed back by the Demon Lord's Army. We're fortunate that the Chosen One has survived, but his defeat has shed light on a particular problem."

The room goes quiet, waiting for the old fart to continue.

"We're running out of time. I hate to admit it, but we don't stand a chance against the Demon Lord's Army in a full-on confrontation. The longer the war continues, the more likely our defeat. Our only hope is for the Chosen One to slay the Demon Lord before his armies lay waste to our kingdom. Speaking frankly, we need the Chosen One to pick up the pace. This latest setback comes at an incredibly inopportune time."

A shadow falls on the room.

"We asked the Chosen One why he attacked the Tower of Duster.

He mentioned that there is a treasure in the tower that he needs in order to bring the fight to the Demon Lord's castle. The Chosen One will have to attack the tower again as soon as his treatment is done. Time is of the essence."

The gruff old man pounds the table in front of him as the rest of us sit in silence.

"So! I plan to lay siege to the tower while the Chosen One recovers. We'll assemble the kingdom's forces, overwhelm their defenses with sheer numbers, and take the treasure ourselves. We can help hasten the Demon Lord's demise!"

A cheer goes up throughout the room. All the unit commanders are worked up into a frenzy.

...But this is a little different from the Chosen One stories I'm familiar with...

In the stories I know, the Chosen One usually gets a purse of gold—a child's allowance, really—then gets sent off to kill the Demon Lord. They're usually not backed up by the might of an entire kingdom.

Well, I suppose it makes sense if you consider the Chosen One is this kingdom's prince. And logically, outside of an epic, it makes sense for a kingdom to mobilize all its resources to fight off an invading Demon Lord.

Unlike everyone else, I'm not actually that pumped about this mission, and I slump back in my chair. If the mission is for the entire army to raid the tower, there probably won't be that much for our squad to do.

"I beg your pardon, my lord...but if we're to successfully lay siege to a tower that repelled the Chosen One, we'll need more than just numbers."

A balding man with a scar over one eye splashes a bit of cold water on the gathering. From what I understand, he's the army's chief of staff. He's one of the VIPs I brought to the verge of tears when taunting the elite knight with my squad's (admittedly inflated) battle results.

"The Tower of Duster is hollow, with a narrow staircase twisting up along its walls. So we'll have to engage the defending demons in a single file along a narrow staircase. The soldiers at the front will fall back as they're wounded, with fresh forces pushing forward. We'll have to grind through it step by step. It might even take longer than a full day to fight our way through… Perhaps you have a better plan?"

The staff officer looks caught off guard by the question, glancing side to side in panic. Looks like he didn't have a plan of his own.

"I…I'm afraid not, my lord."

Hang in there, Pops… Wait, why is he looking my way? I don't have any magic schemes up my sleeve, and even if I did, I'm certainly not going to be putting myself on the spot.

"I cannot think of a better plan, my lord…however, Sir Six has been gaining renown as the commander able to defeat the demons. Not only that, but he hails from a foreign kingdom, possessing insight that we lack. No doubt he has some wonderful tactics to make up for our shortcomings, as he is always so eager to point them out…"

…Well, I guess he kind of took all that criticism personally. I can feel the rest of the eyes in the room turn to me at the suggestion.

Dammit, old man, of course you'd turn to me. You couldn't save your hairline, much less a whole kingdom…

The old fart fixes me with a steely gaze.

"Well, Sir Six, have you any suggestions?"

…I do have one, but to be honest, I'm not sure if this is the right audience for it. The knights in this kingdom are all about honor and chivalry. That's cute and all, but it doesn't really mesh well with tactics employed by evil megacorporations.

"Light it up."

At this point, I've been using my arms as a pillow while I rest my head on the table, just barely looking at the other commanders around me. Everyone seems nonplussed, with several heads tilting to the side.

"You mean to propose setting the tower on fire? It was built with brick and mortar. It's likely impervious to fire."

The question comes from a nearby knight captain, a woman maybe in her midtwenties, who had turned her chair to face me.

"No, not the tower itself. You mentioned that the tower was hollow, right? So what we do is take over the first floor, open up all the entrances, and light a huge bonfire in the middle. It'd be like one of those smoking racks they hang meat in. Eventually, we can cook everything in that tower, from the boss demons on down. It'll be fun!"

....

"Wh-what say you all...? It sounds as though it would be quite an...effective strategy. Yes, quite effective indeed..."

It appears the plan has unnerved the old man, as the confident expression on his face falters.

"It seems a little extreme, don't you think? Even if we're talking about demons here..."

"Still, it *would* keep our losses at a minimum..."

"I can't help but feel this would be crossing a line, not just as knights but as human beings..."

The commanders begin talking among themselves, and the room fills with conflicted murmuring. I sit back and watch the debates unfold, stifling a yawn and folding my arms across my chest.

...A whole ten minutes later.

"Sir Six, we're very grateful for your proposal, but we've decided to go with the frontal assault!"

All the other heads in the room nodded along with the old man's proposal.

2

The tower sits in the middle of a large wasteland, the only building visible for miles around. It's about the same size as a skyscraper, and it kinda looks like it's made out of chalk.

A large number of knights have already been sent inside. Taking advantage of numbers and plenty of floor space, they've already secured the first floor.

Alice approaches the tower, patting the outer wall curiously.

"So here's the deal. We're just going to chill right here until evening."

""...What?""

Snow and Rose look at me like I've grown a second head and blink in confusion. Grimm sits by my side, napping away in her new wheelchair, blissfully unaware of everything as usual.

"Have you lost your mind? The siege is already underway. Not to mention that tower's got demons that beat the Chosen One himself! Imagine the rewards if we were to kill one of them!"

Snow raises her fist toward the tower, convinced she can change my mind with enough enthusiasm.

"Listen, Snow… The Chosen One's supposed to be strong enough to beat any of the Demon Lord's Elite Four one-on-one, right? You're just going to waltz in there and challenge the ones who beat that same Chosen One? Sorry, not interested. There's way too much risk and not enough reward. I'm just gonna take a nap instead."

I yawn, setting my pack down and flopping on top of it.

Then, I gesture vaguely toward the tower. "I mean, look at how many of us are here. One of the units will end this eventually. If the battle drags on until the evening when Grimm's awake, well, we can weigh our options again, then."

I leave one eye open to watch Snow's reaction. A vein bulges in her forehead, and her face rapidly turns a bright scarlet. She really needs to do something about that temper. It's bad for her blood pressure.

"Y-you lazy piece of… I can't believe I ever thought I could count on you! You're just useless to the core! Whatever! I'll go by myself, and I'm sure as hell not sharing any of the reward with you!"

Snow gives me an earful and then storms off toward the tower.

"Um, Boss…? Are you really okay with this? You're not actually going to let Snow go by herself, right?"

Rose casts a worried glance at Snow as she shrinks in the distance. She seems to be wavering between following her and staying with the rest of us.

"It'll be fine. She's plenty strong, and she'll have more than enough backup. I doubt she'll be in any danger, so she'll probably just make her way back here once she's worn herself out."

A few hours later.

"…Hahhh… Hahhh…"

Snow comes back looking like she'd just run a marathon.

"Hahhh… Hahhh… It's…it's just about evening, Six… I-is Grimm still asleep?"

"She'll probably wake up soon, but she's been saying some interesting things in her sleep. We figured we'd let her keep going for a bit."

Grimm, still asleep in her wheelchair, mumbles something every now and then.

"Ohhh… Snow… So bold of you…to beg the commander…to do what he pleases… Grope you, ravage you, anything he wants… Such lewd requests…"

"Wake the hell up, Grimm! Why are you having such weird, totally fabricated dreams?! If you don't wake up right now, I'm gonna give you a five-finger wake-up call to the face!"

Snow starts shaking Grimm back and forth, and Grimm's eyes snap open.

"Ah! But I was having such a lovely, prophetic dream…"

"On second thought, go back to sleep. I'll lop off your head and bury it so you can enjoy your slumber."

"It took long enough for her to wake up! Don't coax her back to sleep! Anyway, Alice, how's it looking? We good to go?"

After I talk Snow down from her murderous rage, I turn to Alice, who has completed her evaluation of the tower's outer surface.

"Looks like the tower's built entirely of stone. Opening a few holes in the walls won't do anything to the tower's structure. Just remember that the wind will pick up as you get higher up. Also, make sure of your handholds—it's easy to misplace your hold in this gloom. Finally, everyone take off your armor, keep your weight down to a bare minimum."

Snow narrows her eyes at Alice in suspicion. "What are you talking about? What are you plotting?"

"Plotting? How rude. We're about to head off and topple this tower."

Snow furrows her brows further. "Wait… You were going on earlier about how you didn't want to risk it. What changed?"

"I said I didn't want to go after the bosses from the front. And while I'm not quite as ambitious as you are, I do want a share of the glory. Especially if I can get them without a lot of effort or danger. As far as I can tell, a few units have managed to reach the top floor and challenge the bosses. Have they been able to land a few blows on the demons? Maybe weaken them a little?"

Snow lets out a derisive snort and shakes her head.

"…You're almost refreshingly treacherous, you know that? …A few have managed to get to the top, but the bosses have had time to prepare. Our forces got wiped out the moment they showed their faces. The enemy is a pair of demons who complement each other rather well. We're still in the process of looking for weaknesses."

Snow is interrupted by the *crunch* of a metallic object being driven into stone. A glance at the tower reveals Alice using a small device to drive iron stakes into the tower's outer wall.

"Oh, not bad at all. They go in nice and smooth. Here, take this, Six."

The device Alice hands me is a compact pile driver. It can drive stakes into even the toughest bedrock.

"...What is that thing? ...Wait, don't tell me you plan to..."

Snow starts sweating bullets as she realizes our intentions.

"All right, let's go. The frontal assault or whatever is taking *way* too long. Right now, the demons are busy fighting the soldiers on the staircase, and the darkness will make it hard to notice anyone climbing the outer walls. Scaling the tower is probably the last thing they thought anyone would try."

3

"Close ranks to the right! Take out the caster first! Minimize the damage!"

"Push! Use your numbers and push!"

I can hear the din of battle through the stone as I continue driving more iron stakes into the tower, leading my squad slowly up the side. The battle raging inside the tower has done a good job of masking our noise.

"This...this is just wrong. This can't be the proper way to besiege a tower...surely..."

Right below me, Snow mutters to herself as she follows behind. She's shed her armor and strapped her sword to her back. The other members of the squad have removed their heavy equipment and join the climb with a light payload.

"Hey, Snow, they probably can't hear you over all the fighting, but try to talk as little as possible. If the enemy finds us here, we're sitting ducks. You can complain to Alice later."

Without my power armor, there's no way I'd survive a fall from this height. Now that I'm a good distance up the tower wall, I take my time in driving in the stakes, making sure that each is secure before moving on to the next one.

The climb feels endless, with only the steadily increasing wind indicating any progress. Eventually, though, I climb up high enough that I catch a glimpse of the top.

"Psst! Six! Hey, Six!" I hear Snow's urgent whisper from below me.

"What is it? And why do you sound so desperate? Wait, don't tell me... Do you need to go to the little knight's room...?"

"No! I-it's not that."

Yeah? I wait impatiently for her to explain.

"...I got carried away when swinging my sword earlier... My arms can't take much more of this. They're starting to tremble..."

"You moron! If you fall from here, that's instant death! And you'll take the rest of the squad with you!"

"I—I know that! I already admitted I got carried away! So what should I do?! I'm seriously freaking out right now!"

Snow looks up at me with tears in her eyes. It's actually kind of a nice change of pace from her usual expression, and I'm pretty tempted to leave her hanging, both literally and figuratively, but Snow's not the sort to beg unless it's an actual emergency. I need to take this seriously.

"Ugh, fine! Give me your hand!"

I bite down and grasp the compact pile driver with my teeth, taking hold of a stake with one hand and reaching down to grab Snow's hand with the other.

"Wh-what are you doing?! Eeep!! Don't just dangle me with one arm! Gyah!"

I ignore Snow's panic and pull her up to my shoulders. In all honesty, this is actually pretty hard on my arms, considering I'm not in my power armor. Sure, I've got cybernetic enhancements, but my physical abilities are basically at the limits of what the human frame can handle. Carrying Snow and her sword one-handed isn't something I can sustain for long.

Mumbling with the pile driver in my mouth, I try to communicate to Snow with my eyes and chin to grab hold of my shoulders.

"Gh... S-sorry."

She might be too tired to continue climbing on her own, but she should still be able to cling to me using her arms and legs.

I confirm that Snow's got her arms wrapped securely around my neck, then resume my climb toward the top floor.

...Hey, wait a second. This is...

"Hey! Tighten your grip a bit. Flatten yourself against me to reduce the effects of the wind!"

"G-got it... Like this?"

A soft, supple warmth presses against my back. The intimate event I was looking for, at long last. I couldn't be happier.

"This is the first time you've been useful today. Hey, if you're going to be dead weight, the least you can do is press your chest against me a bit more."

"Y-you son of a—! At a time like this?! You really are scum, aren't you?!"

"Sh-shut it! Your huge boobs are pretty much your best asset! I'm letting you make good use of them! You should be thanking me!"

"You ass! The moment this mission is done, meet me behind the barracks!"

As we continue our whispered argument, we get to a height where we can climb onto the rooftop. A quick downward glance confirms that the others have climbed up without any problems. I expected Rose to be fine, given her physical strength, but even Grimm, ordinarily confined to a wheelchair, has no problems with the pesky sun out of the way.

Alice, being an android, had no concerns about fatigue, and taking advantage of her near infinite energy, she took the occasional peek through the tower's windows on her way up.

I address the others in a whisper.

"I'll climb up and scout ahead. Join me when I call on you."

Everyone, except for Snow, who is still on my back, nods in understanding.

I drive in the final stake, then poke my head above the edge and sneak a peek.

The sun had set a long time ago, leaving the top floor lit only by moon and starlight. In the gloom, I catch sight of two demons. Standing in front of the staircase is a giant bull-headed humanoid carrying an ax. Standing a fair distance away is a ram-headed demon carrying a staff.

The invading knights were forced to come up the stairs in a single file but faced attacks from both the front and the side. I gotta give credit where it's due. The enemy set up in a good location.

"Now's our chance. Let's call up the others and face them before they notice us," Snow whispers to me from my back…

The two demons, oblivious to our presence, start talking to each other.

"Fu-ha-ha-ha! Hey, brother, how many groups does that make it? I haven't suffered a single scratch yet!"

"Hee-hee, I've lost count, brother. There have been too many. Besides, we already beat the Chosen One. Mere knights and soldiers don't stand a chance against us, no matter how many of them there are."

Still carrying Snow on my back, I stealthily climb up onto the top floor. The demons remain ignorant of our arrival, continuing their cheerful conversation.

"That's true. Since we've beat the Chosen One, I bet we'll get promoted to Elite Four status. I'm sure the Demon Lord's drafting up the orders as we speak."

"Indeed! Come to think of it, we beat the Chosen One when the Elite Four couldn't. We may not have been able to finish him off, but we got him real good. It's not a stretch to say we've probably surpassed the Elite Four!"

"All right, let's gather the others… Um, Six?"

Ignoring Snow, I crawl along the floor, approaching the ram-headed demon.

"Fu-ha-ha-ha! The world is ours for the taking, brother! With the two of us together, we can't lose!"

"Hee-hee-hee! That's right! With the two of us together, we can beat the Chosen One or even the Elite Four! We could probably even give the Demon Lord a run for his money!"

The ram-headed one merrily continues his conversation, still blissfully unaware of our presence. He's standing away from the staircase, glancing down at the battle unfolding in the tower from the ledge near the empty center. I get a bit closer to Ram Head…

"H-hey, Six! We're close enough! Let's hurry and get the others, and then…"

"Fu-ha-ha-ha-ha! Once we beat these fools, we'll gain even greater fame and glory!"

The bull-headed demon lets out a joyful belly laugh.

"S…Six?"

I stand up behind the ram-headed demon, still carrying Snow on my back.

"Hee-hee-hee-hee! Indeed! Our names will echo throughout the world! Just the two of us, Gil the Mighty and Ri—!"

I shove Rista the Windbag off the top of the tower.

"WHOOOOA! HEY! S-Six! Wh-what the hell?!"

"All right, you guys, the coast is clear! Let's get to work!"

I call on the others and wait for them to join us. Snow climbs off my back, drawing her sword and dropping into her fighting stance. She looks at me, her expression torn. I guess she has something to say.

"Hey, Six, don't you think that was a little messed up?! I almost felt sorry for him! I've never heard of anyone kicking a boss off a tower before the actual fight!"

"Wha—?! Where the hell did you all come from?! Cheeky bastards! C'mon, Rista, let's get 'em! We'll use our…"

As the other squad members climb up from behind Snow and me to join us on the top floor, Gil glances from side to side, trying to find his companion.

"...Rista? Hey, Rista, where'd you run off to?"

For understandable reasons, Gil turns his gaze toward Snow and me. Meanwhile, the two of us were looking in the direction that I'd shoved Rista. In a panic, Gil abandons his post in front of the staircase, rushing toward the ledge where Rista fell...

"R-Rista?! Rista!"

"G-Gil! Heeelp!"

I glance down and notice that the ram-headed Rista had managed to grab hold of part of the spiral staircase, hanging off its edge. It's hard to read expressions on animal-headed demons, but if I had to describe what Rista was feeling right then, I'd say it was desperation.

"Damn, I thought he was dead already. Hey, Alice, can you shoot the one clinging to the stairs?"

"Wouldn't be a problem, but why waste the precious ammunition? I bet if you just toss some rocks at him, he'll slip and fall on his own."

I bend down and grab a rock.

"H-hey, stop! Stop, dammit! I won't let you attack Rista!" Gil announces rather dramatically, throwing himself into my line of sight and blocking me from throwing rocks at Rista. "I won't let you lay a finger on him! I don't know where you came from or how we got into this situation, but I'll see to it that no harm comes to him!"

"...Ugh, now I feel bad... Why is he making this difficult?"

Rose lets out a soft whimper, cringing as she looks at Gil bravely putting himself between us and the vulnerable Rista.

I don't know why she's saying that. I'd say this situation is actually pretty cut-and-dried.

"All right, we're going to surround him. The moment he moves to attack one of us, the rest of us will throw rocks at the one hanging on to the stairs."

"Impressive, Six, a wonderful plan. The very model of a Kisaragi employee. Letting him hear his companion's cries of distress so that he can't actually attack anyone was a nice touch."

Glad someone appreciates when a beautiful plan comes together.

"Hey, Gil, was it? Heh-heh-heh, you can move if you want, but I think you can guess what will happen to your precious partner if you do… All right. Snow and I will be on standby with rocks. The rest of you, use ranged attacks to hit him from outside his reach!"

""""Y-yikes…""""

The three squadron members aside from me and Alice cringe and look a bit apologetic as they carry out their orders. Gil the Mighty lets out a cry of despair as he does his best to block the attacks with his ax.

"DAMN IT AAAAALL!"

"—Gil! Gil, are you all right?" Rista the Clever shouts out as he scrambles up the stairs.

"He's alive…but I wouldn't say he's all right."

Gil actually put up a decent amount of resistance. More, if I'm honest, than I expected. By the time he collapsed onto the floor, Rista had managed to pull himself back up to safety. He then gathered his underlings as reinforcements to help the beleaguered Gil……

"You bastards…! You not only shove me off the ledge when my guard is down but then use me as a hostage to beat up on Gil?! Don't think any of you will get out of this alive! You're all dead!"

Rista snarls in rage, glaring daggers at us. I rather casually hold out my palm toward him to stop him from making any rash moves.

"Easy now, didn't you hear what I said? He's alive, but I wouldn't say he's all right. Do you understand what that means?"

As each side prepares to attack the other, and the tension in the room is rising rapidly, I smile disarmingly at Rista. Despite my attempt at putting Rista at ease, the ram-headed demon backs away at my expression.

"…Your precious partner is barely clinging to life. He might make it if you can get him immediate medical attention. So here's my question."

The color appears to drain from Rista's face, and he swallows, tensing.

"How highly do you value your partner's life?"

In response to my question, a familiar voice echoes in my head.

<Evil Points acquired.>

4

Someone's at the door again.

"Six, you there?"

Ah, Snow again.

…Whatever she wants, it's probably not a big deal.

"The gentle and purehearted Mr. Six is off picking up trash by the river."

"Cut the crap! I knew you were here!"

Snow bursts into the room, huffing angrily. It's already well past 2200 hours. It's a bit late for a social call.

"What do you want, Boobzilla? Coming to a man's room at this late hour… Is this a booty call?"

"Stop with that dumb name! What if the others start calling me that?"

"Hey, Boobzilla. Do you want me to give you two some private time?"

"Alice! You too?!"

Snow struggles to get her breathing under control, taking a few moments to rein in her anger. She then thrusts a large leather bag in my direction.

"…And this is?"

I take the bag and peer inside…and I freeze up.

"This is your pay. Base pay plus reward money from your recent victories… I still can't believe it. Climbing the outside of a tower, tossing a boss off the ledge—such ludicrous tactics!"

Noting that I've gone completely still since peering inside the bag, Alice comes to take a look herself.

"…Wow."

"…And the worst part has to be cutting a deal with a demon! Sure, that got us the tower treasure with minimal losses, but taking hostages like that! It's dishonorable! …Hey, why are you frozen like that?"

Snow's suspicious tone helps me snap back to reality, and I confirm the contents of the bag. Gold coins…a mountain of gold coins.

"Um, so Snow. Just how much are these gold coins worth in this kingdom?"

"Worth? Oh, right, I'd almost forgotten you don't remember basics like the value of money. Well, that amount would be enough for a household to enjoy a full year of luxury."

"…Seriously?"

I'm trying to be sarcastic as I numbly grasp the bag, but Snow appears to have mistaken my incredulity for disappointment.

"Mm… I suppose you feel it's not enough. I understand. I've always been prickly about my reward money, too. Still, you have to understand in spite of all your achievements, you're still just a squadron commander. Don't worry, though. Once you've gained some rank, they'll reward you with enough money to make that amount seem like pocket cha—"

Before Snow could finish, I turn to Alice and tell her in Japanese:

"<Alice, I think I'm gonna quit this spy business. I'm going native.>"

"<Hold it. Since you're saying this in Japanese, I'm assuming you're serious.>"

Alice looks at me seriously. The dry wit is gone from her voice.

"<Listen, all right? There was this one time where I'd spent over a month fighting in the Sahara Desert, and when I finally get home, do I get so much as a 'Welcome back'? Nope. Instead, my superior makes me run out and fetch her potato chips. And you know how much I got paid for that month's work? After tax withholding and insurance premiums, I was left with a measly 180,000 yen.>"

"<I'm honestly surprised you didn't quit a long time ago.>"

Snow furrows her brow in suspicion at our Japanese conversation. "What is it, you two? You're speaking in that odd tongue again."

"Don't worry about it. Six was just excited and started babbling in his native language. It was more money than he was expecting."

Snow doesn't look convinced and tilts her head as she listens to Alice.

"R-really? Well, I suppose that's fine, then… Oh, Alice, this is your cut."

"Oh, I appreciate it. It's the first time I've gotten anything since Six gave me my shotgun."

I mean, sure, I suppose she described the shotgun as a present, but she's the one who actually sent the request, using my points as payment. It's not that big of a deal, is it?

Still, despite all that, Alice does carry that shotgun everywhere, almost like a favorite toy. And she seems pretty pleased about receiving her own sack of money.

…Well, if she does consider her favorite thing in the world to be a gift from me, I've got no problems with that.

[Status Report]

Observations indicate that the war between our chosen kingdom and the enemy is continuing to escalate. Skirmishes between the two parties occurring at more frequent intervals.

In recognition of recent contributions to the war effort, the members of our squadron have been awarded a prize consisting of gold coins with a current market value of several million Japanese yen. Repeat, awarded a prize consisting of gold coins with a current market value of several million Japanese yen.

Currently, no major issues or obstacles to carrying out mission objectives.

Will provide further updates at a later date.

Reporting Operative:

Combat Agent 6, Man Awarded Gold Coins Worth Several Million Yen

P.S. Request an immediate improvement to my compensation and position.

CHAPTER 4

How to Defeat a Demon General

1

"I hear the Chosen One's party opened a path to the Demon Lord's fortress using the treasure from the Tower of Duster. That means our enemies have to take the Chosen One seriously. All we need to do is hole up in the castle and defend it until the Chosen One takes out the Demon Lord."

"So it's a question of who succeeds first. The Demon Lord or the Chosen One."

Alice and I are chatting leisurely as we clean and maintain our equipment, until our conversation is interrupted by a knock on the door.

"Hey, Six, are you there?" Snow sounds as ornery as ever.

"I'm here, but I don't feel like dealing with you right now."

"Wow, I think I would have preferred if you'd just made up an excuse like last time! …Ah, maintaining your weapons?"

Snow turns her gaze toward the table, her eyes lingering on my knife. I had been in the middle of sharpening it when Snow barged in.

"...S-say, Six, do you mind if I take a look at that knife? Ever since I caught a glimpse of it, I've wanted to get a better look. It seems like quite the piece."

"...Sure, but you better not run off with it."

I offer Snow the knife handle first.

"This is quite the blade... Is it engraved? If not, do you mind if I do the honors? I wonder where it was made... H-hey, let go! I'm not done looking! You know, I can finish sharpening her for you if you want... Annh!"

Snow's got that dangerous look in her eyes again, and she starts nuzzling my knife. I can't let that continue. I reach over and take the knife back, ignoring Snow's dejected whining.

"Are you gonna tell us why you're here, or did you just come to try to steal my knife?"

"R-right. It was just such a beautiful piece that I guess I lost my head for a bit... Um, the general's calling. He wants to see us in the conference room. It looks like he's got an assignment for us."

With Snow taking the lead, I make my way to the conference room. As I enter the chamber, my heart sinks a little—the only ones in attendance are two grumpy, old geezers: the general and his chief of staff.

The general gestures for me to take a seat.

"Sir Six, thank you for coming. You have, to date, put up quite an impressive list of accomplishments. But most notable is the fact that you are still alive despite your recent encounters with the Elite Four."

"Yeah, I guess all that would be impressive by *your* standards."

"You insolent—!"

The chief of staff scolds me, frowning at my complete lack of modesty or manners.

Why am I here again?

The general appears to struggle with the proper words to broach the subject. Snow, however, has no such reservations and cuts to the heart of the matter with her usual brusqueness.

"Perhaps his lordship has a mission for us?"

The general responds to Snow's prompt with a solemn nod.

"Indeed, that's correct. From here on out, we would like your detachment to…handle major opponents like the Elite Four."

"With pleasure!!"

"Whoa, easy there! Just who died and made you commander?!"

I try to rein in Snow, who's now champing at the bit for another chance at glory.

"Think for once, you brainless worm. An assignment this prestigious doesn't come around often. We're considered equal to the task of handling the enemy's leadership. That, of course, means more opportunities for glory. And that means rewards to match!"

I find myself admiring how true Snow is to her desires. I carefully consider how to convince her that this assignment isn't worth the paper it's scribbled on when the chief of staff launches into grandiloquent praise.

"Lady Snow is correct. Sir Six is among the kingdom's greatest heroes. He has faced down Heine of the Flames as well as Gadalkand of the Earth. He has even done battle with Gil the Mighty and Rista the Clever and lived to tell the tale. No other has ever survived as many encounters with such opponents. If he is not worthy to face them, who in our kingdom is?"

The old man trails off with a heavy sigh, slumping his shoulders.

Ah, that bit of grandstanding definitely clears up a few things.

"…Let me guess, old man. You're the one who pushed this proposal onto the general."

"S-Six! D-don't call him that! His lordship is the second most influential member of…"

Contrary to my expectations, it's the general rather than oldie who responds, speaking right over Snow and cutting her lecture off at the knees.

"That is correct. His lordship, the chief of staff, has a very high opinion of you, Sir Six. He insists you are the only one capable of taking on the leadership of the Demon Lord's Army."

"Oh?"

I can't say I mind the compliment, no matter how excessive, but there's something about the chief of staff's way-too-polite smile that I don't trust.

My time at Kisaragi put me in contact with all sorts of corrupt bastards in power. All of them interested in a single thing, protecting the flow of goodies into their pockets. I can't quite put my finger on why, but the old man seems just as greasy as those guys. I mentally move the chief of staff a few notches higher on my list of potential threats.

"Sir Six, our kingdom desperately needs a hero of your ability. If you feel you need more forces at your disposal, we can swap out the demon-blooded abomination and dark god–worshipping cultist in your unit for proper knights. We'll even promote you from a squadron commander to a company commander. Will you accept?"

As he makes the pitch, the old man lowers his head in a deep bow, exposing his balding scalp to me.

A few days later.

Having formally received our mission, an excessively spritely Snow starts barking orders to the unit.

"Listen up! We've been given the honor of facing the enemy leadership! Failure is not an option! Everyone, stay sharp!"

"Hey, you're still not the commander."

The knights are assembled in formation on a ridge a few miles away from the castle. Our unit's been placed in the very center of the formation. I'm told a detachment of the Demon Lord's Army has invaded this area. There aren't a lot of them, but they're led by Heine of the Flames, one of the Elite Four. And of course, the task of taking on Heine falls on......

"I, Snow, will take on Heine of the Flames, pillar of the Demon Lord's Elite Four! Her head is mine!"

...our unit, of course.

"Six, can't you do something about that woman? When she's excited, she reaches new levels of obnoxious."

As an android, Alice isn't supposed to have any emotions, yet she shoots a look at the giddy Snow that's equal parts weariness and irritation.

"Don't waste your breath; it's pointless. Everyone, listen up. If we run into the enemy, do what you need to do but don't take any unnecessary risks. No point in getting hurt on a mission like this."

Unfortunately, Snow catches my remarks, directing a dangerous glare my way and stalking toward me with a vein bulging in her forehead.

"Why can't you ever take anything seriously?! This is an important mission entrusted to us by the general and chief of staff!"

"Right, the chief of staff. I don't like him. He's shady as hell, I just know it. He's definitely the sort of self-serving bastard that'll do whatever it takes to ensure he comes out ahead."

Snow's expression slackens in shock, and her grip on my collar relaxes.

"A-are you serious? Are you sure you're not talking about yourself?"

"Six, ever heard of a mirror? It's the shiny object that shows you your own face."

"Boss, have you ever heard of a weapon called a boomerang?"

...Okay, so maybe the chief of staff isn't the only person I hate. Seriously, you guys suck.

Standing back and watching the rest of the squad trash-talk me, Snow huffs, putting her hands on her hips.

"Regardless! I won't force you to fight if you don't want to! Just don't get in my way like you did the last time we ran into that woman!"

Oh, I see. It looks like Snow's still salty about the fact that Heine of the Flames didn't even give her the time of day after I showed up last time.

"Hey, Six, what's with the look? Heh-heh, have you noticed anything different about me today? I've brought along the perfect weapon to deal with Heine of the Flames. Take a look!"

Snow draws a sword with a sleek, blue blade from its sheath. The air around it chills immediately, and it's cloaked in a white mist.

"Iceberg the Frost Blade! It's a brand-new sword I had tailor-made for fighting Heine of the Flames. I just had to take out a three-year loan to get it. Grimm, this time we'll make good use of your abilities, too! Hey! Wake up!"

Snow seems really eager to try out her new sword and attempts to shake Grimm awake. Somehow the archbishop is fast asleep in her wheelchair, napping while hugging her knees to her chest.

"...Hey, Alice, what's your take on all this?"

"By 'all this,' do you mean the fact that we've been sent on a suicide mission?"

Standing atop the ridge, I glance off into the distance and catch a glimpse of the Demon Lord's Army.

"So you noticed it, too. Yep, that old fart's trying to get us all killed. I mean, yeah, he almost broke into tears when I tore apart his tactics from that one battle, but I didn't *actually* make him cry. Why would he want me dead?"

"I think that's reason enough to want you dead. I think he also considers you an eyesore. This entire unit is made up of rejects they're looking to get rid of. Ignoring our methods for a moment, we've produced really impressive results. But to them, we probably just look like a bunch of rejects that are hogging all the glory. I can't really blame them for wanting us gone."

Damn. And I've even been on my best behavior this whole time. If I wanted to piss everyone off, I could've thought of a million better ways to do it... Thinking back on it, the old fart said some pretty messed-up things about Rose and Grimm, too.

"Wake the hell up already! Grimm! Gri— Ah."

"Ahhh!!"

Snow and Rose sure are getting worked up over there. I wonder what they're up to.

"Anyway, once we see the enemy leadership, we'll make a show of fighting before beating a quick retreat. I'm still in the process of waxing my shotgun, so I won't even have a weapon today."

"At least bring *something*. If the shotgun breaks, I can just get you a new one. But whatever. We can just let it play out. Boobzilla over there isn't *completely* unreasonable."

"Miss Snow, Grimm made a weird noise when she landed. And her neck, the angle..."

"Wh-what should we do...? J-just put her back in the wheelchair for now! Gah! Oh, crap, her eyes rolled back..."

I approach the pair exchanging urgent whispers near the wheelchair...

"Hey, Snow, wake Grimm up, will you? ...Why are you two carrying her anyway?"

"It's nothing!"

"At all!"

Snow and Rose jump in surprise while carrying Grimm.

"...? All right, well, it looks like the main force is starting to move. It's time for us to get going, too."

*   *   *

The Demon Lord's Army stands defiantly in front of us. In the middle of this huge collection of demons is the brown, buxom beauty herself, wearing a skimpy outfit and a cocky smile. Standing next to her is her griffin as well as…

"…Looks like Heine and her griffin brought a friend. The hell is that thing?"

"…Th-that's a golem. They're automatons carved out of tough boulders and animated by magic."

Snow seems very intimidated by its presence. I can understand why. The golem stands well over two meters in height, is carved out of massive stone, and probably weighs a few tons. Come to think of it, it pretty much looks like a budget version of Gadalkand.

"Magic again? Looks like you can do just about anything with magic. I would really like to do more research into how physics work on this planet. Six, if we run into any incapacitated enemy casters, pick one up for me."

"I mean, I'm curious about magic, too, but just to be clear, we're only supposed to fight Heine, right? The other units are going to handle the griffin and the golem?"

The commanders around me speak up as if catching the tail end of my conversation with Alice.

"Sir Six! Leave the group of high orcs around Heine of the Flames to us!"

"My squadron will take care of that mighty band of ogres! They might be tough, but we'll take them off your hands!"

"We'll take advantage of our speed and go after the ranged enemy units!"

All squads aside from ours hurry into the fray.

"Great. Whole new planet, new kingdom, and I still draw the short straw! Snow! Get Grimm up! We'll have her put an especially nasty curse on Heine!"

"I-I'll leave waking up Grimm to someone else! I need to get my revenge on that woman with this frost blade!"

The fool, completely ignoring my orders, rushes toward Heine with her sword drawn.

"H-hey, Boss? Can I go fight the griffin? I'm curious to see what griffin meat tastes like, and I'd like to try flying. I bet I can do it if I eat enough griffin meat! Need to fulfill Grandpa's dying wish, after all!"

Rose, you too? Dammit, fools all around me!

I watch Rose dash off toward the griffin, then turn my head to look at Alice.

"Leave the task of waking Grimm to me. You can just go ahead and focus on…"

As if in response to Alice's remark, the golem begins advancing toward me, giving a growl that sounds like boulders being ground together.

2

"Heine of the Flames, pillar of the Demon Lord's Elite Four! My name is Snow! Face the wrath of my sword, Iceberg the Frost Blade!"

"So you've come at last, Snow or whatever your name is! Bring it on! Heine of the Flames, pillar of the Demon Lord's Elite Four, shall face you!"

The two armies clash in the center of the ridge where we're positioned.

A short distance away, Heine and Snow face off in a scene worthy of a movie poster.

"Dammit, it's no good! I mean, I half expected this, but bullets won't scratch that thing! Alice! Hurry up and wake Grimm, will you?"

*   *   *

Despite its bulk, the golem moves with surprising agility, closing the distance after my shots bounce harmlessly off its hide.

"Hey, Six, Grimm's not just asleep, she's out cold. She won't be waking up anytime soon."

"Every damn time! Every damn time we need her, she's either asleep or dead! She has yet to do *anything* useful! Seriously, what the hell?!"

I'm starting to think there was a pretty good reason behind putting Grimm in the reject club.

"Guess there's no other choice. Six, buy me some time. I'll order some C-4."

"Whatever, just hurry!"

I yell at Alice, boosting the strength assist setting on my power armor as high as it'll go. I glance around the battlefield for help and notice Snow weaving her way through Heine's fireballs to close the distance.

"SKREEEEEEEEEEEEEEE!"

The high-pitched scream catches my attention, and I glance up. In the skies above, Rose digs her nails into the griffin's flank, biting down on the beast's neck as it tries desperately to shake her off.

Both of them are a little too busy to offer me any support, which means...

"Okay, I put the request in! Six, just hold on a bit longer!"

I feel more than hear the heavy footfalls of the golem as it stands in front of me. Behind me is Grimm, slumped over and dead to the world, and an unarmed Alice waiting for the shipment of C-4. Sure, this isn't the best situation to be in, but for the first time in a long while, I feel a bit of excitement at the challenge.

I'm Agent 6, longest surviving Combat Agent and survivor of countless battles against Heroes!

"Come on, you worthless lump! I'll show you what Kisaragi power armor can do!"

I jump toward the golem, putting all my weight and passion behind my punch!

"……EEEEEOWWWWWWW!! Alice, it's broken! My arm is broken!"

And all I get for the shattered bones in my arm is a crack in the golem's chest. All that excitement and drive? Gone in a little over two seconds.

"You wouldn't be able to scream about it if the bones were *actually* broken. Calm down, your bones are fine."

"That makes no sense!! You're a Lilith creation, all right! Your logic's almost as flawed as hers!"

Yelling at Alice, I duck under the golem's grasp, circle around it, and land a kick square on its back. But the golem barely seems to notice that it was kicked, turning to face me and lunging with both arms outstretched.

I lock my fingers with the golem's, hoping to buy a little time by forcing a contest of strength.

"Hey, Alice, is it me or are the Supreme Leaders taking longer than usual? The hell is going on over there?!"

Alice ponders for a moment, then claps her fist down on her hand in realization.

"My internal chronometer reads 1514 hours. They should be having their scheduled teatime right now."

"Goddammit!"

I drop to one knee as the golem gains the upper hand.

How the hell is this golem stronger than I am in my power armor? Isn't this supposed to be an underdeveloped world with primitive technology? This is where I'm supposed to start a glorious new chapter of my life!

Putting all that aside for a moment, what the *hell* are they doing back on Earth? What kind of evil organization just breaks for tea in the middle of the afternoon?

I redouble my efforts, fighting back a sense of impending doom as the golem looms over me. As I brace myself against the boulder bearing down on me, I let out a hoarse cry.

"Release Restraints!"

Alice turns sharply at my scream of defiance.

"Have you lost your mind?! Cancel that order! The golem's not the only thing you're fighting, genius! Heine will roast you alive during your cooldown period!"

In addition to Alice, a familiar voice in my head chimes in.

<Preparing to release power armor safety restraints. Proceed?>

Ignoring Alice's warning, I hurriedly yell out my reply.

"Yes, proceed! Hurry!"

<With restraints disengaged, the power armor will require a three-minute cooldown period for every one min—>

"Yeah, I know! I accept all the risks, dammit!"

<Releasing safety restraints. To cancel, please issue cancellation order at any point during the countdown. Ten...nine... eight...>

"Hurry! The hell! Up! I can't hold this thing back forever!"

The golem is on the verge of crushing me like a bug, when suddenly...

Something falls out of the sky and slams into the golem. The impact knocks the golem sufficiently off-balance, and I'm able to catch my breath.

A few moments later, the griffin lands a little distance away with a loud thud, smoldering and smelling faintly of charred feathers. Looks like Rose torched it from point-blank.

The griffin writhes on the ground in pain, but Rose seems unfazed by the fall, standing up and dusting herself off.

"Yuck! Boss, that thing tastes gross! I won't be able to eat enough of it to absorb its flying ability. But maybe if I cook it…"

I admit I'm a little impressed that she's already gotten a taste of it.

As I'm admiring Rose's dedication to her stomach—

<Restraints released.>

—The announcement I've been waiting for rings in my head.

"Wroaaaaaaaah!!"

With the true potential of my power armor unleashed, I slowly turn the tables on the golem.

"Huh…? Wha…? B-boss?!"

Rose stands there watching in muted amazement as the multiton golem begins to lift off the ground.

"Six, the C-4's here! Just give me a second to stick it on the golem."

The golem starts kicking its legs against the empty air. Alice approaches with her package of C-4, sticking the plastic explosive onto the golem and molding it into shape.

"Wh-what's that? Some sort of clay?"

Rose stammers out the question. I confirm that the C-4 is firmly attached to the golem.

"RAAAAAAAAAAAAAAAAAAAGH!"

With a loud cry, I throw the golem as far as my power armor and enhanced strength will let me.

"It's an explosive from our country. It may not look like much, but it's quite potent."

"E-explosive? With a fire user nearby?!"

The golem lands with an earthshaking thud, and I take the opportunity to put some distance between us. Alice watches the golem land, detonator already in hand.

"Relax. It only burns when exposed to flame."

"Then how do you set it off?"

As if in response to Rose's question, Alice twists the detonator.

"Like this."

The golem explodes with an enormous *BOOM*, sending rock fragments flying in every direction.

"Ow, ow! I'm getting pelted by golem bits! Alice! Stop using me as a shield!"

With the minute of active use over, my armor enters cooldown mode. Alice takes advantage of the fact that I can't move to use me as shelter from the golem fragments.

"I-incredible..."

As I weigh my options on what to do with this coldhearted pile of junk, Rose just stands there next to me staring at what's left of the golem, evidently unbothered by the rain of shrapnel pelting her face.

"Unh... Can't you wake me up a little more gently...? You seem to be treating me worse and worse..."

The rain of golem shards is evidently enough to finally wake Grimm.

"Ah, Grimm, you're awake. Hey, uh, I'm afraid I can't move for the next three minutes or so. Do you mind shielding me from the enemy until that time's up? There shouldn't be too much to worry about. The other units are taking care of the grunts, Snow's handling Heine, and it looks like Rose took care of the griffin earlier..."

"Heine's actually on her way over here. Oh, and the griffin's up and looking pretty angry."

....

"...B-boss, I want to eat something really tasty when this battle's over."

"I'm not really sure what's going on, but I could go for a good drink myself."

"Okay, okay! Fine! You can have whatever you want! Just help me out here! But, Grimm, you're gonna get it later!"

3

"Hey, Six, looks like we meet again!"

Heine appears before me, her red eyes glinting like flame, as I lay helplessly behind Rose.

She doesn't appear to have noticed that my power armor is on cooldown and that I can't move.

"It's been a while, Heine of the Flames. You seem pretty excited today. Glad to see you're doing so well."

"Of course I'm excited! This is war!! Now let's get this started, Six! We can fight to the death today! There's no one to interrupt us!"

Heine appears satisfied with our conversation, and she's raring to go. In no time, she forms a ball of fire on her palm...!

"Wh-whoa, hold up! What's the rush? I actually had something I wanted to ask you!"

At those words, Heine stops to listen. Good! Need to buy as much time here as possible!

"Something you want to ask me? What is it?"

"What do you eat to get boobs like that?"

Heine throws a fireball in lieu of an answer, which Rose hurriedly swats aside.

"Well, Boss, you can just add this one to your ever-growing list of dumb ideas. Seriously, what were you thinking? Or are you just not thinking at all?"

Damn. Harsh.

"Oh? Swatting aside my flames barehanded? I'm impressed. The knight from earlier was a huge disappointment, but I think I'll have a lot more fun with you!"

Despite having her fireball deflected, Heine looks oddly happy. She eyes Rose with considerable interest.

All right, she's in the mood to talk. This is the perfect opportunity to buy a little more time.

…Or so I thought.

Snow runs toward us, bawling her eyes out.

"Waaaaaaaaah! Six! Siiix! The frost blade! My brand-new frost blade! That bitch melted it! You've got that weird projectile weapon, right? Use it to avenge my poor Iceberg!"

C'mon, don't turn the conversation back to fighting.

"Oh, right! That weird weapon! Whatever, this sounds like more fun! Bring it on, Six! I heard you took the treasure from the Tower of Duster! I knew you'd be able to do it! You're so impressive for a human! Come on, let's get to it!"

I have a woman literally throwing herself at me, and I'm terrified instead of ecstatic!

Heine flings another fireball my way, and Rose swats it down again.

"Six, hurry up and avenge Iceberg! I still have payments to make on it! My precious frost blade! The poor baby I cradled on my bosom every night… The frost blade I waited for ages and ages on a wait list to buy!"

I plead at Snow in silence, tearfully begging her to stop pouring gas on this fire.

"…Hey, Six, why is that girl protecting you? …Wait, you're not paralyzed, are you?"

Dammit! She figured it out.

"Griffin, draw that girl away from Six! I'll use that opening to cook him!!"

"Dammit, Snow! You useless— You'll pay for this, you idiot!"

"What did you say to me?! And for that matter, why can't you move?! Dammit! I can't do much without my sword, especially against that sort of flame…"

If you're that useless without your sword, why the hell did you even bother coming?!

Snow, thrown into confusion by my rage, stands watching as the griffin charges toward us. Rose jumps in front of the oncoming beast and draws in a deep breath.

"Drown in a sea of hellfire…! Sleep for all eternity! Crimson Breath!"

Rose takes the time to recite her little incantation before unleashing her flame breath at the charging griffin.

"Damn! That girl's too well adapted to us! Screw it! Excessive force it is!"

Heine's just about had it with the griffin cowering at Rose's flames, and she raises her arms. Even with Rose in my way, I can feel the heat building as Heine draws more and more fire into her palm.

"Say, Rose, do you really need to go through that little spiel?! Is it really something you need to recite?!"

"I'd rather not say it, either! But I promised Grandpa! I can't help that!"

While I'm bickering with Rose, Heine's flames intensify, turning from red to blue…!

Has it been three minutes yet? It feels like I've been waiting here forever!

"Rose, I believe in you! You can shrug off a little flame like that, right?!"

"Y-yes, the blast lizard meat's given me flame immunity, but Boss, there's a big problem!"

Noting Rose's desperate expression, I uneasily ask, "Wh-what is it?"

"I can't have my clothes burn away in public! And these are the only clothes I own……"

"I'll happily buy you new ones!"

Evidently coming to the conclusion that it'd be best to grab me and run, Rose tries to pick me up.

"Y-you can't expect a maiden to be okay with public nudity just like that...! ...B-boss, why do you weigh so much?! Nrrrrgh! I'm as strong as a one-horned ogre, b-but I can't even get you to budge!"

"The power armor's weight is why I can't move! Just need a little bit longer... Once the suit finishes cooling down, I'll get my strength back. Just hold on!"

Oblivious to our panic, Heine's flames go from blue to a blinding white.

"Make your peace, Six! For your sake, I'll make it quick!"

"Hey! That's one of the lines prohibited by the villainy manual! Rose, we're saved! I bet we're about to be rescued by a brave, elegant heroine responding to my distress!"

As I wander off into my own little world, Rose struggles to move me.

"Boss! Snap out of it! I'm about to get flash-stripped in public! No one will want to marry me! Can I pleeease just run away now?"

"I'll happily take responsibility if that happens, so don't leave meeee!!"

At that moment...

"O Great Lord Zenarith, I beseech thee! Deliver disaster upon this woman! Make her limbs fall asleep!"

Just as Heine prepares to lob an enormous fireball, she freezes in place as though petrified.

"Guh?! Wh-what the hell?! No way...! A curse?!"

Heine's eyes go wide in surprise at her sudden paralysis, while I, also stuck in place, offer thanks to my savior.

"Grimm, you saved my ass! You can be useful after all!"

"Indeed, indeed. Now you, too, have borne witness to Lord Zenarith's power… Wait, just what *did* you think of me until now?"

The long-awaited announcement in my head saves me from having to answer that question.

<Cooldown complete. Power armor reinitialized.>

"Thanks, Rose, I'm good now."

Freed from babysitting me, Rose turns her glare back to the griffin, her true rival.

Heine, too, appears to recover from her paralysis, slumping her shoulders in disappointment.

"Oh, I give up…," she mutters. "And here we were *just* about to test the golem's abilities… Things always seem to go wrong when you're around. Hey, Six, you sure you don't wanna join us? Name your demands. I bet we can meet most of them."

"Quick! Block Six's ears! Or just go ahead and get rid of that woman!" Alice barks out orders, trying to drown out Heine's voice.

"Boss! Talk to me for a bit! Don't listen to the enemy's words!"

"C-Commander! Forget about that woman and let's go on another night date!"

My two subordinates step closer, desperately trying to come up with things to say. At that moment, my senses sharpened by countless battles alert me to danger!

"Whoa!!"

I roll forward, mostly out of instinct, and dodge a lethal blow. Looking back in panic, I see Snow standing, dagger in hand.

"Wha—?! I thought you couldn't move! What are you doing dodging that blow?!"

"What the hell are *you* doing, you crazy bitch?! At least wait till I actually turn traitor!! Seriously, all of you?! Do you really think I'd just happily run off to join the enemy?!"

Man, screw these guys! Just who the hell do they think I am?

"First off, we'll triple your pay. Next, Six, have you ever heard of a demon called a succubus?"

"Yes, ma'am, I'm quite familiar with that demon."

"Hey, Six, stop listening so attentively! Don't answer her that politely! Stop getting baited and draw your gun!!" Alice shouts quickly in a rare display of anxiety.

"...Ugh, seriously, no trust at all. S-sorry to disappoint you, Heine of the Flames. I'm not so easily swayed by riches or women..."

I stand, dusting myself off and reaching for the gun on my hip. Heine smiles invitingly and outstretches her right hand.

"Come, Six, take my hand. I'll get whatever woman you want to take care of you. Teasing succubi, haughty-yet-submissive Lilims, devilishly beautiful vampires, sirens gently cooing in your ear..."

"Grimm! Shut that woman up with a curse! Six can't resist that charm magic much longer!"

"That's charm magic?! I don't feel any magic in the words, though...!"

"<...Sorry, Alice... I think I'm done for...>"

"<Get it together, Six! Also, stop speaking in Japanese! It makes you sound serious!>"

Alice cries out desperately just as a white blur cuts in between Heine and me.

"Gotcha!"

Seeing her opportunity, Snow lunges with dagger outstretched at Heine's arm.

Heine had put out the flames so she could offer her hand to me.

Snow strikes with her dagger, a silver glint flashing in the air. Heine quickly draws her hand backward; the blow glances off her gauntlet, sending a piece of it flying. The piece glows red as it tumbles in the air.

"Ack! My sorcerer stone!!"

All of Heine's attention turns to the stone, as though Snow and I have suddenly ceased to exist.

Heine's gaze falls on Alice, who snatches the gem out of the air.

"...Oh? What's this? Seems pretty important based on your reaction."

"N-not at all! It's n-nothing important..."

Heine's eyes belie her words as she stares desperately at Alice's hands. I stand next to Alice, gazing closely at the gem in her hands.

"If it's not important, I guess we can just hang on to it."

"Agreed. No need to give things back to the enemy. Especially if they're trivial."

"Ah! Um! W-well...that...um...that actually is important...," Heine stammers out after hearing our conversation.

"Oh, that's a sorcerer stone. Magic users need a conduit to cast spells. Usually they use something like a staff, a ring, or maybe a bracelet as a conduit, but it seems that's what the gem is for her. The gem's overflowing with magic. I imagine it must've taken a lot of time and effort to shape it into such a powerful conduit."

Grimm peers at the gem in Alice's hands, looking rather impressed as she describes what it is.

"...What happens to Heine without it?"

"She won't be able to use magic. She could use something else as a conduit, but she won't be able to wield a power befitting one of the Demon Lord's Elite Four."

Alice and I exchange glances, then look back at Heine.

"...Eeep! Wh-what are you plotting, Six? Y-you'll be joining us and bringing that stone with you, right? Right?! Please tell me I'm right!"

Heine's tone grows increasingly desperate, her eyes welling up with tears.

""""Yikes...""""

The other members of the unit back away after seeing our expressions.

4

The sounds of battle around us have ceased. Demons and soldiers alike have given their undivided attention to the sudden event unfolding with one of the Demon Lord's Elite Four. As for what that event is…

"Come on, Heine; it's like you're not even trying! Lean forward and accentuate your cleavage while looking up at me. Oh, hey! That teary expression is perfect!"

<Evil Points acquired.>

<Evil Points acquired.>

The announcer in my head is working overtime as I continue the photoshoot with my digital camera.

"…Just kill me now…"

While glaring daggers at me, Heine follows my instructions and strikes pose after provocative pose in front of the assembled crowd.

"Okay, next let's try leaning back on your arms, spreading your legs, and lowering your hips. Hey now! Get that hand out of the way. Hands *behind* your legs. Ah, those rebellious eyes are awesome! Looks like I'll get a great price for these with the right niche market…"

"*Sniffle…* Waaaah! …*Hic!*"

Heine finally breaks into tears. Rose, looking at her from a distance with the others, winces in sympathy.

"P-poor thing…"

Each time I press the shutter on the digital camera, I hear the announcement. Each time the announcement rings out, Alice nods approvingly at the device she's watching.

"Good work, Six. Keep it up! Drive her deeper into despair. There's nothing quite as satisfying as watching a strong enemy being humiliated. Mmmm… L-look, Six. The mighty Heine of the Flames reduced to heaving sobs…!" Snow stands next to me, hugging her hands to her body and shuddering in delight. "This is for Iceberg! Enjoy your humiliation! Mwa-ha-ha-ha-ha-ha-ha! Bwa-ha-ha-ha-ha-ha-ha!!"

So not only does she let her avarice and ambition drive her decisions, but she gets off on watching the humiliation of her enemies. I've gotta hand it to her. Snow is a piece of work.

Anyway, let's forget about the crazy girl and focus on Heine splayed out in front of me.

"All right, next. Stay in that position, keep that teary look, and give us a smile with double peace signs! …Good, good. Let's move on to the next step… You know, those clothes really do get in the way."

"Eeeep!"

Seeing Heine shy away from my predatory gaze, Rose scoots slowly over to me and taps me on the shoulder.

"B-boss. I—I think going any further would be too far, even if she is an enemy. Why not give her stone back? Once Miss Heine can use magic again, you can have a rematch."

In response to Rose's suggestion…

"Oh, Aliiice, did I ever say anything about giving the stone back?"

"Not that I know of. What you said verbatim was, 'All right, why don't we start with you pressing your boobs together and looking up at me!' You never promised you'd give her the stone if she listened to you. She just followed your directions assuming you'd give it back."

"Th-that's awful…!"

Heine jumps at this exchange, snarling.

"Y-you can't be serious?! You mean to tell me I did all that for nothing?! You're dead… YOU ARE A DEAD MAN, SIX!!"

"Oh? All right, if you can kill me without magic, go right on ahead. C'mon, what are you waiting for?"

"Grrrr… Grrrrrrrrrrr!!"

Heine clenches her jaw, grinding her teeth together in frustration and anger, eyes filled with tears of rage.

"Well, I guess there's no helping it. Do you want this back that badly?"

"A-are you going to give it back?! I beg you, that's a precious— Wh-wh-wh-what the—? What are you doing?!"

I unzip the fly on my power armor and start rustling around. You gotta love how practical the power armor is. It was designed so that you can even take a leak on the go. I snugly tuck Heine's precious object into the space where I keep only my most precious junk.

As a gentleman, I try to make things as painless for Heine as possible. I cross my arms in front of my chest and bend backward, getting into a bridge pose supported only by my neck and legs.

"Come and get it."

"…Six, you bastard! I'll remember thiiiiiiiiiiiiis!"

The sobbing Heine hops onto her griffin's back, trailing tears behind her as she flies off.

5

The pleasant *clink* of glasses coming together rings throughout a small tavern near the castle.

"""""Cheers!!"""""

With the battle concluded, I've brought my squad members to the tavern to celebrate.

"Well, that was quite the outcome, eh, Six? You destroyed the giant golem and, regardless of how you did it, weakened one of the Elite Four and drove her off. I'll never forget the look of despair on the faces of the Demon Lord's Army when Heine ran away! And who made it all possible? Us!" Snow hums happily to herself before tipping her stein back and taking a swig.

"Lately, it feels like we've really been taking the fight to the demons! I mean, before the commander took over, I was getting killed at least once per battle! O Great Lord Zenarith, I thank you for your blessing in letting me wake on something other than the altar of resurrection!" Grimm, taking up quite a bit of space inside the cramped tavern with her wheelchair, offers prayers of thanks to her god.

"Ish sho ghood! Sho ghood! Effer shinsh Boff took ofer, I'fe eafen sho muff delifif fud!" Next to Grimm sits Rose, who happily shovels down food into her mouth as quickly as she can grab hold of it. The crybaby Chimera is clearly still at an age where food takes precedence over beer.

"Yes, that's it! Don't be shy! Sing my praises all you want; I can handle it! …You know, given how well we've been doing, surely some awesome rumors have started to spread about us by now! What should we do if people come up to us for autographs? Oh, what*ever* shall we dooo?"

I use my stein to mime the motions of an eager fan, before cheerfully draining the contents and slamming the empty container down on the table. After taking a few more little sips from her drink, Snow lets out a confident snort.

"This is how it should be! Our squadron has me, the youngest knight in the kingdom's history. At this rate, I'll be back in charge in no time!"

I'm about to remind Snow that she hasn't exactly showered herself with glory while under my command, but a more important question bubbles up to the surface.

"You were the youngest knight once, sure, but that was ages ago, isn't it? How old are you now anyway?"

"Mm? Oh, I'm seventeen. I was knighted at twelve." Snow casually drops the bomb with the ease of someone who does that to conversations on a regular basis. She leisurely tips back her stein again.

"Wait, you're younger than I am? Looking like *that*?! Between your arrogance and your assets, I figured you were at least a few years older than me!"

"Pffffbbbt!"

Snow does a spit take.

"AAAAAHHHH! M-my eyes! My eyes!"

The stream of alcohol nails Grimm right in the face. Screaming in agony, the archbishop clutches at her eyes and writhes her way out of her wheelchair.

Coughing, Snow wipes at the corner of her mouth with her hand and looks at me with a faint flush on her cheeks.

"I—I may be a knight, but I'm a woman, too, you ass! Consider my feelings! What do you mean by 'looking like *that*'??"

"Shut it, you little brat! You've been talking to me like we're equals, and it turns out that this whole time I outranked you AND I was older?! Screw that!"

I sit back in my chair, lounging with an insolent ease, and toss a few coins Snow's way.

"Go buy me some bread. Chop-chop!"

"Not a chance! I'm not your squire; ask one of your servers to go instead! …You wanna be respected for being the oldest? Then stop acting like such a kid! It's high time you got it together as our commander…"

Snow's words are dripping with resentment, but Rose stops inhaling food just long enough to beam at the knight.

"Snow finally acknowledged Boss as the boss!"

"Wh-what?! No! I'm saying he needs to act more responsibly as our commander…"

"Someone get me a towel pleeeease!"

Our antics, while loud, don't hold a candle to the rest of the tavern patrons. The citizens are aware of today's victory, and everyone's in the mood to celebrate.

Wrapped in the night's festive atmosphere, we enjoy an evening of partying.

"Whew… Say, why isn't Alice here tonight?" Grimm asks, her cheeks flushing a faint shade of red as she empties her umpteenth stein. I can't exactly tell them that androids don't eat or drink, so…

"Alice? I sent her home early. Keeping her out at taverns past bedtime sets a bad example."

Snow continues nursing her drink, nodding along with the faintest look of approval. "Feels a little late to worry about bad examples when you're dragging her off to war. That girl's got a nasty mouth on her, but she's got a lot of potential. How do I put this? She's brilliant. Just the other day, I heard a ridiculous story about how she'd read every book in the castle archive in one day."

"I actually saw Miss Alice negotiating with a bunch of merchants at the market."

"*Glug, glug*… Aah! I've seen Alice delivering packages to various healers' clinics around town."

Huh. Seems the android's been keeping herself busy when I'm not looking.

"Merchants and healers? Hey, Six, I've heard a few rumors around town. An increase in the quality of arms and armor. Merchants throwing around money from selling better goods. New medicines no one's heard of… Do you think Alice might be involved with any of that?"

"No clue."

Contrary to my answer, I can see Alice's fingerprints all over these stories. Snow looks a little skeptical about my answer and takes another tiny sip. Well, it was less of a sip and more like she merely touched her tongue to the liquid.

"…Hrmph! Honestly, I don't care where you're from. You and Alice are indispensable members of our squadron. But don't let that go to your head. I still don't trust you! And you're still not my commander!"

"Listen closely, Rose. Snow is what you'd call a *tsundere*. She might act like she hates me, but in truth, she's actually head over heels for me."

"Huh! So the reason Miss Snow is always bugging you is because she likes you, Boss? Interesting!"

"I really will kill you, you know. Don't think I won't. I swear, from the moment I met you…"

"Hey, you! Hot guy tending the bar! Another round!"

They say time flies when you're having fun. This night's flying by so quickly I'm starting to get dizzy…

6

I heave a deep sigh, supporting the half-conscious Six against my shoulder and dragging him out of the tavern. The soldiers we'd shared drinks with look over at him leaning drunkenly against my arm and laugh.

"Thanks for dinner, Boss! It's been a while since I've had this much to eat!"

"My thanks as well, Commander! Now, Rose, you and I are going to go for a little joyride. I feel we can set a new speed record tonight!"

As Grimm gleefully makes an ominous proposal, Rose hesitates, her expression souring.

"Can we not and say we did? My stomach's full and I'm getting sleepy. Can't you just go by yourself? Besides, Grandpa always said that I shouldn't stay out all night."

"Who's going to witness my record if not you? Come along now!

Let's go harass all the happy couples who dare use our triumph as an excuse to get all lovey-dovey!"

"Sigh..."

I watch as Grimm grabs Rose by the arm and drags her along on her self-declared mission. I then half escort, half carry Six back to the castle.

"Yaaaaaaaaaaawn! It's been a while since I drank *that* much! That one barmaid sure was cute, wasn't she? Did you see her reaction when I grabbed her butt? So innocent!"

Six, in full jackass mode, continues like this for some time.

"...At least try to remember you're a commander. Your stupidity is terminal, but I can't have you tarnishing the rest of our reputations!"

"Dumbass! I'm just followin' the etiquette fer a proper Combat Agent! Did you forget to memorize the maaanual? 'Heh-heh, how about you walk that cute butt of yours over this way and pour me a drink?' is the standard compliment for cute waitresses, 'member?"

This idiot is hard enough to understand when he's sober. Now that he's sloshed, he's incoherent.

"Tch... No, don't go that way, you idiot. This way! Hey! That is *not* a bathroom!"

I forcefully drag the stumbling Six back to the barracks. By some miracle, we make it back to the room he shares with Alice.

"Yo, Six, welcome back. Ah, looks like he's wasted again. Just how much did this idiot drink?"

It seems Alice had been eagerly awaiting Six's return. She opened the door immediately after I knocked.

"It was worse than I expected. He demanded they bring the keg, then bought everyone in the tavern drinks, claiming he'd struck it rich."

"He's allergic to saving money. I suppose he can't help that he's a spendthrift. Good work bringing him back."

I feel you've crossed a line of no return when even a child this young has such a low opinion of your character. And yet, this fool claims to be my superior.

"G'niiiiight, Snowy! Thanks for escorting your commander home! Gimme a good-night kiss before you go!!"

"Don't call me Snowy, you drunk moron! Just shut up and go to bed!"

I kick the blathering boozehound into his room. Picking up the pace, I start toward my own quarters.

Honestly... How the hell has he survived this long? He's been insolent and rude since the day we met. Now, I won't deny he can fight, and I admit he has his uses in battle, but "Snowy"? Ridiculous.

"I can't believe him! Thinking he can mock me as he pleases. I'm seriously going to end him one of these days," I mutter.

So I say, but I understand full well I can't do that now that we've fought in the same unit. As much as it pains me to admit it, I'm pretty sure he's...

"Oh? Ending Sir Six? I'm afraid I can't ignore such a remark."

I freeze at the sudden voice before sharply turning in the direction it came from.

"My lord..."

Standing there is the chief of staff, a one-eyed man wearing a hat to hide his balding pate.

"N-no, my lord... I didn't mean it; I was just trying to vent some..."

Given how often I've uttered a variation of that sentiment in public, I don't know why it would be an issue at this point.

The chief of staff holds up his palm, interrupting my explanation.

"Don't worry yourself. I understand how you feel. An insolent stranger blows in from parts unknown and immediately begins running amok and acting a fool. And who gets the blame? You do. Meanwhile, he lucks into a command position, then uses despicable means to rake in the glory. That seems reason enough to want him dead."

The chief of staff doesn't bother to actually listen to me, completing his circle of reasoning and nodding to himself in agreement.

I've never actually wanted him dead, but I can fully agree about his insolence.

"Honestly! He's so insufferable! And he's always finding new ways to get under my skin! It's as though his purpose in life is to annoy everyone around him!"

My alcohol tolerance has always been pretty low, and I've had several drinks at this point. I suppose that's coaxed out the pent-up day-to-day frustration.

"I completely understand your feelings! Every little thing he can think of, he comes and needles me, calling me 'old man.' It would seem that you and I are of the same mind."

The chief of staff stands next to me, placing his hand on my shoulder.

Same mind? A bald-faced lie. I haven't forgotten how this man used to talk down to me. As a lowly knight, my status as a homeless orphan made me a perfect target for his public mockery.

The thoughts go through my head in rapid succession as I glance uneasily at the hand on my shoulder.

"Lady Snow, you've almost certainly produced enough results to return to your old position. Do you not agree that you would be better suited to commanding the Royal Guard?"

"I-if possible, yes!"

Nothing can describe the amount of blood, sweat, and tears I shed in order to rise from slum-dwelling orphan to knight captain.

I suffered countless acts of cruelty motivated by my lowly birth and fueled by envy later on.

To be able to return to my old role would make it all worth it!

…But what would that mean for my current squadron? The recent victories were achieved by the whole squadron, not just myself.

I suppose I could just induct them into the Royal Guard. It would be my unit, and it's my right and privilege to treat Grimm and Rose as equals. I could also make use of Alice's smarts to handle strategies and combat tactics.

...And as for the moron.

You can't rely on a single thing that goes on in his brain or comes out of his mouth, but he's a better fighter than I am. It'd be cruel to leave just him out, so I'll include him in my unit!

I don't know what my expression looked like at that moment, but the chief of staff nodded at me with a satisfied smile.

He's kept his hand on my shoulder for an uncomfortably long time, but I don't want to upset him by pointing that out. I can take out this frustration on someone later, maybe on the moron...

"Excellent, excellent. Lady Snow, you look quite pleased as well. I'm sure you're sick of fighting alongside that demon-blooded abomination and crazy disaster cultist as well. I understand, I understand completely."

My brow twitches at those insults to my comrades, but I somehow manage to contain the anger. That flash of rage coupled with my tendency to lash out at provocation are the reasons why the moron can mock me about my quick temper.

"On a related subject...Lady Snow, you mentioned in front of His Majesty that Sir Six was a foreign spy."

I'd forgotten about that. I vaguely recall saying something along those lines.

"I'm afraid that was a misunderstanding on my part. I don't believe that man is capable of something as subtle as spying. If anything, he's the kind of person who would forget his mission if he grew too comfortable in his target country, and he would probably end up settling in."

That's definitely my gut reaction. There's no way that fool could manage something as complex as espionage. He'd make a horrendous spy, drawing far too much attention to himself.

...Still, the chief of staff seems unconvinced.

"I believe it's too soon to say. That man won those victories, after all. It wouldn't be a stretch to assume that he might be smart enough to hide his true nature... You're observant and intelligent. Moreover, your loyalty to this kingdom is unparalleled. So I wish to ask you a favor. Can you subtly monitor Sir Six's activities? I want you to find evidence that he's a spy. Regardless of the truth of the accusations."

Slumping my shoulders while walking down the hall, I sigh and think back to the chief of staff's request. Find evidence that Six is a spy in exchange for promotion back to Royal Guard captain. The chief of staff made it abundantly clear that he didn't care if the evidence was genuine, meaning he planned to set Six up for a fall either way.

Despite the kingdom facing annihilation, the chief of staff is more worried about his career.

"...The chief of staff. I don't like him. He's shady as hell, I just know it. He's definitely the sort of self-serving bastard that'll do whatever it takes to ensure he comes out ahead." Suddenly Six's words come to mind, and they're much more credible now.

There may be some hypocrisy in the statement, but I can't shake the feeling that the moron is still the better man.

I let out another deep sigh, shoulders still slumped, as I approach Six's room. In my hand, I carry a leather pouch containing reward money for Six. The chief of staff happily gave me the errand.

"'It'll give you a reason to meet with Sir Six,' he says. Ugh... If I go to his room at this hour, I'm never going to hear the end of it."

...Oh, well. I guess I'll give up on the Royal Guard billet.

If I keep fighting with the current squadron, I'll eventually have a real opportunity to win back my rank.

Standing in front of Six's door, I take a deep breath to calm my emotions.

"But seriously, like, what do I do? If the king asks me to take Tillis as my wife and rule the kingdom, should I do it? Does this kingdom even allow polygamy?"

I still can't understand how the hell his mind works.

"Don't know, don't care. Tillis seems like quite the beauty to me. Are you not content with just one wife?"

"It's not *about* being content. Think about it! My squad's nothing but hot babes! What if on the night before the wedding, one of the squad members came up to me? 'Commander! The truth is, I've always…!'"

…S-seriously! What is wrong with his head?!

"…I thought my wealth of prior knowledge on these scenarios would prepare me for any situation. I guess I've got a lot to learn."

"Is that so? Well, I have no idea what you're talking about, but you're pretty good at getting things done when you actually try. Give it your best effort."

I'm starting to feel a lot of sympathy for Alice. She's the one stuck caring for him.

"If my wife ended up being someone like Snow, I bet every day would be something new and exciting."

I feel the blood rushing to my head at the remark. I take a deep breath, preparing to launch into a venomous tirade as I reach for the door…!

"…That reminds me. I need to keep the Kisaragi Supreme Leader route open. Let's start wrapping up our spy activities. The reward for this last mission was pretty impressive. We probably have enough to finally establish that base…"

"Six, it's good that you're happy, but you need to keep it down. At least use Japanese when talking about—"

The leather bag of coins given to me by the chief of staff lands on the floor with a loud thump.

[Status Report: Update]

Primary survey of target planet status—completed.

Alice and I are switching primary objective to establishing a base of operations.

Secured sufficient funds to purchase a base of operations through local currency investments conducted by Alice.

Will provide update when a location suitable to serve as a base of operations is identified.

…No major obstacles anticipated in acquiring a base of operations.

Reporting Operative:
Combat Agent 6

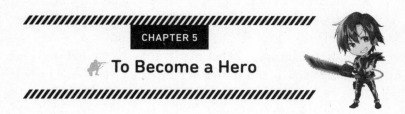

CHAPTER 5

To Become a Hero

1

"…What did you say?"

Bursting through the door, Snow clenches her hands into fists and casts her eyes downward.

"A spy? Is that what you've been all this time?"

…Oh, crap. She's the last person in the world I needed to hear that. And it looks like she caught the whole conversation.

Okay, let's think. How the hell do I get out of this one? Should I just play dumb?

I mean, I'm already supposed to have a head injury from battle. I don't think I can keep any more of these stories straight.

Oh, I know! This problem is best solved by acting pissed off myself! Of course!

"Barging in without so much as a knock? What are you, an ape? What if I had been doing something *private*…? Were you hoping to walk in on me changing, Boobzilla?"

"Really, Snow, you can't take the words of a drunk so seriously. At this rate, you'll end up getting conned by some random scumbag. That's why Six is so good at..."

Catching my intention, Alice starts to follow up but trails off as she notices Snow is still staring at the ground. Her whole body is trembling.

"...It's over, Six. Just give up."

Seriously? If I give up here, they'll cut my head off for spying. I have no intention of losing my head without a struggle. I've gotta think of a way to convince Snow...

"I won't ask who you really are. Think of it as thanks for all you've done for us."

Snow clenches her jaw, tightening her grip until her knuckles go white.

"I'm giving you one chance to leave quietly, so get out. I don't want to see you ever again..."

Snow speaks in a deflated whisper. She never once looks up from the floor.

"Yippee, I'm first! I call this room! Whoo-hoo! This bed is huuuuuuuge!"

"No fair, Six! Fine! The first- and second-floor bathrooms are mine."

Alice and I have rented a house to serve as a temporary base of operations. It's a small house on the outskirts of town, but it's pretty well suited to serving as a villain's hideout.

"Wh-what? You have no need for bathrooms! At least let me have the second-floor bathroom!"

"I'll consider giving you a bathroom if you hand over this room."

Alice and I explore the house, going through each room and claiming them.

"This room's right next to mine. Right, this'll be Astaroth's room. I'll just go ahead and write her name on the door. If our rooms are nearby, I should be able to catch the occasional glimpse of her after a bath."

"...Right. Well, knock yourself out. Oh, Six, I almost forgot to mention. While you were off playing knight, I went ahead and completed resource and life-form surveys of the surrounding area."

Well, that explains where she'd been disappearing off to. I was wondering what she had been up to when I wasn't watching her. Good thing, too, since I'd completely forgotten about that part of our assignment.

"Huh. I guess you are pretty high spec after all."

"Thank you for that, ex-knight-captain-obvious. I should mention I've also made some local connections by selling a few new material and medicine recipes. All within reason, of course. I also made a little money doing commodity speculation using our funds. We've got a decent amount saved up."

Whoa, really?

"Miss Alice, spare a coin or two for poor old Six? I went a little too far with my spending. The rent on this house cleaned me out."

"...You should have a little more shame instead of begging an android for money. Anyway, this took a little longer than expected, but we can start on the last stage of our mission."

Right, our final task on this planet.

"...Yeah, good point. Is the basement a good place for the teleporter back to Earth?"

"Yeah, if we spruce it up a bit, we can fit a small teleporter. Why don't we have them start sending the pieces today?"

It's a really important task, but it feels a bit anticlimactic.

Once the teleporter is assembled, we can call more Combat Agents in from Earth and start our invasion of this kingdom.

Once there are enough of us, the Demon Lord's Army won't stand a chance. This planet will be crushed by a combination of the Kisaragi Corporation's modern weaponry and sheer material resources.

"Hey, what's wrong, Six? You can tell me if something's bothering you. I was designed to support you, after all. The least I can do is lend a listening ear if you need one."

Alice falls into the bed, all but her face being buried by the covers, and turns her head to face me.

"…It's nothing specific. I'm an operative for an evil organization. After everything I've done, it'd be weird if I had any hang-ups about this place. The moment I get back to Earth, I'm going to drink ice-cold beer until I pop. All the alcohol here is lukewarm, ugh. When I get home, I'm going to make the Supreme Leaders pay my bar tab. As for this backwater kingdom with no electricity or gas? I won't miss it. With all the accolades I've earned here, I can be promoted right to the top!"

As I think of the bright future waiting for me back on Earth, Alice seems to lose interest, turning to stare up at the ceiling.

"…If you say so. Anyway, Six, I'm going to start on renovating the room and assembling the teleporter. Stay out of my way for the next month or so. Wander off for a bit and enjoy yourself."

…A month?

"Wait, why do I have to wait that long? Surely it doesn't take that long to put a teleporter together."

"…You really don't listen, do you? I explained it to you when we first got here. It takes at least a month after assembly for the connection to Earth to stabilize."

Oh yeah, I vaguely remember an explanation of that sort.

"…That leaves me with a *lot* of free time…"

"Right. Which is why I want you to spend it somewhere else so you're out of my way… That reminds me. It looks like the Demon Lord's Army has been making some odd moves lately. The Chosen One or whatever has driven one of the Elite Four into a cavern. The other Elite Four are taking advantage of the Chosen One's absence from the capital, and they're gathering their forces. They're probably plotting to take out the kingdom of Grace while the Chosen One's busy elsewhere."

Where the hell does she get her information…?

Hmm… The Demon Lord's Army, huh…?

"That's what they get! Time for that bitch to regret driving me away! I mean, sure, the whole spying thing is entirely my fault, but given all the results we produced, the least she could do was hear me out!"

"You do realize espionage is usually a capital offense, right? The fact that she didn't bother asking any questions and simply kicked us out was probably her way of saying thanks. Anyway, if by chance, the Chosen One loses again, this kingdom's coffers will take a serious hit… Are you okay with that?"

Alice's expression is flat, but I feel like she sees right through me.

"…Wh-what are you talking about? I'm no Hero. I'm not bailing them out."

That's right, I'm a Combat Agent for an evil organization.

It's completely against our philosophy to put myself at risk to help others with nothing to gain for myself.

I suppose I might consider it if that bitch comes to me and begs for help.

Putting aside that insolent brat, Rose and Grimm were my subordinates, too.

But that's not really enough reason to help them.

I go silent for a while as I struggle with conflicting emotions.

"Hey, Six…," my partner, the high-spec evil android, says, turning to me. "The thought of a competitor getting in the way of your invasion target pisses you off, doesn't it?"

The supposedly emotionless android looks over at me with an impish grin.

2

"Odd movements from the Demon Lord's Army?"

"Yes, Boss. From a scouting report. Scouts say there's a good chance the enemy will invade within the next few days."

"…I see. Thank you, Rose… Oh, also, you don't have to refer to me as 'Boss.' You can go on calling me Miss Snow."

Rose breaks out in a happy grin.

"…Understood, Miss Snow!"

…If I were as straightforward as she is… If I could deal with things more flexibly, could I have at least listened to what he had to say instead of just driving him away?

I shelve that bit of self-doubt and address my knights.

"Split into two groups for a training exercise. We'll fight with the assumption that we're facing the Demon Lord's Elite Four."

My loyal subordinates roar their enthusiasm and quickly begin organizing.

…This wasn't how I wanted to come back to this unit…

I think back to the events that led to my reinstatement and can't help but frown.

Once Six left, the chief of staff, convinced that it was my doing, happily signed the reinstatement papers putting me back in charge of the Royal Guard.

That's not why I drove him off. I know I'm particularly attached to money and prestige, but I can't feel happy about being reinstated this way.

…Not that this is a new revelation, but times like these are when I want to curse my own personality.

I guess my irritation is showing itself on my face again. Rose hesitates before she approaches me to speak.

"…Um, Miss Snow, there's another report…"

"What is it? Good news? Bad news?"

I'm not certain I can stomach more bad news.

"I-I'm not actually sure… It's um… Well, lately, it seems a pervert has been spotted creeping around at night."

"…Oh, is that all? That's a job for the town guard, isn't it?" I reply.

Rose looks decidedly uneasy.

"The witnesses say the pervert wears a spiky suit of black armor…"

3

"Well, hellooo there, little lady! Wanna see a magic trick? Keep your eyes on my pants now! Behold! The zipper goes down without me lifting a finger!"

"Ahhhhhh! You pervert! S-someone heeeeeelllllllp!!"

A girl out alone this late at night. What are her parents thinking? I watch the girl run off, listening to the familiar announcement of my Evil Points racking up as I zip up my fly.

"Hmph. How irresponsible. Makes you worry about the future of this kingdom… Whew, that makes six for the evening. Who's next? Ah, how about that girl wandering near the alley?"

It's long past nightfall and nearing midnight. I follow a girl who appears to be walking alone down a dark alleyway for some reason. There isn't a single other person around. Now's my chance.

"Hee-heeeeeeee! Look at meeeeee!!"

"Ahhhhhhhhhhh!!"

I spread my arms and position myself in front of the girl.

"Now, little lady, can you work up the courage to unzip my fly?"

"Ahhhhhhhhhhh! It's a rapist!!"

Terrified by my sudden appearance, the girl curls up into a ball on the ground.

"Heh-heh-heh-heh-heh, don't worry, I don't plan to touch you. All you need to do is scream and run away! No time to waste! If you don't run now, my fly will come down even without your help!"

"Ahhhhhhhhhhh! You're lying! You plan to do way more than touch, don't you?! You'll use sweet words to lower my guard, then drag me off into the shadows. Then you'll violate me and make me into your sex slave!!"

This reaction is a little more extreme than I was expecting, so I try to calm the screaming young woman.

"Relax, there are reasons why I can't touch you! Now, get up and run away, or I'll show you something that'll *really* make you scream!"

I let out the creepiest chuckle in my arsenal before placing my hand on my fly and inching ever closer.

"Lies, all lies! You're going to kidnap me and use me as an outlet for your raging libido, day after day! Oh no! I twisted my ankle trying to run from you, and now I can't get up! Nooooooooooo!!"

"Um, when exactly did you try to run? Much less twist your ankle? …Listen, I'm not going to kidnap you, and I don't actually touch civilians. I just wanted to creep you out…"

"Noooooooooo! Lies! There's no way you can resist touching such a beautiful girl like me! I bet you're going to drag me off to a beautiful white house by the sea miles away from anyone else, keeping me as your sex slave and forcing me to have at least three of your children! The first will of course be a boy! Then we'll have a girl! What would you want for the third?!"

Who the hell is this girl?! Is this really happening?!

"No, no, listen... Wait, this is weird. I'm not getting any Evil Points... Hey, you. You're not actually resisting, are you? I only need you to look, honest."

I try my best to get through to her, but the girl has absolutely no intention of listening to me. She just keeps violently shaking her head from side to side.

"Noooooooooo! Just looking? Nooooooooooo!"

"Looooooooooooooooook!!"

"...Well, if you insist."

While struggling to figure out what to do with the girl in front of me, I relax as I hear a new voice behind me, and I turn around.

"Oh? You actually want to see? In that case, feast your eyes upon my—"

Sure enough, Snow is standing right there.

"Feast my eyes upon your what...? Go on, then. What were you going to show me?"

Having helped up the girl I had been trying to frighten, Rose joins Snow and looks at me pityingly. Snow, meanwhile, stands with her arms crossed. She's glaring at me with such cold contempt that I have to suppress the shiver up my spine.

"...I'm very sorry, ma'am," I say in a voice so tiny that it sounds like the buzzing of a mosquito.

"No reason to apologize. You're going to show me something, right? I'm telling you I'll look. Rose, go to that tavern and gather up a crowd for me. He's about to put on a show of some kind. Now, go ahead and show me! I'll take a long, hard look at that pathetic little thing."

"I'm sorry! Please, please forgive me! But take back what you said about it being pathetic!"

"...So? I'm well aware that you're a disgrace to humanity, an idiot, a pervert, and utterly beyond saving. So tell me how you ended up here. You can explain, right?"

In the back alley, without another soul around, I'm sitting on my knees with head bowed in front of Snow.

"U-um... This is all part of making preparations against the Demon Lord's Army..."

"...Do you really think I'm that stupid? What sort of harebrained excuse is that?!"

Snow reaches for the sword on her hip...

"It's true! I'm not lying; I swear it's true! I need to do this! You can ask Alice if you want!"

"Are you out of your mind? How in the hell does your perversion tie into the Demon Lord's Army?!"

Goddammit! She's actually using logic!

Is there really no way out of this...?

"I'm telling the truth! I swear! I'm not lying!"

"Quiet! I've heard enough. The serious parting, all that second-guessing, and *this* is what I catch you doing?! I feel like an idiot for actually being depressed!"

"P-please calm down, Boss, Miss Snow. U-um...wh-why did you quit anyway, Boss? Miss Snow wouldn't tell me..."

Rose hurriedly restrains Snow from drawing her sword. Huh, that's kind of a surprise. I figured Snow would've told everyone why we'd left.

"I couldn't stand Snow's constant sexual harassment. It was getting worse by the day. She kept grabbing my butt every time I passed her in the hallway. Let the rest of the castle know that's why I left."

"Just who do you think I am anyway? Don't try to spread idiotic rumors! Enough! I can feel myself growing stupider just by talking to you. I'll let you go this time, but if I hear more rumors of your perversion, you're dead!"

With that, Snow turns on her heel...

I shout at her back.

"I hear the Demon Lord's Army is invading soon! If you want my ultrapowerful assistance, then apologize for your shitty attitude and beg for it!"

"Like hell I'm going to do that! I see your talent for enraging people hasn't gone anywhere. Do you want to die that badly?" In a fit of anger, Snow twists back around, hand on the hilt of her sword. "You know, I thought I told you I never wanted to see you again, and yet here you are! Fool!"

"Y-you're the one who came looking for me, you idiot!"

"Miss Snow! Boss! Will you two calm down? You sound like children!" Rose tries desperately to stop our argument.

"Rose, he's not in command anymore. Stop calling him Boss. We're done here!"

Snow spits out the words like she just took a bite of something nasty before turning away from me again.

"I hope you get so angry you have an aneurysm!"

"You son of a—!"

"If you two don't stop, I'm going to take a bite out of both of you!!"

4

A few days later.

"Hey look, it's the Fly!"

"Hey, Fly! Unzip your fly!"

Children follow me, chanting taunts as they fling rocks at my back.

"Oh, look… That's the guy everyone's talking about…"

"…Want to talk to him? He might unzip his fly for us!"

I hear some young women, students probably, exchange whispers a little distance away.

"U-um… I'll take this one and that one…"

I do my best to ignore all the hushed gossip and order my food from the lady at the skewer shop.

"A chargrilled lizard skewer and a rat skewer, right? That'll be six copper."

I count out the coins and hold my hand out toward the lady…

"Eeep!"

…………

As I stand there with the coins in my outstretched hand, the lady looks contritely toward me, then lets out a soft giggle.

"S-sorry. Um, I thought you were going to unzip your fly and take the money out from there."

"Waaaaaaaaaaaaaaaah! Alice! Listen! Everyone in the city is being so mean to me!"

I rush into Alice's room crying.

"Hmm? What's wrong, Fly? Did it get caught in your fly?"

"Stop calling me Fly!"

Thanks to a wanted poster put up by Snow, I'd become famous as the neighborhood pervert. I hear a voice from outside the window.

"Hey, Fly! Come on out! Show me your magic trick!"

"You damned brat! I'll pants you in front of everyone and reveal you as Captain Commando!!"

I prepare to jump out the window after the kid, but Alice grabs my arm as she continues writing on a sheet of paper on her desk.

"Stop that, Fly. If you get in trouble now, you'll actually be arrested."

"Don't call me the Fly! Dammit, and to think I was doing this to prepare for the fight against the invading army!"

Yes, that's right. The flashing was something I was doing to earn Evil Points.

"I mean, yes, I told you to go earn some Evil Points, but I didn't expect you to earn them that way, Fly."

"Stop it with the Fly!! And as for the bastards in this city, once the battle is over, I'll show them that I'm not just a pervert!"

"I didn't think you'd actually admit that you're a pervert... All right, I'm just about done."

Alice sets down a map and some forms on the desk and turns to me. Chewing on the meat skewers I bought, I take the seat across from her.

"For starters, we'll need a lot of anti-personnel mines. We should also get a few anti-tank mines for the really big demons."

I let Alice figure out how to spend the Evil Points acquired over the past few days. I could have done it myself, but I figured I can trust the high-spec android.

"We've got a little over five hundred points right now. I'd like to keep around two hundred points in reserve. So we can spend three hundred. Let's have them send three anti-tank mines, with the rest of the points going to anti-personnel mines."

"Never thought I'd see the day when I spent Evil Points on land mines. What a waste..."

Ordinarily, Evil Points are used to get powerful weapons that can't be bought with money. Anti-personnel mines are cheap. Depending on the type, you can buy multiple without breaking the bank.

"Think they'll send us mines if we offer our gold coins?"

"Probably not. The Supreme Leaders don't care about money as

much as they care about having you rack up evil deeds. The plan probably goes something like this: You commit a steady stream of evil
deeds, then something really atrocious, and ta-daa! You're a villain-
ous Supreme Leader."

Eh, I suppose that's been the case since I was still on Earth.

"Do they really think I'm capable of heinous evil deeds?" I let out
a soft sigh, thinking about the three top Supreme Leaders.

"Hey, however bad you are at it, you'd actually managed to rack
up a pretty decent amount of points. Of course, now that everyone recognizes you as a pervert, and Snow's put you on notice, you won't be
able to earn more this way... Still, you did really well given how petty
your deeds were and how little time you had to do it."

"Um...are you praising me or insulting me? I can't tell."

Alice starts writing down the equipment to be teleported over.

"All right. Let's go over the rest of our plan. If the Demon Army
invades while the Chosen One is away, the Demon Army's going to
win. That's the worst outcome for us. We'll have to abandon this base,
and this kingdom is the largest in the area. Once it goes down, no one
will be able to stop the demons. If they keep going and invade neighboring countries, it doesn't matter where we go. We won't have any
breathing room to put our teleporter together."

Where the hell is the Chosen One anyway?

"It takes a month to assemble the teleporter and stabilize the connection, right?"

"Right. If we rush it, we might manage three weeks, but we want
to avoid that if possible. I never want to deal with an unstable teleport
again. So a month to be sure."

Wait...?

"'Again'? Wait, was your first unstable teleport the time you were
sent here with me? What was our actual chance of success on that trip
anyway?"

"At any rate, we need the kingdom to repel the upcoming invasion and then maintain a safe environment for us to assemble the teleporter. But as it stands, the kingdom will lose if we don't intervene in some fashion. We'll still probably end up relying on the Chosen One, but we need to buy enough time for him to get here. Therefore, we'll be installing mines and traps and using guerrilla tactics to slow the advance of the Demon Lord's Army."

"Don't change the subject. Just how risky was that first teleport? Come on... Guerrilla warfare, huh? That brings back memories. We set a lot of traps back then, too. I wonder how the tiger man and chameleon man are doing these days? They saved my neck more than once in those jungles."

If those two were here, this fight would be a cakewalk...

"Ideally, we could have Kisaragi send us some reinforcements. Unfortunately, the Supreme Leaders dislike throwing employees away on one-way missions, so they probably won't authorize reinforcements unless there's a way to get them back to Earth."

"Uh, they sent me here without any guarantee I'd get back safely..."

Alice spreads out the map, pretending not to hear me. "All right, let's figure out the enemy's invasion route. I mean, it's pretty obvious based on this area's geography and the size of the enemy army..."

"...Hey, Alice. Do you think the Supreme Leaders secretly hate me? They don't, right? I'm a Supreme Leader candidate after all..."

Alice completely ignores me and stands up.

"Right. Let's bury the mines around here, where human hunters aren't likely to go. There's only so much we can do, but let's go and thin out the advance units of the Demon Army while we wait for the Chosen One to get back."

"C'mon, Alice! Tell me I'm right! Please? Please?! Pretty please??!"

5

The next day.

"That should do it. The camouflage is perfect. Hey, Six, I'm all done here. Hurry up and dig the next hole."

Alice hums a song to herself as she sets the mines.

"...*Hahhh... Hahhh... Hahhh...*"

Exhausted from the work, I can't even manage a coherent reply. I toss my shovel aside and slump onto the ground.

"Y-you...you need to remember...that I'm still human... There are limits to how much work I can do... L-lemme rest for a sec."

We started a little past dawn, and now it's currently around noon. I've been digging nonstop since we got here.

"We're already in enemy territory. Given that it's broad daylight, it's only a matter of time before they see us. Suck it up. We're almost done," Alice says.

I drag my heavy limbs, pick up my shovel, and resume digging. "C-come to think of it...since you can't get tired...why don't we have you dig the holes...and I bury the mines...? It'd be...way more efficient."

Alice sits with her knees to her chest, watching me gasping for breath as I dig.

"It's a precaution. There are a lot of demons with sharp noses. If you touch the mines, you might leave your scent on them. So long as you're just digging, even if they detect you, they won't detect the mines. And if they want to make it to the kingdom, they have to come through here. There's no way around it. Furthermore, can you remember where every mine is buried? Mine removal after a war is basic etiquette."

"...This is slave labor..." An idea occurs to me, and I call out to Alice. "Hey, Alice, save a mine for me. I have an idea."

As Alice looks over at me curiously, I take an object from my pocket and hold it out. It's the sorcerer stone we took from Heine of the Flames.

"Let's put this on top of the mine trigger. I figured we'd have to sell or destroy it, but this is way too good an opportunity to pass up."

"Oh, come on. Surely she won't fall for something so obvious. She'll just send an underling to go fetch it. I mean, the probability that Heine's the first one to find it is pretty low anyway. Considering the possibility the sorcerer stone ends up back in enemy hands, we're probably better off destroying it right now."

Alice looks closely at the stone, as if considering our options.

"It's fine. If some other demon picks it up, that's at least one less demon to worry about. And the blast should take out the stone, too. Besides, just imagine the look on Heine's face when it blows up in her grasp. I get chills just thinking about it!"

"...You've definitely got the right personality for this line of work."

By the time we finish our work and get back to the city, the mood of the place has changed completely. The people walking by all look a little pale, and everyone is gloomy. A good number of people walk with eyes downcast, avoiding eye contact.

"Something's wrong. They weren't this gloomy even when there was a mysterious pervert on the loose."

"Hey, can you do me a favor and forget that ever happened...?"

Alice's callback aside, there's something wrong with the city's mood. I approach a nearby woman.

"Um, excuse me, do you mind if I ask you something?"

"Yes... What is—? Eeep! Th-the Fly..."

....

The woman clams up and backs away as soon as she recognizes me.

"I'm sorry about the pervert accompanying me, ma'am. Also, everyone here looks really sad. Is something wrong?"

The woman is still staring at me and twitching in fear, but she eventually lowers her guard thanks to Alice's innocent little girl act.

"Y-yes... There's been an unsettling rumor surrounding the Chosen One... It seems he's been missing in action ever since his encounter with Faustless of the Wind, one of the Demon Lord's Elite Four... On top of that, the demons are taking advantage of the Chosen One's absence and gathering their forces. And this town is their next target..."

6

"According to the information I've gathered, the Chosen One fought one of the Elite Four and was close to beating him. However, this new enemy, Faustless of the Wind, used a spell called Random Teleport and took the Chosen One with him. As you might guess from the name, the spell teleports the targets to a random destination."

Back at our hideout, Alice and I hold an emergency meeting.

"This teleport spell has the ability to transport you pretty much anywhere. The destination remains unknown. Think of our first teleport on to this planet. It could be somewhere in the sky, out at sea, or even the middle of the Darkwood. The probability of survival is close to zero."

"I've never even seen this Chosen One in person, but I feel for him. I could've been in his shoes if something fudged my teleportation. Well, in my case, I was probably guaranteed a pretty high success rate, right?"

Sure, it's not directly related to me, but if I consider that the very same thing could've happened to me, I can't help but feel sympathy for the Chosen One.

"...........Right."

"Why did it take you so long to agree?"

Okay, so it seems my situation was a lot closer to his than I thought.

"Anyway, isn't the Chosen One supposed to beat the Demon Lord according to the prophecy or whatever? I'm not really one to believe in something so unscientific, but I'd heard that things were proceeding as expected, more or less. I wonder what happened."

"Hey, don't change the subject... But you do have a point. It's basically unheard of for the Chosen One to just disappear in the middle of the story. The Demon Lord showed up, and the Chosen One was identified by a mark on the hand. Sounds like that shady prophecy's been right up till now."

Alice goes quiet and appears to be lost in thought.

"...Hey, Six, you like games and novels where there's a Chosen One, right? I don't have any entertainment-related data in my memory, so can you tell me how those sorts of stories usually go? Does the Chosen One appear out of nowhere, display superhuman abilities, and defeat everything in his path?"

"Hmm? Nah, they usually suffer at least one defeat. Something along the lines of losing to a powerful opponent, engaging in self-reflection over their weakness, training to overcome their weakness, and getting their revenge on that opponent. The whole 'hero's journey' thing actually requires a failure here and there. Are you saying this Random Teleport is one of those necessary failures? Like, the Chosen One will undergo intense training wherever he ended up and come back stronger when the kingdom truly needs him?"

I guess that could happen. Maybe he'll encounter a mysterious old man at his destination and learn a new finishing move.

Ignoring the part about being teleported into the middle of nowhere, losing and getting stronger is a key part of the narrative, no matter the medium.

"...No, probably not. The Chosen One's already suffered defeat once, remember? He got beaten by those two boss demons at the Tower of Duster. If things had gone according to plan, the Chosen One would've trained to beat those two and eventually defeated them and

Whatever-His-Name-Is of the Wind with his new ultimate techniques. Thinking back to the tower assault, if we hadn't gotten involved, I'm not sure the kingdom's knights would have been able to win. The Chosen One was probably supposed to defeat an enemy that the entire royal army couldn't, thus inspiring the masses. However…"

"…Wait, are you saying that we screwed up the narrative by clearing the tower ourselves? That makes it sound like it's my fault. I mean, fate is tougher than that, right? Right?! …Hey, you're supposed to be a genius, right?! Well, use that big brain of yours and find a way to fix this!"

I'm nearly overwhelmed by the feeling that I may have just caused the mother of all plot derailments. I grab Alice, shaking her by the shoulders in the hopes that a solution might fall out.

"There are multiple potential fixes. *How* we fix this depends on what methods you're willing to employ."

"Let's hear them."

Alice raises her index finger.

"You go commit some unspeakable act of evil that earns you an enormous number of Evil Points. In the meantime, I'll request access to the restricted stock of biological and chemical weapons. We then use your newly acquired points to obtain them."

……

"Any other ideas?"

Alice's middle finger extends to join her index finger.

"I attack the Demon Lord's fortress on my own, then taunt the nearest enemy. They attack me. The ever-so-slightly dangerous reactor core embedded within me goes off. The Demon Lord's fortress, the Demon Lord himself, and everything within a few miles of it are vaporized."

"Plan rejected, you dumbass! Is there absolutely no way for us to solve this peacefully?"

I wait for Alice to raise another finger and present option number three, which she doesn't do.

"Nope. Let's say through some miracle we stop the invasion currently underway. That doesn't change the fundamental math. Our ace in the hole, the Chosen One, is gone. Which means even repelling multiple attacks will be futile in the long run. Any resistance we tried to put up would be a drop in the bucket."

"......Which means our remaining option is......"

Alice and I exchange nods.

""Let's ditch.""

Time to cut our losses and close the book on this place.

7

"Wait? Why are you leaving my favorite pillow? What's with all your luggage anyway? Leave that behind and pack my pillow."

"Don't be absurd. All my items have enormous value. Each of them could be traded for a mountain of ratty pillows like that one."

Alice and I pack our belongings and make preparations to leave the city.

This kingdom is done for.

Sure, I'd be lying if I said I had no regrets, but I gotta look out for number one. Besides, everyone I know here is strong. I'm sure they'll all be fine.

"Hey, Alice, what are we going to do with the assembled teleporter? We can't use it yet, right?"

"Technically, it's already connected to Earth, but the teleport space is still unstable. Considering the distance between this planet and Earth, even the smallest misalignment could have catastrophic consequences. We were lucky to appear in the air. There's no surviving being teleported to the bottom of the ocean, for example."

You know, the more I learn about the risks of teleportation, the more it seems like a miracle that I made it to this planet at all.

"……Don't worry. This planet's teleport coordinates were calculated, then double- and triple-checked by the finest minds at Kisaragi. That's why I was carrying a parachute. Typically, the hard part is the first teleport. So as long as I make it through in one piece, everything that comes afterward is merely a formality. It's fine if we leave the teleporter here. Once we establish a new base of operations, we can just have Kisaragi send the parts for a new one."

"Don't try to read my mind. I won't be taken in by your pretty words! If you were telling the truth, then that means we could've been teleported *much* closer to the ground!"

As we're in the midst of preparing our escape, I hear knocking on the door accompanied by several voices. But we don't have friends or acquaintances who would visit us at this house. Which means…

"Damned kids! We don't have time for this! I'm going to strip them and toss them in the girls' bathroom!"

I loudly stomp my way down the stairs and forcefully throw open the door—!

"It's been a while, Sir Six. I was hoping we might have a word."

Standing there, smiling and surrounded by a large retinue of soldiers, is my former employer, Princess Tillis.

In Tillis's personal chambers atop the royal castle…

"I refuse."

After being dragged to the castle against my will, I only had one answer for Tillis.

"…But…I haven't even asked you anything yet…"

Tillis looks up at me, thinning her lips in distress.

Save it, princess. Nothing, not even those doe eyes, could sway me.

I already heard from Snow. Just like Alice had already guessed, Tillis was, in fact, the de facto ruler of this kingdom.

"I already know what you're gonna ask me to do. You either want me to fight the Demon Lord's Army, hold off the Demon Lord's Army, or become your lover. Sorry, princess, but you'll have to look elsewhere. I've already got my hands full."

"Um...perhaps your last example was a bit..."

The soldiers had dispersed the moment we arrived at the castle. Which meant that the only occupants of this room were me, Alice, and Tillis.

I remain alert. There's no guarantee that Tillis isn't preparing a trap at this very moment.

"Sir Six, tell me, are you familiar with this object?"

Tillis places a backpack on the table in front of me.

Wait...

"A parachute?"

"Quiet, you idiot."

"So this object is called a parachute? Fascinating."

Tillis politely lets on that she noticed my slip of the tongue with a knowing smile and faint nod.

Alice's face contorts into a scowl as I stare blankly at the parachute. How the heck did it end up here? It was heavy as hell, and we didn't have much use for it after we landed, so Alice just left it at the landing site.

"On the day that a mysterious object was seen falling from the sky, our knights found this near the spot the object would have landed. I could not, for the life of me, figure out what it was for, but it appears you, Sir Six, even know what it is called."

Tillis says these words with a smile, but there's a definite edge lurking beneath her tranquil expression. I do my best to suppress a shudder as the temperature in the room feels as though it's dropped a few degrees.

What's she getting at?

"Allow me to be blunt, Sir Six. You are a spy, an operative sent from another nation, are you not?"

Straight to the point! A point aimed straight at my throat, no less!

"I don't really know what you're talking about."

"I see. Then I'm afraid we have no choice but to torture you until you do."

"I'm sorry—I lied. I admit I'm a spy. Please forgive me."

"Well, that was fast! Tell me, Six, what was it like growing up without a spine?!" Alice snaps after I reveal my complete inability to offer any resistance.

For whatever reason, Tillis doesn't reprimand me and instead chuckles with faint amusement.

"...Um, are you not going to arrest us?" I ask, suddenly worried at the mildness of Tillis's reaction.

"I wasn't planning on it, no. I did, however, have one request for you."

Tillis then gazes intently at us, expression turning somber.

"You mentioned that the two of you came from beyond the Dark-wood, yes?"

Technically, we came from beyond this planet, but she's not wrong, so I nod.

"You two appeared in this kingdom soon after the mysterious fly-ing object was sighted. That means you two have some method of flying. Your story about coming from beyond the Darkwood gains credibility in that case."

Tillis looks at us with a faint look of triumph at her observation, and I don't have the heart to tell her the hypothesis is wrong. Oblivious to my thoughts, Tillis gazes at us with a serious, somber expression.

"This kingdom...in all likelihood will fall tomorrow. Once we're gone, there will be nothing left to stop the Demon Army from digging their claws into the neighboring kingdoms. So I have a request for the two of you."

"I'm listening."

She meets my gaze directly.

"The kingdom's knights and soldiers... Their lives, their battles, their ends... Will you stand and bear witness to it all until the final countryman breathes his last? Then tell the people of your nation that there was once a kingdom called Grace. That the people of this kingdom stood and fought the Demon Lord's Army until the bitter end. Then please use their example, their sacrifice, to call the other nations together to resist the Demon Lord... I have no great powers or magics of my own, Sir Six. With all my influence, the only thing I can do is ask that future generations remember my people."

Tillis pauses, catching her breath and straightening in her seat.

"Please, I beg of you."

Before me, a nobody from who knows where, Princess Cristoseles Tillis Grace sets aside her royal status and bows her head deeply.

8

It's currently a little past 2200 hours. The world outside is already dark, and the air is alive with the sound of chirping insects.

"Well, damn... How the hell am I supposed to say no to *that*? ... Should we just make a run for it now? Nah, I guess it'd be best to wait until the Demon Lord's Army is here and then slip away during the chaos..."

After soaking in the barracks bath, I mutter to myself as I head to Tillis's room.

"Well...in the worst-case scenario, Tillis said she'd find a way to get us out of here..."

Tillis has requested that Alice and I escape by air once the Demon Lord's Army breaches the city walls and begins invading the city. Unfortunately, with my current point total, there's no way I could requisition something like an airplane.

…And at that exact moment…

"Hey! It's the boss!"

Rose's sharp eyes catch a glimpse of me just as I'm exiting the bath, and she cheerfully calls out to me from across the hall. She politely nods in my direction as she wheels Grimm toward me. Grimm's eyes twinkle with amusement.

"Commander! I heard you left because you couldn't stand Snow's sexual harassment any longer, so what are you doing here?"

"Grimm! I told you not to believe those rumors! They're vicious lies he's been spreading!"

Snow makes her presence known, barking angrily as she stalks up next to the other two.

"Tillis asked that I stay in the castle until tomorrow. But she did give me permission to run away if things get too hairy."

"That's great! Boss, if you're defending Princess Tillis, we'll have nothing to worry about."

I see they've convinced themselves that I've been hired on to protect the princess. Given Rose's high-spirited giggles, I can't bring myself to tell her the truth about Tillis's request. Instead, I just smile.

"…If Her Highness requested your presence herself, it's not for me to question it…but this adds a new type of concern. Six, you better not spread any of your ludicrous lies to the princess, or worse, sexually harass her! Got it?"

"When you put it that way, I can't say I'm not tempted."

"Don't even think about it! I'm serious this time, understand? You better not try it!!"

I smile as I look over the three of them and ask the question that's been bugging me all evening.

"Where are you lot going to be stationed tomorrow?"

Based on how our squad was treated in the past, I'm worried they're going to be positioned right on the front lines.

"Hmph! Not to worry. Grimm and Rose are members of the Royal Guard. And just as the name implies, the Royal Guard is going to be guarding royals like the king and princess. Tomorrow we'll be the last line of defense, positioned by the front gate."

I admit I feel a bit of relief at knowing my acquaintances won't immediately be in harm's way.

"Don't you dare die on me tomorrow. If things get desperate, forget about the kingdom and run, all right?"

In response to those words…

"Don't be ridiculous!" Snow cries. "We're the Royal Guard! We'd sooner choose an honorable death than a disgraceful retreat! Isn't that right?!"

""Uh.""

…………

"We'll do our best tomorrow!" says Rose. "And, Boss, if things get too dangerous, take Princess Tillis and get out safely, okay?"

"I'll be awake tomorrow, so don't worry about me! I refuse to die single! I'll definitely survive and find myself a wonderful groom!" Grimm adds.

"You two! What do you mean, 'Uh'? Y-you'll stay, right? You'll be here with me until the very end, right?"

Well, if this scene is any indication, I think they'll manage somehow.

"…What are you smiling about? Quit it, it's disturbing. And just so there's no confusion, I'm only tolerating you because the princess wants you here. *I* still haven't forgiven you."

All I was doing was enjoying a moment of pride over how tough my subordinates have become, and she's calling my smile disturbing?

"What's your problem? How do you even walk from place to place with your butthole puckered so tightly all the time? That's why Heine of the Flames won't take you seriously."

"Y-you son of a...! Do you know how much these two worried when I ran you out of the castle?"

I pretend to pick some wax out of my ear with my pinkie instead of paying attention, letting out a sigh at the predictably short-tempered Snow.

"Yeah, yeah. I repent, or whatever."

"............"

Snow draws her sword without a word, and I drop into a defensive crouch and start backing slowly away.

"Ah-ha-ha-ha-ha! You never change, Boss. Even when we can't be sure we'll live to see tomorrow, you're still butting heads with Miss Snow... I think I finally get it now. You're like an old married couple! I'll try not to get in your way from now on."

Rose claps her hands together happily, laughing in delight.

"You know...your flirting is kind of obnoxious...so obnoxious, in fact, I'm tempted to curse you. I mean, Snow, you were so dark and depressed after the commander left, and now look at you! You're practically giddy."

"Now that you mention it...Miss Snow *is* much more animated."

"Fine, if that's how it's going to be, I'll take on all three of you! It'll be a warm-up for tomorrow. All three of you need some discipline!"

And then, as if signaling the start of her discipline regime, Snow slashes at me with her sword.

Rose doesn't bother to stop Snow and instead watches with a smile.

"You know, I think I like our squad best when Boss is in command. It's just...comforting."

"I can't say I dislike it, either. The commander may be a hopeless pervert, but he's generous with the tabs."

I dodge another slash as these two happily make comments next to me.

"Whatever! One of you stop her! What'll you do if I die before the battle?!"

The peaceful night wears on.

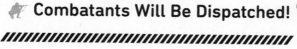

Combatants Will Be Dispatched!

1

The city of Grace spreads out in front of the royal castle.

The lord general calls out to the knights assembled in a defensive formation in front of the main gate—

"Okay, everyone! I'm sure you've all heard the news by now. The Chosen One is missing after his battle with Faustless of the Wind! I know how many of you feel! The disappointment! The despair! But I stand here to remind you, the Chosen One is missing but not lost! So long as this kingdom remains, so long as we stand and protect our homes and families, we will be the light that guides humanity's final hope, the Chosen One, back to us! Now is the time for us to stand! Show the demons that they have more to fear from humanity than just the Chosen One!"

The general's speech stirs the morale of the defenders, drawing a defiant cheer from the assembled knights and soldiers.

Tillis watches over the proceedings from her balcony with a somber expression.

"...Sir Six. How should we expect the enemy to proceed...?" Tillis asks.

As for me......

"I'm serious! I saw the unicorn use its horn to hike up the girl's skirt! The knight in charge of caring for them was being harassed! Unicorns are a bunch of good-for-nothings! I bet they're just pervy old men in costumes!"

"All right, all right," Alice snaps. "I'll listen to that story later. I'm in the process of writing a letter to explain our situation and hopefully get some support. Stay out of my way."

I've been trying to explain the shocking truth I witnessed in the stables.

"U-um...Sir Six?"

"I bet those cold-blooded Supreme Leaders won't make any exceptions. C'mon, listen to me. This is a pretty important issue. If there are unicorns here, they've clearly got horses, too. So why not just use horses?! There's actually no need to bother with these pervy unicorns at all!"

"Why are you telling me this? I can't do anything about it. I've done a survey of the local fauna, and there's all sorts of odd creatures that make no evolutionary sense. Then there's the fact that legendary and mythical creatures actually exist here. We'll be here a while if we start listing off every little thing that's wrong with this world. Then there's the whole issue of all these ridiculous phenomena like magic and curses......"

You know, from my point of view, an android like you strikes me as plenty ridiculous, too...

"......Am I correct in assuming you have an interest in magic? I can demonstrate some simple magic if you'd like."

"Really? Lemme see!"

"Oh? I'd like to see as well."

Feeling excluded from our conversation, Tillis offers to demonstrate her magic.

In front of the gate, the kingdom's knights stand and patiently await the Demon Lord's Army.

2

"All right, is everyone ready? Time to take over this kingdom once and for all! The Chosen One is gone! There's no one left to..."

As she fires up her band of demons, Heine hesitates mid-sentence. A face appears in her mind, the face of the only man who still poses a threat. The pillar of the Elite Four erases the image from her mind with a quick shake of her head.

"There's no one left to stop us! Let's raise some hell! Go teach those humans the true meaning of fear!"

In response to her cry, the army of demons, now swelling to over twice the numbers of the kingdom's defenders, stomp their feet in unison, sending tremors through the ground.

"Hey, Heine, with this many demons, do you really need my prized golems? The Chosen One's gone. Hell, I bet you can take care of a puny human kingdom like that on your own......even with your low-powered magic conduit."

The one mocking Heine is the other pillar of the Elite Four leading the army, Gadalkand of the Earth.

With the Chosen One gone, the army of demons is driven by the belief that there's nothing left to fear from the humans.

The rank and file are convinced that even in her weakened state, Heine will lead the demonic horde to victory, trampling right over the demoralized army of the kingdom.

"Don't get cocky, Gadalkand. I told you, they've still got the bastard who made a fool out of me. Honestly, I'd prefer to fight the Chosen One over him. The Chosen One's strong, sure, but that bastard's unpredictable. So there's no harm in being a little overprepared. He did struggle against a single golem, so the ten we're taking along should be more than enough to deal with him."

"...Ah, the bastard who destroyed my golem. Heine, leave that one to me. I'll break him into tiny pieces, just like he did to my golem."

Heine sighs at Gadalkand's words. *To think I have to rely on a hot-blooded moron like him.*

......At that moment, disaster strikes.

With a thunderous blast, the golem leading the column explodes in a shower of fragments.

""Wha—?!""

Heine and Gadalkand stare, dumbfounded by the sudden event.

"Wha...wha...what the hell just happened?! Heine, is it him?! The bastard who killed my golem?! Impossible! We're still in Demon Army territory!"

Gadalkand, ordinarily overflowing with confidence and possessing a stony calm, hurriedly scans his surroundings, a faint panic creeping into his demeanor.

Seeing Gadalkand's panic actually helps Heine regain her composure.

"Keep moving! You'll make yourself a target! Magic powerful enough to blast a golem apart can't be launched from a distance! Damage and range for spells are inversely related! If you want damage, you lose distance, and if you want distance, you give up damage! You need to be up close to do that much damage! The enemy can't be far! Find them!"

Heine's calm, rapid directions calm the chaos rippling through the demonic ranks.

The demons begin to disperse, spreading out to seek out the enemy, however......

Both Heine and Gadalkand are thrown into confusion as a string of blasts goes off throughout the demon ranks.

"Whoa, whoa, the hell is going on here? Since when is it this easy to fling high-grade magic? Our demons are getting blown up left and right! Just how many of them are there?!"

"Cerberuses! Bring several of the Cerberuses! Sniff the bastards out!"

As Gadalkand shouts in disbelief, Heine issues further orders.

"...Lady Heine! We're sending the Cerberuses out to sweep for the enemy, but shortly after they start sniffing around, they refuse to move!"

"Lord Gadalkand! A golem! We've lost another golem!"

"What the hell?! Dammit! Be on alert, you bastards! Keep your eyes peeled and proceed with caution! The enemy is hitting us from somewhere. Stay alert! Withdraw the golems! They're nothing but walking targets right now!"

As Gadalkand barks out orders, Heine focuses to track the flow of magic, seeking the unseen enemy.

......There's a strong magic signature nearby.

It's powerful, but there's something *familiar* about it......

"......This feeling... It's my sorcerer stone!"

Which must mean he's here.

All the pieces suddenly click into place for Heine. Ignoring the demons, she starts running toward her sorcerer stone.

If she can find the stone, she'll find him as well.

"...What the...?"

Heine arrives at her destination to find no one; just her sorcerer stone sitting on the ground.

She glances around, senses primed to detect anyone who might be lurking nearby, but she finds nothing.

Inching closer to the stone, Heine surveys her surroundings once more. Again, she finds no one nearby.

"...You're there, aren't you, Six? What is the meaning of this?"

More explosions ring out along with the screams of demons caught up in them. She can hear those sounds off in the distance, but there are no voices coming from her vicinity.

The sorcerer stone sits right in front of her.

No matter how hard she tries, Heine can't feel a human presence nearby.

Could this have been placed here by Six as an apology?

With the Chosen One gone, does he actually want to defect to the Demon Army?

Whatever the truth of the matter, it'll remain a mystery until she actually meets him.

"...Oh...my...my precious sorcerer stone...!"

Heine ecstatically reaches out to recover the conduit she had spent many long years pouring magic into......

3

"Very well, here we go! With my power, I will only be able to do it once, so please watch carefully! In the name of the Goddess of Water, Aquans, I summon you!"

<Evil Points acquired.>

"......Hmm?"

"What is it, Six?"

I tilt my head in response to the sudden announcement, and Alice turns to face me.

"Hmm? Oh, I just acquired some Evil Points out of nowhere. Remember those brats calling me the Fly? I tossed some porn into their houses where their parents could find it. Guess they just got caught."

"…You did what? Against children…?"

At that moment, I hear the splash of water.

"Did you see? That was the spell used to summon the spirits of water…!"

I turn to the source of the sound and see Tillis standing there in front of a puddle, breathing raggedly but looking quite pleased with herself.

"Sorry, I missed it."

"I'm afraid I missed it as well. Do you mind doing it again?"

"Oh…"

For some reason, Tillis stands there looking crestfallen.

Gazing down at the city from the balcony, there's no sign of the enemy. It's long past the expected arrival time of the Demon Lord's Army, and it's closing in on 1500 hours.

"They're a little late, aren't they? Maybe they won't show up today."

"No, they're probably just held up by the minefield."

Oh yeah, I forgot about those.

Still, I've got no complaints. Really, the later they are, the better. My promise is to stay here until 2000 hours. Once that time passes, I've got no intention of letting anyone complain about my departure.

…The waiting continues, and even the tension among the knights stationed in front of the gates starts to slacken.

Then a vague shadow appears in the distance. The Demon Lord's Army arrives at last, bloodshot eyes boiling with rage.

"Sir Six! Look! The captain of the sixth company is bravely charging alone into the enemy!"

Neither force is gaining or losing much ground.

The demons push forward, trying to make the most of their numerical advantage. For their part, the outnumbered knights maintain their disciplined ranks, working together to take down demons as they approach one by one.

In spite of all the doom and gloom before the battle, they're more than holding their own against the larger force.

"Huh. At this rate, we might not even have to run. Uh, just so we're clear, Tillis, you won't turn around and execute us as spies if we get through this, right?"

"Whyever would we do such a dishonorable thing? True, we did put you in a single room to save on costs, but we wouldn't stoop to such depths."

....

"Wait, you put Alice and me into the same room to save money?!"

"Sir Six, you'll be departing this castle tomorrow. No need to dwell on the past."

"'No need to dwell on the past,' my ass... You might look like an angel, but you're a damned cheapskate!"

As Tillis and I argue, Alice looks to the battlefield and coolly makes an observation.

"...The front line's breaking."

"Oh! Oh, heaven help us......"

Tillis shoves me aside and leans forward to get a better view of the battle.

The soldiers are fighting with grim determination in their eyes. Tillis stands there offering prayers to the gods in their name. In the middle of all that, Alice and I are bored out of our minds...

"Hey, Alice, how about some tic-tac-toe?"

"And what is that, exactly?"

Alice and I spread out a sheet of paper atop the rug. Tillis glances over at us, biting her lip as if she has something to say.

"I thought you were supposed to know everything. Tic-tac-toe is a game where you take turns filling X's and O's into a grid. First one to line up three in a row wins. You up for it? We can bet a gold coin per round."

"You serious? You think you can beat me with a lowly human brain?" Alice says in a slightly exasperated tone.

"Let's even up the rules, then. How about you give me an extra move every five turns?"

"Not a chance."

...Time passes steadily.

"Oh no...! Even the fourth company has broken!"

"There. Looks like I win."

Alice marks in a large X on the sheet in front of us.

"Hey now, you know that tic-tac-toe is best of nine, right? You've only got one win."

"Cut the crap."

The battle rages on in spite of the dying light, and fire glow begins dotting the landscape here and there.

Demons have the advantage in night combat. I guess they're lighting bonfires to minimize the enemy's advantage?

"Sir Six, I'm afraid it is time to make preparations to leave. The enemy is approaching the main gate."

Tillis speaks with a solemn look in her eyes. I glance up from the game.

"I guess it's about time... All right, we'll get ready."

"Hey, Six, it's your turn. I'm playing with this dumb handicap, so the least you can do is hurry the hell up."

Tillis looks at me, half standing in a crouch, apparently at a loss and holding back tears.

"You really are something... You won't even turn to watch them fight."

Her tone is exasperated now. I look up at her and dust off my hands.

"It's because I believe in them. Snow, Rose, and Grimm. They still haven't seen any action. And I know those three are strong. After all..."

I grin.

"They're my subordinates," I say confidently.

"Hey, Six. You've got nowhere else to go. Fork over the gold already."

4

"Rose! Grimm! The enemy's isn't here yet, but stay alert! We're counting on you to take out their heavy hitters!"

Screams and the sounds of battle ring out from all around us.

"I'm ready. Leave them to me!"

"I'm sleepy...b-but I must remain vigilant...! Once this is done, I bet Snow will buy me tons of drinks... Stay awake...stay awake... The s-sun's almost fully down... I just need to keep my eyes open a little longer..."

I'm moved by Rose's confident response, even as Grimm's muttering gets a little unsettling. I make a note to wine and dine them both once this is over.

A soldier arrives at our post where the Royal Guards, under my command, stand as the last line of defense in front of the city's main gate.

"Lady Snow! Where is Lady Snow?"

The soldier is pale, raising his voice in near panic before he finally locates me and dashes in my direction.

"Lady Snow! Golems! The enemy...they had seven stone golems in reserve! They waited for the fighting to go on long enough for the knight companies to be exhausted... Then they sent in the golems.

They've forced their way through our lines, and they're heading straight this way."

Seven golems?!

"Grimm! Will your curses work on them?!"

I hear the sound of wheels clattering against the cobblestones, and Grimm appears next to me. She gazes intently at the golems steadily making their way toward us.

"We're nearing Lord Zenarith's time. I might not be able to destroy them, but I can certainly stop them in their tracks! Look at these! I had the city guard confiscate these paired rings from a bunch of couples, using the defense of the city as an excuse!"

Normally, Grimm is super-unreliable, but I'm seeing a whole new side of her today. I'll pretend I didn't hear anything about the confiscations.

"Good. Everyone, form a defensive wall around Grimm. Those of you with hammers and maces, be ready to clobber the immobilized golems!"

Just as I give the order to my subordinates…

"Not happening! You guys stay out of this!!"

The ground rumbles as the seven stone golems stomp toward the gate. Standing upon a golem's shoulder is a pillar of the Demon Lord's Elite Four, Heine of the Flames.

"Finally, some familiar faces. But I'm afraid I've got no time for you small fries. Bring out Six. I'm here for him."

Heine's body is covered in wounds, so many that I feel a brief pang of sympathy. The pang is short-lived when I see her expression. There's no trace of pain there. Just rage. Pure, burning rage.

"Six? He's not here. I, Snow, will be your opponent today. Draw!!" I cry.

At my challenge, Heine turns her gaze to me, her eyes flaring with anger.

"You?! You're nothing! You're not even worth the effort of killing.

But *that* bastard?! There's no way I can let him live after the humiliation he's caused me! I'll kill him if it's the last thing I do! Using my precious sorcerer stone as bait... I bet he's sooo proud of himself for that one, huh?"

I don't have a clue what she's talking about... I guess that idiot found yet another way to incur her wrath.

I take a touch of satisfaction in the knowledge.

"It doesn't matter if I'm nothing! I can't...I won't let you get to Six. Her Highness has tasked him with something important. Grimm! Do it!"

"O Great Lord Zenarith, I beseech thee! Deliver disaster unto this stone doll! May its soles be sewn to the ground!"

Grimm unleashes her curse before I finish giving the order.

The paired rings in Grimm's hand are offered to the dark god as a sacrifice and vanish in a flash of light.

The golem's feet freeze in place. Unable to stop its forward momentum, the golem collapses with an earthshaking thud. Seeing their chance, the soldiers armed with blunt weapons close in and clobber the golem, reducing it to rubble.

"O Great Lord Zenarith, I beseech thee! Deliver disaster unto this stone—"

"You really thought I'd let you do that twice?! I may have lost my primary sorcerer stone, but I've got a spare! And it'll be more than enough to take you out!"

Heine's arm erupts in flame as she flings a fireball toward Grimm, but a small shadow jumps in to protect the archbishop.

"O Great Lord Zenarith, I beseech thee! Deliver disaster unto this woman! Forever take away her ability to wield flame magic!"

Sheltered from the flames by Rose, Grimm places a large parcel on her lap and points her finger at Heine. The parcel, filled with paired rings, is bathed in light as Zenarith claims them for a sacrifice. Hearing Grimm's words, Heine's eyes go wide, throwing her arms up in a reflexive gesture of defense.

"...It f-failed...? Holy shit, that scared the hell out of me!"

Producing a flame from the tip of her finger, Heine howls in relief.

"You! Whores like you who draw the eyes of men just by existing! I hate you most! If I had a little more courage, I'd risk the backlash and curse those udders of yours to fall right off!"

"Wh-what the hell are you talking about?! Don't call me a whore!"

Still, the threat of the previous curse appears to have put Heine on her guard as she climbs down from the golem and backs away.

Grimm doesn't suffer anything even if her ability to use flame magic is lost from a curse backlash. With the large number of sacrificial objects on hand, Grimm will probably be able to take away Heine's flame magic with enough attempts.

This realization drains the color from Heine's face, and she puts another golem between herself and Grimm.

"The hell are you doing, Heine? Stop playing around with these maggots! Just kill that woman already!" Gadalkand appears from the flank, forcing his way into the center of the fight. "...Huh? Hey, you... You look a lot like a lady I killed not too long ago... Eh, whatever. You're dead either way."

He lifts his metal club, stifling a yawn as he prepares to take a swing at Grimm. The sickening crunch and the image of Grimm's headless body flopping to the ground replay in my mind.

"T-take that!"

Rose lets out a rather weak battle cry, unleashing a flying kick at Gadalkand's head.

"...Hmm? Did you just do something?"

Gadalkand takes the blow without so much as flinching, reaching up and theatrically scratching the spot Rose kicked as if it were a bugbite. Then he pounces at Rose with a speed that ought to be impossible for a creature his size, landing an open-handed blow on Rose's shoulder.

Rose is tossed like a rag doll by the impact, and Gadalkand seems to forget about her, turning his attention to the only thing standing between him and Grimm. Me.

"...Move."

A single word. An order.

This demon...this pillar of the Demon Lord's Elite Four. He doesn't even regard me as the enemy.

As I grit my teeth in frustration, I hear a *whoosh* as a jet of flame cuts through the air, hitting Gadalkand and engulfing him in flames.

"Guh! You little brat! I forgot you could do that!! You miserable runt! You know you can't beat me. Even if you have mixed blood, your demon blood's gotta be screaming at you to run. It's not like these vermin are treating you well, are they? You can join us once this is over. Now get out of my way!"

Buffeting his wings to blow away the flames lapping at his stony skin, Gadalkand turns to look behind him.

Rose stands there with blood trickling from her temple, hands balled into fists while one arm wipes the soot off her chin with a sleeve.

"Heh-heh-heh... I know I can't beat you, and yeah, I have mixed blood...but I'm also a Combat Agent trainee, so I'm afraid I have to keep fighting, even if I'm scared. Also..."

I notice a faint tremble in her voice.

"Grandpa told me on his deathbed that if I ever made friends, I should stick with them, no matter what...!"

With that, Rose assumes a fighting stance against Gadalkand.

"Heh! Fine. Then hurry up and die!"

He brings down his club toward Rose, shattering the stones below and sending fragments flying in every direction.

Instead of giving herself breathing room, Rose dashes toward the large demon, punching at Gadalkand's gut with all her might.

The sound of a hard object being hammered rings through the area, and Gadalkand's face twists into a grimace.

Her flame breath requires her to hold a deep breath for a few seconds, making it impractical for use while dodging hits at close range.

Rose dodges Gadalkand's powerful swings, exploiting each

opportunity to land a blow on him in return. The soldiers and knights stare at the battle between superhuman fighters from a distance, unable to provide any meaningful support.

The same applies to me.

A girl who is younger than me, smaller than me, and suffered much worse treatment than I've ever endured. She's matching Gadalkand, blow for blow, in defense of Grimm.

If I joined the fight against Gadalkand, I would only be in her way. With my sword, I wouldn't be able to so much as scratch him.

So what's left for me to do...?

What good is the reputation that comes from being the youngest to achieve knighthood, an elite member of the Royal Guard, and all the other accolades if I still lack strength?

The other pillar of the Elite Four, Heine, cautiously avoids getting in Grimm's line of sight and continues scanning the surroundings as if still expecting to find Six here on the field.

The steady stream of arrows fired at her is swallowed by the flames burning around us.

"O Great Lord Zenarith, I beseech thee! Deliver disaster unto that woman!"

Grimm points her finger at Heine, prompting the demon to hurriedly seek cover behind a golem.

"Don't you point at me, you crazy dark-god cultist! Golem! Shield me!"

"D-don't call Lord Zenarith a dark god! Dammit, I'll put a curse on you that makes you irresistible to orcs!"

...It's time to make up my mind.

Even if I'm consumed by flame, I should be able to get at least one strike in.

How ironic that I, the one most concerned with money and glory, would find myself facing the honorable death every knight longs for.

The hand gripping my sword hilt trembles, but I convince myself the shaking is from excitement, not fear.

At that moment, a voice intrudes into my thoughts.

"I'm not entirely sure what it is that you're planning to do, but I wouldn't recommend it. Just a warning from the Archbishop of Undeath. Dying is truly awful."

Just as I make my peace with my decision, Grimm pauses in her efforts to deter Heine. She sounds more sober and serious than I'd imagined her capable of being.

Rose shouts over her shoulder, still with her back to me as trades blows with Gadalkand.

"I can't hold him forever! Miss Snow, please go to Her Majesty and tell her to evacuate to safety!"

At the desperation in her voice, I remember what I should be doing.

Knights of the Royal Guard are here to keep the royals away from harm.

Going to Princess Tillis and finding a way for her to escape is consistent with our duties. Still, there's no reason that I should be the one to do it. After all, I'm the one in charge right now. Which means...

"We'll be fine. Off you go to the castle! Even if the princess needs to defect to another country, it's better that she have more than just the commander go with her. Snow, you need to go and make sure he doesn't try anything funny with the princess."

Which means these two are telling me to run.

How pathetic. How powerless.

I, who once joined in with the other soldiers to mock these two as rejects, am now being defended by them. In spite of everything, they're trying to find a way to let me escape.

......There's still hope.

He's still here. If anyone can find a way out of this mess, it's him.

But who am I to beg for his help? Me, the very person who drove him out of the ranks.

I recall something he said earlier.

"I hear the Demon Lord's Army is invading soon! If you want my ultrapowerful assistance, then apologize for your shitty attitude and beg for it!"

If it means I can save these two, I'll gladly apologize. I'll happily beg and stroke his insufferable ego. But will he actually help us under these circumstances?

As I stand there, trying to sort out my jumble of thoughts and emotions, Rose is knocked back toward me, landing on all fours. Her tail straightens, and she snarls at Gadalkand.

Her back, turned to shield me from the enemy, a back belonging to a little girl desperately forcing down her anxiety so that she can keep fighting, is the last straw. I know what I need to do and turn on my heel.

"Drown in a sea of hellfire…!"

I hear her voice from behind me.

"Sleep for all eternity! Crimson Breath!"

I start running toward the castle.

5

"N-no, I'm not moving from this spot! If my countrymen die, I'm dying with them!"

We're still in Tillis's chambers at the top of the castle.

"Stop struggling and come on! Look, let me explain why I decided to stay as long as I have! You said you wanted me to tell the other countries that this kingdom was here and to get them to band together to fight the Demon Lord's Army. Screw that! Do it yourself! Even if the kingdom is destroyed, if a member of the royal family survives, you've won! If you need help leaving descendants behind, I can help you out with that once we're safely out of here!"

"Your last point is ridiculous! I'm your employer! I order you to let go of me! S-someone! Someone help!" Tillis yells as I hoist her over my shoulder like a piece of luggage. So far, no one from below is coming up to stop us.

Of course, that's because the castle's master, the king, asked me to help Tillis escape.

Still, this wasn't how I pictured things going. I didn't expect them to have so much trouble fighting the demons.

I probably tempted fate by going on that little spiel about how they were my subordinates.

There's no way to win here. It's time to go.

"All right, let's get out of here, Alice!"

"Roger that!"

"Wait, please! Please set me down, Sir Six! Are you really ready to accept what's about to happen? Once the castle falls, everyone you know in this kingdom is going to die!"

Tillis attempts to convince me, still struggling on my shoulder.

"Now, now, there's a perfect sentiment for times like these. Everything's fine... They'll live on...in our hearts."

"Well said, Six, now let's go! We don't have much time!"

"What is wrong with you twooo?!"

I carry the sobbing Tillis in one arm, heading to the hallway to make our escape. But just as we reach the staircase to make our way down...

"Combat Agent Six!!"

The voice belongs to Snow, dashing up the stairs. Her hair's a mess, and she's having trouble keeping her breathing under control.

After shouting my name, Snow stands in front of the staircase, trying to catch her breath.

"Can you make this quick?" I ask her. "We're kiiind of in a hurry."

"Snow! Stop this man! Order him to set me down!" Tillis shouts.

Snow, her breathing ragged, looks at the floor and says, "S-Six, right now seven golems, Heine of the Flames, and Gadalkand of the Earth are attacking the main gate."

"Yep, already aware of that. Saw the whole thing from the balcony. Now get out of the way, we're really pressed for time. If we're going to get out of here, we need to go with everyone else in the city. The sheer number of people raises our chances of escape!"

"It's almost kind of impressive how casually you say that." In contrast to my building panic, Snow appears to have calmed a bit, continuing in a detached tone. "I can't do anything about them. Rose and Grimm are buying time, but they probably won't last much longer."

After hearing that, my legs pretty much turn into cement.

"To the enemy, I'm nothing. Less than nothing. They won't even consider me an enemy."

A slight tremble enters Snow's voice.

"…I've been swinging a sword since I was a child. My birth, my upbringing, my sex… I've worked hard to forge an identity beyond those labels. I've practiced every waking moment of my life so that I could beat anyone who came my way."

I listen to Snow's remarks without comment. She's being so sincere that I couldn't toss out a witty remark if I even had one.

"If it's an apology you want, I'll apologize a thousand times over. You can do whatever you want to me. So please…"

Snow raises her head and looks up at me before bowing deeply.

"I beg you! Lend me your strength! I'll do anything within my power! If it's money you want, I'll give you all that I have! You know how greedy I am! I have a lot of it piled up, especially if you add in my sword collection!"

"Six, ignore her! It's time to go. We need to use your remaining points to buy a ton of stun grenades and a motorcycle to escape on. We can't waste resources helping them!"

I'm almost convinced by Snow's plea when Alice's words snap me back to reality.

"What am I supposed to do with money under these circumstances? And do you really understand what you're saying when you say you'll do anything? Leave me alone; I'm just a commoner! You made sure I wound up this way! It took you way too long to come crying to me! Just how stubborn are you?!"

"Look at her! Snow's debased herself for you, and you react this way?! I've truly lost any shred of respect I had for you!" Tillis shouts from my shoulder and starts struggling again.

I ignore her and step forward, passing Snow as I make my way toward the stairs.

Snow grabs my arm.

"Not like this... I don't want us all to go down without a real fight..."

The disappointment, the anger—I know how all this feels.

I can't remember the number of times I lost to Heroes and their crazy-strong abilities.

I'm not a mutant with awesome special abilities. My cybernetic enhancements are half-assed and outdated.

I wanted to scream at her, tell her that she's not the only one dealing with how unfair the world is. That she needed to accept it. Then I look at her face.

In all the time that I've known Snow, she's never, ever shown a shred of weakness to me.

Yet now, as she gazes up at me, her eyes are filled with tears.

".........Please......Commander."

She calls me "Commander" for the first time.

Her voice is trembling like a child fearing a scolding from her parents. Snow clings to my arm, her voice ragged with desperation.

".........Commander......please save Rose and Grimm...!'"

6

"You really are a half-assed villain, you know that? Buckling to your conscience at the very end. No wonder you're still a lackey despite being with Kisaragi from the beginning."

"Oh, shut up! I know all that! I'm weak willed and a pushover and whatever the hell else you have to call me. Just have them send the goddamn anti-materiel rifle already!"

Back to Tillis's chambers and on to the balcony. As night begins to fall, I start kicking at the balcony's railing.

"C-Commander! Aren't we going to the gate? What are you planning to do from here...?"

I vent a bit of my frustration at Snow, who's been following me like a newly hatched duckling. "Use your head! We don't have time to head back to the gate. So we're attacking from here! ...And how much longer are you gonna cling to my arm?! It's not like I'm gonna run off as soon as you let go!"

"Oh...!"

Snow lets go of my arm and watches me continue destroying the balcony.

"Sir Six! I have no idea what you plan to do, but do as you please! You're perhaps the most stunning man in the kingdom right now!"

For whatever reason, Tillis decides to cheer me on while I ravage her balcony. Just as my line of sight clears up, Alice yells in my direction.

"...Hey, what's going on here? We're short on points! I made sure to leave a little over two hundred points, but now we don't have enough for the rifle. What the hell did you use your points for?!"

Oh, shit...

"Um, well......you know how there's nothing to do here? Well, last night, I sort of......"

"You spent those points, didn't you?! On what? Porn?! You wasted those points the night before an invasion?! YOU IDIOT!"

I'd really like a hole to crawl into right about now.

"I had no choice...! It was the middle of the night! And there's no convenience stores or anything around here!"

"Wh-what is it? Is there a problem?" Snow asks.

Alice lets out a weirdly human-sounding sigh. "I was just thinking that this idiot's nothing but comic relief even at the very end. I guess we've got no other option. Hey, Six."

"Yeah?"

Alice points her finger to the stairs. "Go downstairs and punch that useless king in the face."

"On it!"

"No, don't!"

"Why?! What did Father ever do to you?! Snow! Stop them!"

The two of them scramble to get in my way.

"Let go, will you? I'm not doing this because I want to! It's an emergency."

Snow lets go. "...Do you just need to hit someone?" she asks, gazing intently at my face.

"Hmm? Well, it doesn't have to be hitting. Just something they don't like."

"...Understood."

Snow closes her eyes. "Hit me."

"..........What?!"

What the hell is she saying?

"J-just hit me! ......I don't quite get it, but you need to do this right now, right? Then hit me! Or…well…if it has to be something I don't like…y-you could fondle my boobs or do anything else your heart desires!"

Snow's face goes beet red at her statement, and everyone else just goes absolutely quiet.

"U-um, wait… Y-you can't just suddenly offer……"

Alice interrupts my awkward babbling.

"Do it, Six, we're running out of time. If you don't want to hit her, just grope her or kiss her or whatever!"

"B-but wait… I can't…"

Alice pushes me forward toward Snow.

Snow's face remains flushed, and her eyes are tightly shut. I place my hands on her shoulders, and she reacts with a slight tremble.

Tillis swallows a breath, looking over at us intently and blushing. "…I-is he going to…?! Is he going to kiss her?!"

Tillis covers her face, as though her modesty and decorum won't let her watch the rest of this spectacle, but it's clear she's still watching from between her fingers.

What the hell is going on? Here we are in the middle of a life-or-death struggle…and now this!

"Do it, Six! Aggressively! Kiss her and shove your tongue down her throat! Hurry up, you wimp! Do it!"

Alice is starting to get on my nerves. Well, so is my heart, with all that rapid beating. What should I be doing? Goddammit, why is Tillis looking over at us?! You're a princess, aren't you? You shouldn't be watching this sort of thing, you perverted little brat! As for you, Snow, why are you just standing there? And why are we taking so long to do this? It's not like we're middle school students. It's just a kiss! Are we sure I'm actually going to get points given the circumstances? I mean, this is starting to look awfully like we're both consenting adults! Goddammit, gaaaaaah, what am I supposed to do; if I kiss her, I won't get the points, and if I start groping her breasts, she'll let out a little coo like "Mm...," and goddaaaaaaaaammmit, what am I supposed to dooooooooooooooooooooooooooooooooooooooooooooooooooo oooooooooo?!

"Aaaaaaaaaaaaaaaaaaaaaaaaaah!!"

Something snaps inside my head, and in that moment, I reach forward and pull down...

...Snow's panties.

Yes, in an instant, my hands disappear beneath Snow's skirt, grab hold of her panties, and drag them down to her ankles.

Every person on that balcony, plus Alice, who technically isn't human, freezes in place, staring at me, mouths agape.

I don't think I'll forget the look on their faces for as long as I live.

<Evil Points acquired.>

7

"Get off me, dammit! Obnoxious gnat! Hey, Heine! Peel this bug off me, will you? I can't shake her off!"

Gadalkand lets out a frustrated roar. Rose is clinging to his arm with all four limbs and biting into his shoulder. The giant stone demon tries to shake her off, repeatedly slamming her into the ground.

"Oh, stop whining and hold on a minute! I'll be done here in a second. Hey, dark-god cultist! Your curses require a sacrifice, right? I noticed those rings of yours are disappearing each time you cast a curse! Looks like you're running on empty. You're no match for us. Hurry up and bring Six to..."

Heine stretches her hand out toward me, as if preparing to cast a spell.

She's interrupted mid-sentence when something annihilates a golem's torso, blasting Heine off its shoulder and onto the ground.

Everyone in the area goes stiff, caught completely off guard by the sudden turn of events. A faint *crack* rings through the air and reaches us a heartbeat later.

"Wha...wha-wha-wha-wha......?"

Knocked onto her butt by the first blast, Heine stares in open-mouthed shock when a second golem's torso explodes in a rain of fragments.

"The hell is this?! Heine! What the hell is going on...?! And you, *get off me!*"

Gadalkand peels Rose off his arm while directing his question at Heine.

"I—I—I don't...I don't know...what just...what......"

Another golem is reduced to a shattered hulk, followed by the same sound a few seconds later.

It must be coming from afar.

The attacks are probably coming from so far away that the sound isn't keeping up with the attack itself. Like thunder after a flash of lightning.

"Whatever it is, we can't just stand here. You lot! Get in the air! Once you're up there, fly as fast as you can!"

Gadalkand issues the orders, beating his wings and rising into the air himself. Heine, too, calls down her griffin circling above and hurriedly hops on its back.

Just as they lift into the air, another golem shatters, followed a few heartbeats later by the sound.

"Gadalkand! The castle! They're hitting us from on top of the castle!"

"...*What?!* How the hell are they attacking us from that distance?!"

Gadalkand curses loudly as a fifth golem breaks into fragments. His tirade is cut short as he stares mutely at the golem's destruction.

"...Gadalkand, your warriors can fly and can hold their own against anyone. Gather the strongest ones you've got! We'll go assault the castle and take out the bastard attacking us from there!"

"...You boys, with me! We'll hit the castle directly and take 'em out!"

Heine and Gadalkand circle once overhead, then fly off toward the castle.

The sixth golem is blasted into fragments, leaving one more.

"...There they go."

"...Yes, indeed. I'm sure the commander can do something about them."

I flash a reassuring smile at Rose.

"...Really? You really think the boss'll take care of this instead of running away?"

".........P-probably?"

As the final golem is shot down, the soldiers around us let out a cheer.

"Wow... The boss did all this, right? This probably sounds weird coming from a Chimera, but I wonder what the heck he's made of."

"Yes, he really is a mysterious man... But more importantly..."

I look around at the large group of demons encircling us.

The golems and the two pillars of the Elite Four are gone, but we are still vastly outnumbered. The enemy slowly closes the distance between them and the soldiers standing guard.

In response, Rose lets out an intimidating snarl.

"Krrrrsssshaaaaaaaw!"

The demons stop briefly in their tracks but then continue to close the gap...

"Ee-hee-hee-hee..."

I smile my most predatory smile, wheeling myself forward and bringing my chair to a stop in front of the assembled demons.

"Ah-ha-ha-ha-ha-ha-ha! In this world, all living things eventually die...but I? I have overcome death a thousandfold. I am the Arch-bishop of the Great Lord Zenarith! Know my name, for it is Grimm Grimoire! Those among you who seek death, step forward! Allow me to demonstrate the true power of my dark blessings!"

At my sudden monologue, Rose's eyes go wide in surprise.

"Wh-what's going on?! And what's with that monologue?!"

"I rarely have anything to do at night, so I've been practicing for a time like this."

"Cheater! I—I...I wish I had something cool to say, instead of the silly things my dying grandpa made me promise I'd say...! Um, let's see... Hear me! My name is Rose! ...Um...uh..."

As Rose continues her stilted attempt at an improvised monologue, I turn back toward the demons, showing off the last few remaining sacrificial items with a flourish.

"Brace yourselves! You shall now taste the true power of the God of Undeath and Disaster!"

"What she said!"

8

"Bwah-ha-ha-ha-ha-ha-ha! Power! Absolute power! The Demon Army is *nothing* next to my power!"

With each crack of my rifle, the golems far below shatter.

Well, okay, it's actually too dark to see if my shots hit anything.

"Focus. Stop laughing and relax. You're making it hard to aim," Alice chides me. I exhale and relax while she adjusts the rifle barrel to compensate. "Good. Fire."

Another shot rings out. Another golem goes down.

Ordinarily, I wouldn't be able to hit anything that far away in this sort of darkness.

Which is why I'm leaving the aiming to Alice. As a high-performance android, she's equipped with night vision. So I can just focus on pulling the trigger.

"...I-incredible... Um, may I ask why you didn't just use this from the start? I imagine this would have made the fights up to this point much easier." Tillis tilts her head in curiosity.

"I'm the type of guy who doesn't really like spending reward tokens on OP weapons and buff accessories in video games."

"That's why you can't take advantage of opportunities and end up stuck as an errand boy for the Supreme Leaders. All right, fire."

Another bang. The powerful recoil from the anti-materiel rifle ripples through my body.

"...Every shot makes the spot where you punched me hurt even more," I grumble.

"Shut up. Drop dead." Snow clutches her knees to her chest, sulking a short distance away.

".......You're the one who said I could do whatever I wanted."

"Shut up. Drop dead."

".........All right, fire."

Another bang rings out, shattering the last golem.

"All right, that should even up the odds a little."

"Shut up! Kill yourself!"

"There's still the two members of the Elite Four to take care of, but I don't see the— Wait, are they the ones flying around over there? It'd be one thing if I could aim *and* fire, but we can't hit them if I'm stuck aiming for you."

"But we can't have *you* firing this rifle. The recoil would rattle you to pieces."

"Shut up. Drop dead."

Alice suddenly pipes up as she watches the Elite Four members from the balcony.

"...Hey ...Hey! They're coming straight for us! Everyone get inside, now!"

Heine, mounted atop her griffin, and Gadalkand with his band of demons are gliding through the air toward us.

I shoulder the rifle, then go over to Snow, still sulking in the corner. I grab her by the hand and pull her into the room.

"Oh, come on, get over it already! All I did was pull down your panties! It's not like I got a good look afterward!"

"Shut up. Drop dead."

With the great crash of shattering glass, the griffin and the demons charge into the chamber!

"There you are, Six! You're dead! There's never been anyone dumb enough to mess with me as many times as you have! You were behind all those explosions earlier, weren't you?! And then you went and blew up my precious sorcerer stone!" Heine snarls in rage as the ten or so demons who charged into the room let out a bloodcurdling scream.

"Ohhh, I thought you looked familiar. You're the pathetic bastard who was cradling that dead lady and bawling! Did you bury the body properly? Or did you keep it around as a plaything? Either way, it looks like you're the bastard who took out my golems, huh? I'm about to make you wish you were dead. If you'd like, I'll even let you slit your throat with your own knife. I'm merciful like that. Now then, you've got two seconds to die, so hurry up and get dying! One! Tw—"

As Gadalkand begins his hyper-clichéd countdown, I unshoulder the rifle, take aim at him…and fire.

Gadalkand apparently sensed the danger and jumped out of the way as soon as I aimed the barrel at him. The shot takes out the demon behind him instead. The bullet goes straight through its head, punching a hole in the wall behind it. The sight of one of their own being reduced to pebbles silences the screeching band of demons.

Behind me to the right, Alice loads her shotgun and takes aim, while to the left, Snow brandishes her sword.

Standing a few feet behind us, Tillis calmly stares down the demons.

"Is everything all right?" a soldier calls from the door. He probably heard the sound of demon bits hitting the floor from below.

Snow shouts a reply. "The demons are here! Go and defend His Majesty!"

Gadalkand listens to the exchange with a casual air, whistling tunelessly as if trying to taunt us.

"...Well, damn, that's some weapon you've got there. I gotta admit, you gave me a scare when you pointed that thing at me. What the hell is it?"

I slip another round into the chamber of the single-shot rifle, keeping my eyes locked on Gadalkand.

"...Oh, this? It's a neat little toy known as an anti-materiel rifle. It's designed to take out hardened targets like you from the safety of a balcony... Oh, that reminds me. Remember that woman you were talking about earlier? She's still alive. You just met her earlier. And you actually taunted me, convinced that you'd killed her! Ha, what a moron! Are you sure you're not just some third-rate demon that fell ass-backward into power?"

My words wipe the smirk off Gadalkand's face.

"...You wanna die that badly, asshole? I'll—"

"'—gladly grant that wish for you.' Seriously? Does that pea brain of yours only have room for tired clichés? You want your head squished like you did to Grimm? No? Then take that horde of yours slumming around out there and get lost!"

I lightly wave the barrel of the rifle toward him. Gadalkand assumes a fighting stance.

"...All right, listen up, boys. It looks like that weapon can only manage one shot at a time. He's a sitting duck after each shot. Otherwise, he'd have blown us all to bits by now. Close the gap and jump him all at once. Don't stop even if he blasts the guy next to you. You'll get him."

Dammit! This one's not as stupid as he looks.

"Six, I'll take care of the underlings. Do something about Heine and Gadalkand."

"Not calling me commander anymore? That was quick. How long are you going to hold the underwear thing against me? Anyway, fall back. I'll show you your commander's real abilities. Hey, Alice! Get me the R-Buzzsaw!"

"...I beg your pardon? You're gonna take them on by yourself?! You idiot! You are already..."

As Alice launches into her explanation, the demons begin moving.

"Six! I can at least deal with the grunts! I can help!"

Snow won't back down, choosing instead to stand by my side.

Sigh. This woman. I thought she'd gotten over that stubborn streak, but nope, she's still the same, even at a time like this.

The demons tighten the circle around Snow and me. Behind them, Heine begins gathering flames in her hand.

It looks like the griffin's a little too big to fit into the room, so it's waiting out in the balcony.

"Alice, hurry up! Please, I need that thing ASAP!"

At my desperate urging, Alice sets down her shotgun and scribbles onto a sheet of memo paper.

"Fine, but you're on your own now!"

As if prompted by Alice's remark, the demons pounce all at once.

I turn my rifle barrel toward Gadalkand, but unlike the other demons, he jumps to the side.

I turn the rifle toward the nearest demon and pull the trigger, taking it down.

As if taking advantage of that moment, another just barely streaks past me.

Sparks fly as a demon's claw grazes the torso of my power armor.

I kick one of the pouncing demons, using the momentum to jump back and dodging a second fireball thrown my way. As I land, an enemy grabs the rifle barrel.

Two more rush me from the side.

"Six! Duck!"

As soon as I do, something grazes the top of my head.

Looking up, I see the two demons howling as they rear back with sword slashes across their faces.

"Wh-what were you planning to do if I didn't duck?"

I try to contain the panic in my voice as Alice shouts at me.

"It's here, Six! Grab it!"

The space in front of me hums and ripples with blue-and-white electricity.

When the static storm fizzles out, a familiar weapon is waiting for me.

I let go of the rifle, which still has a demon clutching at the barrel, and grab the weapon in front of me with both hands.

I flip the switch and slash at the demon holding my rifle.

The demon tries to block the slash with the rifle...

The sound of a rapidly vibrating blade cutting through hardened metal rings through the air.

The demon and the rifle both fall to the ground, cleaved clean in half.

"...H-hey! Wh-what the hell is that...? ...Where did it come from...?"

Gadalkand mutters in shock; the demons around me, catching sight of their companion being hacked in half, halt their advance and back away.

"This? This is a piece of cutting equipment called the Anti-Armored-Vehicle Omnidirectional Vibrating Blade Bad Sword, Type R. I've taken to calling it the R-Buzzsaw, for short. See, where I come from, *Bad Sword* and *Buzzsaw* sound pretty similar. It's perfect because they're both handy tools for slicing up weaklings like you," I answer Gadalkand, lifting the all-purpose chain saw with both hands and getting ready for battle.

I don't really understand the mechanics, but an internal engine rapidly vibrates the blade, allowing it to slice through armored objects from tanks on down. It's definitely my favorite weapon out of the entire Kisaragi arsenal.

I take the R-Buzzsaw's external power connector and plug it into my power armor. That lets me add the power armor's output to the blade.

It won't last more than a minute, but this move's allowed me to take out countless numbers of Heroes.

Now I can't lose.

"Release Restraints!"

With that command, an announcement echoes in my head.

<Releasing power armor safety restraints. Proceed?>

"Six, isn't that the ability you used against the golem? The one that paralyzed you? Are you sure you want to use that with this many demons and two of the Elite Four surrounding us…?" Snow shouts in surprise.

"Proceed."

The announcer continues in response to my answer.

<With restraints disengaged, the power armor will require a three-minute cooldown period for every one minute of activity. Continue?>

"Alice! Stop him! Isn't that supposed to be your job?!" Snow is still yelling.

"Yes, continue."

The announcer begins counting down at the command.

<Releasing safety restraints. To cancel, please issue cancellation order at any point during the countdown. Ten…nine…>

Everyone in the room is frozen in place. The air is thick with tension.

* * *

"Siiiiiiiiiiix!!"

Sensing her opportunity, Heine tries to lob a fireball at me, but Alice thrusts her shotgun at her and diverts the blast.

<Six...five...>

I glance over at Alice as the countdown nears the end.

"GO GET 'EM!!"

My partner throws me a thumbs-up, evidently forgetting she's an android and grinning from ear to ear.

<Restraints released. >

"I'm Combat Agent Six of the Kisaragi Corporation! This world doesn't need *two* evil organizations! I'm gonna end you here and now!"

"Bring it on, human! I'll rip you apart and feed you to the ogres!"

Having grown tired of waiting, Gadalkand rushes forward while swinging his club. I jump forward to attack, pushing my body to the limit.

"Snow! Stay back! I'm going to take these bastards out with my Finisher!"

The club and the R-Buzzsaw meet mid-swing.

"?!"

My R-Buzzsaw slices easily through Gadalkand's club, right down the middle, and I continue the downward swing without missing a beat.

"H-hey, wait!"

Letting the momentum carry my blade in an arc, I slash again at Gadalkand.

He utters a frantic plea and tries to shield himself with his arm. Both his remark and his right arm are cut off by my attack.

"H-hey, Six! What the hell is a Finisher?! P-pay attention to your surroundings!" Snow stammers in a panic.

"G-Gadalkand?! Hey, you! Stay back! Get away from him! Hurr——!!"

I use the momentum of my swing to spin in place, planting my heels in a point. Using them as a fulcrum, I become an unstoppable whirlwind of death. As I spin, my blade lashes out at everything near me.

"Ah......ahhhhh!! Ahhhhhhhhhh!! AHHHHHHHHHHHHHHHHHHHHHHH!"

Heine lets out a high-pitched scream as she watches her companions get drawn into the whirling blade and chopped into fine paste.

I'm spinning too quickly to actually keep track of who is getting caught up in the attack.

"Wai— Six!...... S-stop.........! Y-you're going to kill me, too......!"

Things that move, things in black.

"Eeeeep!"

I can't tell who's screaming what. I'm just mincing everything that catches my eye with my whirling sword.

The cooldown process begins, and I finally stop moving.

Around me lie the scattered pieces of what's left of Gadalkand and his lackeys.

"Ahhh... Wh-wha-wha-wha......what-wha-wha-wha...?"

Heine sits cowering in the corner of the room, backing away in terror, her legs refusing to let her stand.

"...Sniff..."

Behind me, Tillis plops to the ground and starts to sob.

"Good work!" Alice chirps. She had taken cover by the wall sooner than everyone else.

"........."

Nearby, I see Snow assuming a turtle pose. She's covering her head with her arms, and she's curled up into a ball.

Noticing the silence that has fallen over the room, Snow peers out cautiously from her crouch, and I catch her tear-filled eyes.

"...Y-you...y-y-you...you, you! Six, what were you...? I thought I was going to...! I really thought I was going to die! Look at this massacre! One wrong step and I would have joined them on the ground in several pieces!"

"I did say I was gonna use my Finisher."

"...Next time, give me ten seconds' advance notice..."

Snow still looks on the verge of tears, sniffling loudly as she stands and wipes at her nose with her sleeve. She then looks over at the shell-shocked Heine.

"...Now then, what do we do about her? Are you going to splatter her across the walls with that weapon of yours?"

"Eeep!"

Snow probably meant that as a joke, but Heine takes it seriously. She goes deathly pale and begins to tear up.

It'd be a while before I could use that move anyway. My armor's still on cooldown.

Evidently, Heine's in no state to think that deeply about the circumstances.

"Well, I suppose there's no reason to let her live..."

Alice looms over Heine, meaninglessly pumping her shotgun and chambering a new shell with a loud *ga-chunk*.

"A-ah...ahhh...!"

A thought comes to mind as I watch Heine cowering, teary-eyed, in the corner of the room.

"Now, Heine…"

"Y-yesh?!"

As I call over to her, she answers in a frightened falsetto.

"…I'm willing to overlook your role in all this…"

The silence lingers in the room.

"…*Hic… Sniffle…* Waaaaaah…!"

For some reason, Heine suddenly bursts into tears.

"H-hey! Why are you crying?"

"…S-Sir Six… Sh-she might be a demon, b-but…please…! Such a punishment is…!"

"…W-well, I do feel bad for her, but we don't have a lot of options. Heine of the Flames, I'm sorry. All you can do now is, well…make your peace…"

"Okay, you two, let's have a little chat. All I said was that I'd be willing to overlook things…"

I guess my pervy day-to-day behavior caused them to fear the worst for Heine.

"So, Six, does that mean you're just going to let her go?"

"Of course not."

At my immediate answer to Alice's question, Heine's face shifts from abject horror to crippling despair.

"It's not gonna be that bad; don't worry so much! I haven't even done anything, but now I feel like an asshole! At least wait until I've done something before you react so negatively!"

"…Th-then…wh-what do you want me to do…?" Heine asks haltingly.

"How about a truce? A month should be fine. Those are my terms. If you accept, I'll let you and your underlings go home."

With that, I flash her my best roguish smile.

9

"...Was it okay to let them go with just a truce?"

Snow seems dubious as we watch Heine hop on her griffin and lead the massive horde of demons away from the city.

"If they actually wait a month, it'll be plenty. I've got a plan... Still, we actually got through it. Oh, from now on, remember I'm *Mr.* Six to you lot. Make sure you thank me once a day. I mean, that's the least you can do, given my contributions, right? Especially you, Snow. You promised I could do anything I want to you, right? You know what happens next, don't you? Go get in the bath and make yourself all nice and squeaky clean for me."

"...Say, I should go down and thank all the soldiers on behalf of the kingdom!"

"Hey, Six, when your suit cools down, we need to talk about something. I'll be waiting downstairs."

Tillis and Alice, hearing my words, make their way out of the royal chambers.

"...This is fine. I'm not lonely. It's not like I wanted them to stay or anything. I'm used to this. Snow is plenty," I mutter to myself as the room becomes emptier.

"...Um, Six. I mean, C-Commander... I know this is going to sound awfully convenient for me, but I need to ask a favor of you..."

Snow says this without her usual confidence, kicking at the floor, then bending down to pick something up.

"...Well... It's just that, as a knight, I'd like to continue riding a unicorn... I'm sure you're well aware of the criteria for being able to ride one... I know I'm being selfish..."

She cradles the object she picked up in her arms and approaches me as I remain immobilized.

Is that...?

*   *   *

Oh Lord, it's Gadalkand's head.

"…I'm sorry, Commander. Don't feel pressured one way or the other. This is just a request…"

"What are you doing? Why'd you pick that thing up? Put it down! Don't come any closer!"

Snow knits her brow, frowning apologetically. "C-could we… well…wait a while longer before we sleep together…?"

"Stop! What are you doing?! It's not good to play with corpses, even if it's an enemy! Stop! You're too close! It's creepy! Really, really creepy! Gadalkand's head is freaking me out! I get it, I get it, I understand! We're even! No need to worry about the promise! J-just stop! I don't wanna kiss Gadalkand!"

Hearing those words, Snow finally tosses Gadalkand's head aside. I growl in irritation and vent my frustration at her.

"Unbelievable! I figured it'd be something like this! You're just like Astaroth! All women are the same! They use you when they need you; then when it comes time to return the favor, they cry and change the subject! Idiot! Moron! Ever since the day we met, I haven't liked you one bit! Just leave and join the—"

Something soft presses against my lips, cutting off my fiery rant.

Snow's quieted me with her own lips.

Even if I wasn't still on cooldown, I'd be too shocked to move. Snow pulls away with a blush on her cheeks.

"Forgive me… This is all I can do for now…"

My brain still hasn't finished processing the sudden event, and I remain silent.

"I—I don't dislike that y-you like me… And I'd be lying if I said I wasn't flattered by your desire to bed me… But I just don't understand this whole love and hate thing. Even so…"

Snow's white skin flushes pink.

"I don't hate you as much as when I first met you. I'm still very inexperienced, but…I'd like to take the time to think through my feelings for you…"

She looks at me with a soft, gentle smile.

…………?

"Wait, what the hell are you talking about? Why are you making it sound like I'm in love with you or something? Creepy!"

………

"…Huh?"

"No 'huh' about it. How did you get it in your head that I loved you? I don't remember ever saying anything to that effect."

Snow tries to process my words and looks at me in confusion, as though she doesn't understand what I'm saying.

"…B-but I thought you wanted to s-sleep with me…"

"Well, yeah. Your face and body are definitely my type, so I just wanted a quick fling. No strings attached. Yikes, don't make me say this out loud. I thought it was obvious. As for dating you? Give me a break; I'd never want to go out with someone like you. I mean, you're quick to draw your sword and attack me, your ambition outweighs everything else, and you're cheap as hell. What exactly is there to like about you? And really, you think you can get away with just a kiss…?"

As the words come flying out of my mouth, I note a sudden change in Snow's demeanor and clam up.

"Haaaa……aaaaa……aaahhh……"

Snow has gone from blushing like a bride to taking deep breaths while holding back tears.

She looks like she's trying really hard to contain something.

It reminds me of how a toddler pauses before going into a full-blown crying fit.

Snow's hand trembles, and her armor rattles slightly as she reaches for her sword.

"...Calm down, Snow. Let's talk this over like grown-ups. Look, I can't move right now. If you lose control and attack me, I'm going to die."

"Haaaa......aaaaa......aaahhh......"

Snow appears to understand what I'm saying, doing her best to hold back the emotions that threaten to overwhelm her. Her body shakes as she fights to hold it all in.

Unfortunately, for all her efforts, her hand slowly grasps at the hilt of her blade...

"Hold it in just a little longer, Snow. I'm sorry; I was being way too harsh. But you know, if you kill me after making me go through all this effort, it'll completely ruin the taste of victory. You can contain this; I know you can! Just take deep breaths and count out prime numbers."

"O-one...three...f-five...s-s-s-seven..."

<Cooldown complete. Power armor reinitialized.>

I take off in a mad dash toward the stairs. Snow gives chase, screaming and crying at the same time.

"Raaaaaaaaaaaaaaaaaaaaaaaaaaaaaaaaaaaaaaah!! Ahhhhhhhhhhh hhhhhhhhhhh!!"

Snow's war cry sounds like a giant tantrum.

I urge my legs to run faster as the berserker chases me through the castle.

"Release Restraints! RELEASE RESTRAINTS!!"

I let out a hoarse cry as I flee.

"All right, I guess we're done here."

It's gotten quite late. Just before midnight, by the look of it.

With the Demon Army gone, there's no reason for us to stay here.

"Sir Six...thank you for all that you've done. I didn't expect you to go to such lengths for our kingdom. Truly, you have my gratitude."

"If you really are thankful, there are ways you can show your appreciation, you know? Make sure you put my name in this kingdom's history books and let future generations know what I've done."

Tillis smiles, then nods a bit shyly at my remark.

I've grown so used to seeing her as the malevolent power behind the throne that the sudden change in mannerisms catches me off guard.

...Or maybe it's just the sudden relief as her kingdom is saved from the brink of extinction that gave me a glimpse under her mask.

With such an incompetent father as a king, she probably feels an added responsibility to be strong for the kingdom's sake. That probably manifests itself as the whole iron-fist-in-a-velvet-glove persona.

The princess pauses a moment, pursing her lips like she's about to say something.

"...Um, Sir Six. I'm aware that you have *another* mission to attend to. However, do you think I could perhaps convince you to become a knight of this kingdom once again...?"

In response to Tillis's halting request, I slowly shake my head.

"Well. Honestly, I'm tired of this knight stuff. Babysitting these weirdos was exhausting."

Tillis smiles sadly, as though she anticipated my answer. She can't quite keep all the disappointment hidden, however.

As for two of my former subordinates who hear the remark...

"Weirdos?! Are you talking about us?! How rude! Don't make me bite you, Boss!"

"So you do all those things with me, Commander, and you're just going to walk away...? Take responsibility for what you did to my body!"

"Phrasing! Watch the phrasing, Grimm; you're giving people

the wrong idea! I bought you a new wheelchair, and we went for a few joyrides! That's it— Ow! Rose, I'm sorry I called you a weirdo! Stop biting me! Stop!"

I peel Rose off my back before she can chew on me anymore, and then I make preparations to leave.

"…………"

There's a silent Snow standing behind me.

"…? Well? Say something. You're kind of intimidating, just standing there without a word."

Snow continues to stare at me in silence. I guess she's still mad about earlier.

"…Hey. Are you really never coming back?"

Great. She finally speaks, and those are the first words out of her mouth.

"You don't need to threaten me. I'll stay far away unless invited!"

In response to my usual banter, Snow takes a deep breath.

"…S-so are you going back to your country?"

"Of course. A certain someone here is likely to take my head off my shoulders if I stay. Besides, we've pretty much accomplished our objectives."

Snow nods her head briefly. "……I see."

"…Just spit it out already! Where's your usual spice? If you have something to say, just say it. I need to go meet Alice soon."

Snow clenches her hands into fists, pursing her lips. "…C-currently, our kingdom's taken heavy losses in our war against the Demon Lord's Army. So we're currently seeking people who can command units or fight battles."

"…………And?"

She pauses, as if weighing whether to say the next part. "…I don't care what you are or who you really are anymore. If you don't want to be a knight because you want to avoid annoying subordinates like me, well…we could hire you as a mercenary……"

The longer she continues, the tamer and more hesitant Snow's words become.

Seems she still feels a little guilt for driving me off that first time.

"So you want people who can fight?"

"Y-yes. But that doesn't mean we'll take just anyone......"

When did she lose that confidence and sass anyway?

......Sheesh, she's a handful however you look at it. I can see why she'd get demoted to the reject squad.

A brief glance shows me something else.

Snow's not the only one giving me puppy dog eyes and begging me to stay.

Everyone around me, from my two former subordinates to Tillis herself are looking at me with hope and anticipation in their eyes.

Geez, these people really are needy.

Of course I'll fight. It's my job. And there's plenty of battles waiting to be fought on this planet.

This kingdom needs people who can fight, huh?

Then I should take full advantage and corner the market.

I turn to the women in front of me and say in my best sales rep voice:

"One Combat Agent, at your service!"

10

The time is late, well into the night and closing in on early morning.

I knock on a particular man's door.

"......Who is it?"

"Me. It's me."

At that response, the man opens the door without any semblance of caution.

"Who is it? Gear? Pomegranate? I haven't called you; I'm busy right now..."

"What's up, old man? It's me, your favorite person in the world!"

The chief of staff stops his questions in mid-sentence, hurriedly trying to slam the door shut. I stick my foot out and use my boot to keep the door from closing.

"Gaaaaaaaaaah! Ow! Ow! My foot!"

Hearing my scream, the chief of staff throws open the door in a panic. I casually walk in, and Alice follows a few steps behind me.

"Wha...? Wh-what are you doing?! You can't just barge in here!"

I ignore the chief of staff's angry sputtering and glance around the room.

"...Well, well, things sure are different at the top. A lot of expensive stuff you've got here, *milord.*"

"Hey, Six, this is some really good furniture. Even a quick estimate would put their total worth in the millions."

Whoa, really?

"...I'd be tempted to let him go if he gave us all his furniture..."

"I can't have you being that easily swayed."

The chief of staff seems to be struggling to follow our conversation. "Hey, now! What the hell do you two want at this late hour?"

"Well, well, that's an interesting change from your usual tone. Is this how you really talk?"

"There's an easy way to spot the small-time crooks. They can completely change their manner of speaking at a moment's notice. He's a stereotypical petty villain, Six."

The chief of staff looks down, as if resisting an impulse. "......What do you want?!"

"...Well, you see, Snow told us everything. About how you got her to investigate us because you didn't like me."

"Indeed. Evidently, you hooked her by offering her a promotion, which led to her wandering to our room and overhearing a sensitive conversation. She kept apologizing for it."

At that, all the color drains from the chief of staff's face, leaving him white as a sheet.

"...Uh, well... Um..."

"There's no way that's true, riiight? You were so quick to praise me and call me a Hero at those meetings. Isn't that right, old man?"

The chief of staff's face lights up, and he pounces for the rope I dangle in front of him.

"Y-yes, that's right! Sir Six is a Hero of the kingdom! Why would I hate such a man?"

"Good point... It must have been a misunderstanding on Snow's part," Alice agrees, and the old man nods enthusiastically.

"Yes! Yes, of course! That's correct! ......Hey, wait. I recall Lady Snow saying that she wanted to kill you, Sir Six. That woman, she's a commoner from the slums. If not for the war, she wouldn't have ranked much higher than private. She got lucky and won her promotions, but I have no doubt that her ambition tempted her to do more. She probably hoped to take my place by pitting you and me against each other..."

"Damn, seriously? That's messed up! Oh, hey, you know about that girl Rose? Apparently, she's been on the hunt for some weird rock her grandpa wanted her to find. Something about it being his dying wish. I heard she's being worked for almost no pay! Who came up with that idea? It's genius!"

"If we're going there, the whole idea of gathering a group of rejects from the army and using them as expendable troops is impressive, too. A true masterstroke."

At our words, the chief of staff grins widely. Pleased as punch.

"Why, those are my ideas! Princess Tillis is a capable administrator, but she's much too sheltered. She's incapable of discarding the unworthy. So I chose to help reduce her burden, you see. I didn't gain the chief of staff position for nothing. Not to toot my own horn here, but this whole plan went rather well..."

....

"Hey, Alice, can we stop now? Like I said from the start. He's not worth recruiting."

The chief of staff's eyes widen in surprise at the sudden shift in my attitude.

"Right. I'd never met this old man or had a conversation with him, so I thought there might be some hope. But this guy's not evil. He's just an opportunistic little worm... What's wrong, Six? Does your chest hurt?"

"Urgh. I don't know why, but those words just hit me right here..." I press my palm against my chest.

"...Wh-what is the meaning of this?! Why the sudden change in attitude...? ...I don't know what triggered it, but I apologize if I offended you. What say we forget about the past and discuss the future...?"

The chief of staff begins to offer excuses, which Alice interrupts by slamming something down on the desk.

The object on the desk is...

"Wh-what is this?"

...a lotus root.

"It's the edible rhizome of a lotus plant. Not only can you eat it, it's got some medicinal uses."

"...A-and?"

Alice presses her expressionless face toward the chief of staff. "How would you like us to shove this entire thing up your ass?"

"Eeep! Wh-what is this girl saying?! D-didn't anyone teach you not to play with your food?"

Alice didn't look like anything other than a young girl, but her mannerisms and tone were as effective in the art of intimidation as those of any evil corporate operative. The chief of staff's face twitches anxiously.

"I wouldn't dream of wasting food. Once we're finished, it will be cleaned, cooked, and consumed. Of course, I can't eat, so you'll have to do the honors."

"Wha...? Wh-wha...what are you...?"

As the chief of staff backs into a corner, I tear off a length of an item I'm carrying in my hand.

"...J-just what is that...?"

The chief of staff grows curious about the item I'm holding.

"This? This is a tool used for punishing balding men. In some regions it's referred to as duct tape."

"Eeep! S-stop! What are you doing?! Please don't!"

Looks like the chief of staff cares about his hairline after all; he keeps backing farther toward the wall with his hands shielding his scalp.

"Don't worry so much. All I'm going to do is stick this on your head and peel it off. See? Easy."

"P-please don't! I'll do anything! Do you want money? I can give you money! I'll give you all that you ask for. So please don't!"

Alice picks up the lotus root, then approaches the chief of staff, completely immune to his pleading.

"Hey, old man, if you're gonna dabble in evil..."

I tear piece after piece of duct tape, storing it on my wrist before finishing Alice's warning.

"...And if you're planning to entrap someone, you'd better be ready to go down yourself... This is a show of thanks for how you treated my subordinates. So... Lotus root or duct tape? What's it gonna be?"

The chief of staff just gives a tense, weeping smile.

<Evil Points acquired.>

*   *   *

After leaving the chief of staff's room, we make our way toward the hideout to pick up our luggage.

"…You know, Six, even though you're a meathead, your latest plan has my praise."

I raise a brow at Alice's comment.

"Hmm? What 'plan' are you talking about?" I ask back, confused by her praise. "And stop calling me a meathead."

"…Wait, that wasn't part of a plan? Everything we've been through?"

"…?"

Nope, don't understand what she's getting at.

"You made a promise with Snow, remember? About hiring Combat Agents?"

"Oh, that. Right. I promised Snow that we'd stick around and fight whoever we needed to fight, at least until we can get back to Japan. Though, since the truce with the Demon Army is supposed to last a month, we might not even have to fight before we leave. How's that for an impressive plan?"

In spite of being an android, Alice lets out a sigh of exasperation.

"…Look at your current Evil Point balance."

…190 points.

"…Huh? There's a lot more than I thought. How? How did I get this much for pulling down Snow's panties and bullying a baldy?"

"Look closer. Notice something next to the total?"

I take a second look.

…………-190.

"Uh…what?"

"Don't 'what' me. You requested the R-Buzzsaw even though you didn't have enough points, remember?"

?!

"Since your point count's negative, if you get back to Japan, the retribution squad's going to grab you and subject you to some pretty rigorous punishment."

So our corporation's got this division called the retribution squad.

Normally, Evil Points are accumulated by completing evil deeds. However, if you rack up enough good deeds or tarnish the reputation of the organization by doing something embarrassing, you'll start losing points.

Once your score hits negative figures...

"...I've heard the punishment is terrifying."

"Seems like the punishment is customized for the victim each time."

......*Shit, shit, shit, shit. What do I do?!*

"Alice! I don't want to go back to Japan!"

I grab Alice and shake her in a panic. She stares at me as though she's watching a particularly interesting new animal.

"Huh, you really weren't doing it all on purpose, then...? Okay, here's the plan, Six. Stay here. Even once the teleport connection is stabilized, stay here and keep working as a hired Combat Agent. Earn yourself enough Evil Points and head back to Japan only after you get them back up in the positive."

"Perfect! Still, if there's a month between now and the connection stabilizing, that should be plenty of time to get myself in the black again."

I mean, I actually raised more than that in a shorter period of time. And that was just a few days ago!

"Hey, Fly, you're forgetting that there's wanted posters of you all over the city. You're basically on parole."

Oh, crap!

"Listen, will you? I'll write the report this time. I'll come up with some reason why you can't leave yet. I'll stay here with you as you accumulate points."

"All hail Queen Alice!"

I cling to Alice. She in turn starts patting my head as though reassuring an overgrown child.

"All right, all right. Now start thinking up new ways to acquire points."

"You got it, partner! I'll start by meeting up with my squad members and stripping all of them naked!"

As I turn to head back to the castle, I hear Alice's voice.

"H-hey, are you serious? And what's this 'partner' business? I'm a support-type android..."

Alice is giving her usual complaints, but I'm too preoccupied with figuring out how to acquire points that I don't quite make out all her words...

"...Partner, huh?"

...But I could've sworn I heard her mutter one last thing with a hint of satisfaction.

Epilogue

"...What's this?"

Astaroth holds out a single report to Lilith, one from the pile she had been sorting through.

"That's Alice's proposal. It's a marvel of logic and practicality."

At Lilith's cheerful response, Astaroth lightly massages her own forehead.

"But this type of work... This is something Heroes should be doing. It's unbecoming for members of an evil organization."

"Now, now. This'll give our Combat Agents plenty to do once we finish conquering Earth. It's not a bad proposal. Besides, once we drive off the competition and corner that market, we can then turn around and invade the planet ourselves. Until then, why not just send a few Combat Agents and focus our efforts on consolidating our hold on Earth."

Astaroth begrudgingly responds to Lilith's proposal

"...I suppose we have no choice. Looks like the conquest of Earth will take a while longer anyway, since the holdouts are being a bit more stubborn than anticipated. Not to change the subject, but..." Astaroth turns her gaze to a corner of the conference room. "Combat Agent F18! Combat Agent F19! You know why you've been summoned, yes?"

"Please wait, Lady Belial! It was the Chosen One's fault this time! I was busy carrying out my evil schemes when he showed up to interrupt me!"

"Faustless, you windbag! You weren't carrying out any evil schemes! It was just some petty crime. Lady Belial, I was only trying to keep him on task!"

Two men stand in front of Belial, making their excuses to the Supreme Leader. One of the men was best described as a mutant, while the other had the unmistakable aura of a Hero.

"Silence! None of this changes the fact you were fighting each other. You know internal conflict is forbidden. Also, get it through your thick skulls. He's not the Chosen One anymore, he's Combat Agent F18. And he's no longer 'whatever of the Wind,' he's Combat Agent F19! If you keep going on about Chosen Ones, you'll end up an irredeemable weirdo like Agent Six! As for this 'of the Wind' nonsense, you only get to use titles like that if you're a Supreme Leader. Understood?"

""Y-yes ma'am!"" the pair of trainees answer in unison, snapping off a sharp salute.

".......Just what are those two? That one reminds me of a Hero, and the other seems like a mutant."

"Them? From what Belial was saying, they suddenly appeared on her lawn and started brawling. As the story goes, she smacked both of them until they shut up, then recruited them as Combat Agent trainees. From what F19 said, he was trying to teleport to Something-Something of the Flames but wound up on Belial the Great Flame's lawn instead... or some such nonsense."

......

"So Belial's started bringing in stray heroes and mutants instead of just cats and dogs? ...First, Agent Six says he wants to stay on that planet and now this. What's gotten into them......?"

"...From the reports, it sounds like there are a lot more women than men on that planet due to the war. And almost all those women are gorgeous by our standards. I want to head over there, too. There are too many tempting things on that planet. It's a whole new world!"

Lilith's breathing becomes a bit labored toward the end of her speech as she walks out of the room.

"...H-he'll come home eventually, right? He's not going to get married over there and insist on staying, is he? ...B-Belial, I'll leave the reports here. Lilith, Agent Six will come back, right?!"

Astaroth dumps the sheaf of reports on the desk and hurries off after Lilith.

[Final Report]

Successfully acquired local base of operations.

Ready to accept Combat Agents and mutants.

Due to his own insistence, Combat Agent 6 will continue carrying out his survey assignment.

Discovered solution to the shortage of assignments for Combat Agents after conquest thanks to Agent 6's suggestion.

The proposed solution to the Combat Agent assignment shortage is detailed in attachment titled "Combatant Temporary Service Dispatch Project."

Current local conditions means invasion plans should be put on hold at this time.

Recommend invading only after local competitors are eliminated.

Currently, approximately 80 percent of this planet remains unexplored and undeveloped. As detailed in separate report, there are a large number of mysterious geographic features such as ancient ruins and giant forests that require further study.

Can confirm the presence of anomalous artifacts that exceed current Earth technology.

Considering all factors noted above, final recommendation is to begin planning a conservative invasion and exploration plan.

End report.

[Combatant Temporary Service Dispatch Project Overview]

Dispatch Combat Agents to develop undeveloped lands and conduct local fauna surveys.

Destruction or assimilation of local competitor Demon Lord's Army.

Investigate unconfirmed anomalous artifacts and ruins on planet.

Conduct extermination of local fauna at the behest of local inhabitants.

The Kisaragi Corporation should accept contracts to carry out these tasks and operate a labor dispatch agency utilizing the corporation's Combat Agents.

For local branch manager, recommending Combat Agent 6 due to strong level of trust and support among local inhabitants.

Final Reporting Operative
Combat Agent 6's Partner, Alice Kisaragi

AFTERWORD

If we haven't met before, it's nice to meet you.

It's Natsume Akatsuki, part author, part NEET.

Thank you for picking up a copy of *Combatants Will Be Dispatched!*

This is a rework of a piece I'd written up for the novel submission website So You Want to Be a Novelist.

It was originally written before my other series, *Konosuba: God's Blessing on This Wonderful World!*, and after a long, complicated history, it's finally seeing publication.

If I was to describe the plot in a single sentence, it would be "Lowly Combat Agent for an evil organization is sent off to the middle of nowhere."

It's a little hard to classify, but I suppose it has elements of the *sentai*, sci-fi, and fantasy genres.

At its heart, it's a comedy.

Anyway, for this work, the goal isn't to defeat the Demon Lord and win world peace.

Six and his partner Alice, sent off to this unexplored planet, will be getting into a lot of different adventures, developing the world with modern and advanced technologies, fighting the Demon Lord's Army, running from local life-forms, and solving the various mysteries hidden on the planet.

Even I'm not sure what'll happen from here on out. I hope you'll strap in and enjoy this journey with me.

This time, while struggling to get this book out the door, I had the help of a particular author who read the manuscript and left me all sorts of feedback and comments. I won't mention his name, but many thanks to you, Tappei Nagatsuki.

I also want to thank everyone involved in getting this book produced, from the wonderful illustrator Kakao Lanthanum to my editor, sales staff, designers, editors, and everyone else.

I'll most likely be giving them a lot more headaches to deal with not just for *Konosuba: God's Blessing on This Wonderful World!*, but I'm in the process of writing more books in this series, so I'll go ahead and apologize in advance here.

I know we'll get some complaints from people telling me not to cause the problems in the first place, so sorry about those!

I feel like I'm apologizing to a bunch of people every time I turn in a manuscript.

And I know this is all at the end, but finally, to all the readers who've picked up this book and given it a read, thank you so much!

Natsume Akatsuki

HAVE YOU BEEN TURNED ON TO LIGHT NOVELS YET?

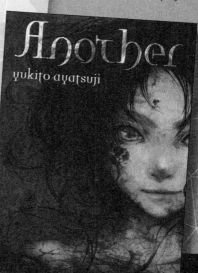